Red Summer

A NOVEL

CASSIDY HUDSPETH

Copyright © 2023 by Cassidy Hudspeth

All rights reserved.

No part of this book may be reproduced in any form or by any electronic or mechanical means, including information storage and retrieval systems, without written permission from the author, except for the use of brief quotations in a book review.

Editing/Proofing: Jenni Brady

Cover Design: Sam Palencia at Ink and Laurel

*To those who have never felt good enough—**they're** just not good enough for **you**.*

PLAYLIST

GETAWAY CAR – TAYLOR SWIFT
ON PURPOSE – SABRINA CARPENTER
STARVING – HAILEE STEINFELD, GREY, ZEDD
GOODNIGHT N GO – ARIANA GRANDE
CRUEL SUMMER – TAYLOR SWIFT
MAIN THING – ARIANA GRANDE
NONSENSE – SABRINA CARPENTER
NOBODY – SELENA GOMEZ
BLUE – TROYE SIVAN, ALEX HOPE
HURTS SO GOOD – ASTRID S
ENCHANTED (TAYLOR'S VERSION) – TAYLOR SWIFT
ILYSB (STRIPPED) – LANY
ARMY – ELLIE GOULDING
THINKING OF YOU – KATY PERRY
TILL FOREVER FALLS APART – ASHE, FINNEAS

dow, adjusting the strap of her purse on her shoulder, her phone buzzed with a message from her best friend.

WREN: *How is your date? You haven't sent me any deets.*

Ophelia laughed softly under her breath, whisking open the bar door as she typed back.

OPHELIA: *I bailed as soon as he said he wanted a girl just like his mom.*

WREN: *Do I need to come get you? The last thing I want is for you to end up on one of those true crime shows, Lia.*

She rolled her eyes as she walked into the bar, observing the dimly lit scenery around her. There were pool tables in the back surrounded by burgundy-colored booths and an old-looking jukebox in the corner. The wooden floors were faded, and the baseboards were tattered, but something about it still felt inviting. It was oddly quiet inside for a Saturday. Only a few stragglers sat at the bar, but she preferred it that way. Admittedly, it wouldn't have been her first pick for a night out, but she'd make an exception tonight.

Tequila was calling her name.

As Ophelia searched around for a bartender, she hopped into one of the bar seats and tapped her fingers lightly against the wood. Pursing her full lips, she swung her feet patiently as she waited.

CHAPTER ONE

Ophelia Clark was so over the male population.

She was wholly convinced that there wasn't a single specimen left on the planet capable of relationship material. It was stereotypical to say that it seemed as though they were all identical, but from her experience, it always wound up ending because of the same continuous cycle of *bullshit*.

They either had a secret girlfriend, couldn't manage to hold a decent conversation, or thought that sending unsolicited dick pictures was the way to a girl's heart.

Or, in her current situation, she ended up getting dropped off on the corner of some random street because there was no way in hell she could continue riding in a car with a guy who had just talked about how much of a momma's boy he was for the last ten minutes straight.

Flicking her blonde hair over her shoulder, Ophelia huffed as she twirled on her heel away from the car as it drove off, not daring to even give it another glance as she proceeded to walk along the sidewalk. She decided her night was turning around, however, when she glanced up to see the glowing light of a sign that read *The Beer Lounge*.

As she examined herself in the reflection of the glass win-

WREN: *Hello? I didn't mean literally, bitch, don't make me come find you. I have your location.*

She didn't even have time to snicker or respond to her worried friend before a tall, bearded guy rounded the corner of the liquor shelves towards her. His dark hair sat in ruffled waves along the top of his head, brushed up slightly, connecting with his full beard that complimented his structured jawline. He was undoubtedly older than she was; his face didn't possess any of the round, babyish cheeks that guys her age carried. His blue eyes were almost the same bright shade as hers, crinkled ever so faintly in the corners, and immediately falling on her and giving her heart palpitations.

It was quite ironic that she was just mentally swearing off men forever, only for this attractive, muscular man to appear and cause her to practically have a stroke. And by muscular, she meant *muscular*. She could tell how brawny he was beneath his black leather jacket.

Did she mention he was wearing rings?

Fucking rings.

OPHELIA: *Can't talk. At a bar with a hot bartender. See you tonight.*

WREN: *NO. Don't come home, get laid!*

Struggling to hide the smile that threatened to creep on her lips, she stuffed her phone into her purse as she straightened up in her seat. Locking eyes with the mystery man as he stood in front of her, she gulped. He towered over her in the chair, so she could only imagine how tall he'd appear if she stood from the bar stool. His pink lips twisted as he gnawed at them from the inside, studying her for a few moments.

"Got an ID?"

His voice was *deep*.

Ophelia wanted to scoff, but she pulled her driver's license out anyway. Sliding it across the bar towards him, she tapped her finger on the birthday teasingly. "Just turned twenty-one this year, mister. I'll have a shot of tequila."

His thick eyebrow raised dubiously as he slid the ID back to her, turning to grab the bottle as he poured the clear liquid into a tiny shot glass.

She ogled at the size of his back while he was turned around, just barely getting a glance at his butt before he twisted to face her again. Sitting the shot down in front of her, his lips formed a thin line.

It was a *nice* butt.

"Want to open a tab?" he asked quietly as she downed the glass.

Ophelia nodded as she flashed him a toothy grin, handing the glass back over. "Keep them coming. It's been a long night."

"Did you drive?"

"No. I walked, kind of." She twisted her hair up into a pastel pink clip as she spoke. "It's a long story."

Just by looking at him, he didn't seem like he would be the quiet type. The jacket, the rings, the beard, or the faint outlines of tattoos that she could see just above the collar of his shirt. It all screamed hot, bad boy. Even his voice—she could break out into a sweat just picturing what it would sound like whispering into her ear.

"You walked," he repeated firmly, placing the shot in front of her. "By yourself?"

The familiar warmth spread through her chest as she downed the second shot, silently hoping the faint buzz would start not long after.

"Well, I was on a date," she sighed, running her fingertip around the rim of the glass as she stared down at it. "But he started to show me pictures of his mom and talking about how he wanted to be with someone who reminded him of her, and uh—*yeah*, it was kind of weird. So I had him drop me off at the corner outside."

She would always ramble when the buzz kicked in. It was a fault that she hated about herself since she had her first taste of alcohol. The words would fumble from her lips like vomit before she could cram it back down, locking them up tight and throwing away the key. But as she peeked up at him, she saw the remnants of a smile on the corners of his lips before he whisked out a white rag to start cleaning some glasses behind the bar, and her worries dissipated as quickly as they had formed.

"You know, for a bartender, you're not very talkative."

He flicked his tongue along his bottom lip before a faint smile flashed across his features. "How do you plan on getting home?"

"I haven't thought that far ahead," Ophelia admitted sheepishly, taking her bottom lip between her teeth.

For the smallest second, she could have sworn his eyes had flickered down to her lips. It was so quick that she wasn't sure if she had just made it up, but it made her heart lurch inside of her chest, nonetheless.

"Do you live in LA?"

She shook her head. "I grew up here, but I live in Georgia on campus right now. I'm staying with my friend for the summer."

"Georgia is pretty far," he said as he pressed his hands against the bar, his head cocking slightly as he looked down at her.

"Yeah, that was on purpose."

He nodded understandingly as his eyes studied her briefly.

Ophelia was an only child who grew up on the outskirts of Los Angeles with her parents, who were both world-renowned surgeons that were never home and only paid attention to her when it was to lecture her. The moment she graduated high school, she moved to Georgia for college, eager to get as far away as she could from her condescending parents. Across the entire country seemed far enough. She would only come back during the summers for Wren, her best friend since they were practically in diapers.

"Does your friend live within walking distance?" he asked curiously, a concerned tone to his voice, as he filled her shot glass for the third time.

The buzz was behind her eyes now as she threw her head back and let the warm liquid fall down her throat.

"I'll just call an Uber." She shrugged, swaying in her seat as she smiled.

He somehow seemed displeased with her answer, his eyebrows furrowing together as he watched her hesitantly. He filled the glass again despite his reluctant disposition. With the liquid courage pumping through her, she couldn't help but ogle at him, observing his broody face and attractive hands as they moved around.

Quite *large* hands.

She wondered what they would feel like wrapped around her—

"You don't feel weird getting a ride from a stranger by yourself?" he asked, glancing over his shoulder at the clock that hung on the wall. "At almost midnight?"

"They're usually nice, old men."

He hummed.

"You're skeptical," she assumed, fighting the urge to smile.

"*I* could take you home."

Her mouth popped open faintly at his words, her fingers holding the full shot glass as she watched him throw the rag down and nod at the other guy working behind the bar, signaling for him to come over to them.

"You don't have to do tha—"

"Sean, could you take over until I get back?" he asked his coworker, interrupting and ignoring her statement altogether.

Sean was a few inches taller than her quiet, new friend, who she thought was pretty tall himself. His black hair was buzzed almost to the scalp. His eyes were the same color as his skin, a rich brown that was smooth in the dim light of the bar. It was a beautiful contrast to the bright smile that he flashed toward his friend. Glancing between the two of them, the corners of Sean's lips twitched.

"Sure thing, Jam."

Jam?

His name was Jam?

As he began to exit from behind the bar, Ophelia hurriedly gulped down the remaining tequila, her eyes falling on his dark jeans and leather boots now that she could see him in full view. Not to mention the size of his thighs.

Holy smokes, he was hot.

Even if his name was Jam.

"That's enough tequila for one night," he said lowly, a hint of amusement lacing his words, as he held his hand out to help her hop down from the tall bar stool.

"But I opened a tab," she whined softly.

Who was she kidding? She had to hold herself back from hopping into his arms and telling him to whisk her off into the moonlight. Maybe her failure of a date earlier was only meant to bring her here, to the quiet bar with the bartender that looked like he just walked out of *Vogue*.

"Don't worry about it." He shook his head. "It's on me. Let's just get you home safely, yeah?"

Hesitantly peeking down at his outstretched hand, Ophelia grabbed her purse before putting her hand in his as she hopped off the stool. His other hand hovered behind her lower back, agonizingly close to touching her as he led her from the bar until they were outside in the fresh air.

Tugging her phone from her bag, she typed out a quick text to Wren as she followed in step behind him as he led the way.

OPHELIA: *Hot bartender is giving me a ride home. Thought you'd like to know so you can stalk my location and make sure he doesn't take me to an abandoned field to murder me hehe*

Her eyes widened as they came up on a matte black motorcycle, observing him through her gaze as he threw his leg over it to sit down. Of *course*, he owned a motorcycle. She should have guessed it earlier from the jacket and boots.

If she wasn't already drooling, she was now.

"This is yours?" She hiccuped timidly.

He nodded, looking back at her. "I hope that's okay."

"More than okay," Ophelia enthused with a laugh, hopping on the back as she encircled her arms around his broad waist. "Let's go."

Her tiny arms almost didn't fit around his toned abdomen. She intertwined her fingers tightly together as she pressed her cheek against the cool leather of his jacket. He smelled of sandalwood and hints of musky vanilla; the scent swirled in her spinning head, making her feel even more intoxicated.

"Are you ready?"

"As long as you drive responsibly—because I may be slightly inebriated, and I'm barely hanging on here," she teased, squeezing him around his waist. "Then I think I'm ready."

She felt a faint rumble of laughter reverberate through his body as she pressed against him, making the corners of her lips turn up as the bike roared to life.

Shouting the address over the loudness of the motorcycle, a giggle escaped her lips as he sped off, her loose strands of hair whipping wildly around her face as they flew down the streets of Los Angeles. Her sweater rippled in the wind, the breeze cool against her skin as she let her head fall back—her eyes closing as a content smile permanently etched onto her lips.

She was on the back of a hot bartender guy's motorcycle. This wasn't something that she normally did. This would be the first time she'd agreed to be chauffeured on a stranger's bike in her entire life. The whole night had taken a turn in a direction she hadn't expected—getting dropped off at a random street and willingly accepting a ride home from a stranger. But maybe this is exactly what she needed; something completely out of character.

Any ounce of doubt that rested in the back of her mind disappeared completely every time his hand left the handlebars of the motorcycle and rested gently on her intertwined ones. He was making sure she still had a good grip around his waist. It would only last long enough for the excitement to settle in before he took it away again. But it was quite possibly the sweetest thing anyone had ever done.

The trip ended entirely too soon, causing disappointment to seep through her veins as they came to a gradual stop in front of Wren's apartment complex. Unlatching her fingers from around his waist, she climbed from the back of his bike as she blew her hair from her view.

"Well, um, *Jam?*" she questioned tentatively, squinting playfully at him. "Is that your real name?"

A breathy laugh escaped his lips as he let his head fall briefly, his nose scrunching cutely as he lifted it back up. "Jamie. Um, James. Jam is just something Sean has called me since we were kids."

"Hmm." She hummed sweetly, nodding her head. "Jamie. *James*, thanks for the ride home."

"No problem," he said.

His eyes searched hers for a few moments, his lips parting just barely as he glanced down at her upturned ones.

"Thanks for not murdering me."

He raised his eyebrows as a strangled sound left his mouth, his fist pressing to his lips as he tried to cover it with a cough. "You thought I was going to murder you?"

"It was a joke, bartender boy."

"Yep. I knew that."

"I'll see you around." Ophelia grinned. "Maybe?"

A smile formed that matched her own as he continued to peer at her, making her want to squirm under his stare as her stomach did somersaults.

When he didn't say anything, she took a few awkward steps backward, waving her hand in the air as she said, "Goodnight."

"Goodnight, Ophelia."

In the few tiny seconds that he had glanced at her license earlier, he had taken the time to see what her name was. The notion only made the somersaults transform into full-blown butterflies as she swallowed the thick lump in her throat, watching him drive off before she turned to walk inside the apartment building.

Perhaps she wasn't over the *entire* male population.

CHAPTER TWO

SCRUNCHING UP HER NOSE in embarrassment, Ophelia ducked her head to avoid looking up at Wren's critical stare.

"Let me make sure I understand this correctly," Wren stated, crossing her arms in front of her chest as her tongue flicked out to wet her lips. "You rode home on the back of this handsome bartender's motorcycle just to say *goodnight*? Did you at least get his phone number?"

Her green eyes squinted down at Ophelia, who sat perched on the couch in her apartment, as she blinked rapidly in disbelief. Her bright red hair cascaded down to the middle of her back, not a strand out of place.

"I may have been all mind jumbled from the four shots of tequila, Wren," Ophelia said gently. "I couldn't exactly think straight, okay?"

She didn't need Wren to remind her of just how dumb she was. She felt it this morning when she woke up and realized that she didn't get his number. His obvious attractiveness and her inebriated state were to blame for that. How could she even begin to get her thoughts together with him smelling all delicious and stuff? Ophelia could still practically smell his cologne inside of her nostrils, as though it had been imprinted there.

She wasn't complaining.

"But he didn't ask for *your* number, either," she mumbled, placing her fingers on her chin meticulously as she began to pace back and forth in front of the sofa.

"Exactly." Ophelia huffed, blowing the strands that had fallen loose from her braid away from her face, throwing her hands in the air. "What if he wasn't into me? He probably was just trying to be nice by driving me home."

"He remembered your name, Lia. It's because he was into you or because he plans on murdering you and hiding your body in his basement or something."

Ophelia rolled her eyes as she snickered, pushing up from the beige-colored couch as she placed her hands on Wren's shoulders to shake her gently. "I didn't get serial killer vibes, I promise. You watch too much *Forensic Files*."

"And I'll be more prepared than most people if someone tries to kidnap me, won't I?" she asked, sticking her nose in the air jocosely.

She loved her best friend for many reasons, but this one was probably her favorite. Wren was either urging her to get laid, which, according to her, was for Ophelia's own well-being, or being overly protective at all costs. There was no in-between. Her exuberant friend was like a safe space, someone that anyone would feel comfortable with as soon as they met her. The moment she had met Wren as a child, they were instantly attached at the hip. They were soul sisters.

"Haven't I taught you anything?" she continued, tearing Ophelia from her train of thought. "You're a bad bitch and you *need* to put yourself out there. Get the hot bartender. Make your move."

"And what if he rejects me, Wren?"

Wren glanced crossly at her. "Have you seen yourself?"

Always her biggest hype woman.

"That's not the point—"

"If you don't get your ass back to that bar right now—" Wren paused, a smile forming along her lips. "I'll drag you there myself."

Ophelia groaned quietly, throwing her head back as she sighed. She had to muster up the courage to even attempt to think about walking out of the door.

Wren noticed her hesitation, however, playfully swatting at her butt as she shoved her towards the front door. Her emerald irises narrowed at her, silently telling her to *go*, before reaching past her to turn the knob and nudge her once more.

"I don't want to seem desperate."

"Think of it as you being confident," Wren urged. "Men love when a woman is confident in what she wants."

"What if *he* doesn't?"

"There's only one way to find out, babe."

"Okay." Ophelia surrendered with a sigh, hurrying out of the door before she could swat at her again. "I'm going, *jeez*."

"Love you," Wren cooed sweetly in a sing-song voice.

"Yeah, yeah, I love you more."

Swallowing the thick, cottony wad of saliva in her throat, Ophelia stared up at the familiar sign outside of the bar.

The sun was just beginning to set, and the sky had different hues of pink and orange that cascaded along the streets and buildings of downtown Los Angeles. She could see the luminescence against her skin in her reflection in the window, reminding her that she was only donning a lousy hoodie and some cut-off jeans.

If he wasn't interested before, he definitely wouldn't be now.

WREN: *YOU'RE A BAD BITCH*

Grinning down at the last-minute confidence boost from her friend, Ophelia straightened her shoulders. Sucking in a deep breath, she whisked open the door and walked inside the bar before she could manage to psych herself out.

Her heart felt like it was doing cartwheels inside of her chest as her eyes fell on James standing behind the bar, chatting to Sean as his nose scrunched slightly. His shoulders shook as he laughed at something his friend had said. His smile made heat pool in her stomach, all warm and rich like honey.

He looked even more scrumptious than last night if that was even remotely possible. He donned another leather jacket. This one was different—it had silver chains linked to the front pockets and a silver zipper to match. The black t-shirt underneath fit tighter on him than the one before, and the outline of his muscular chest was more prominent.

And as if the rings weren't hot enough, he wore a gold necklace that hung low against his torso.

Focus.

She approached the bar timorously, brushing her loose strands of hair behind her ears as she cleared her throat. Sean's dark eyes were the first ones to land on her, a knowing smirk forming on his full lips not long after, before James turned to see who he was looking at.

She held back a giggle as his eyes did a double take, his mouth parting slightly.

"Hi," she greeted softly.

"Hi," he mumbled unsteadily in response.

He was either taken aback because he was glad to see her again or because he thought she was a full-blown stalker.

Glancing over at Sean, who gave him a suggestive eyebrow raise before he nodded once, James gave him a friendly pat on the back as he walked out from behind the bar. Towering over her, his blue eyes stared down at her, studying her momentarily before a sheepish grin spread across his lips.

"You look surprised," Ophelia teased.

"I am, actually."

She tilted her head sideways as she peered up at him. "How come?"

"I'm..." he trailed off, a breathy laugh escaping his lips as he looked down at the ground. "*Old?*"

Mortification flooded through her as she realized that maybe he hadn't initiated anything last night because he thought she was too young. James didn't look that old, but perhaps age gaps weren't his preference. They normally weren't hers, either, but she would be willing to make an exception for the man standing in front of her.

"I wasn't asking for your hand in marriage, James," Ophelia quipped lightheartedly, fiddling with the sleeves of her hoodie as she spoke. "I came to see if you wanted to go somewhere with me?"

She wanted to cringe at how nervous she sounded, but she shoved the thoughts back down as she focused on Wren's voice inside of her head.

There's only one way to find out.

"Go somewhere? Uh—" He paused, peeking over at Sean who was distracted by a customer at the moment. "Yeah, we can go somewhere."

"Should you ask if that's okay?"

"Nope," he chuckled, his hand grasping hers as he tugged her towards the door, making her heart jump inside of her chest. "Let's go before he sees me sneaking away."

The pair snickered simultaneously as they tiptoed quickly outside of the bar, James pulling her down the sidewalk until they were completely out of view of the windows. She was slightly disappointed when he dropped her hand, rubbing the back of his neck as he peered down at her with amusement in his eyes.

"Are you sure this is okay?" Ophelia asked softly, taking her bottom lip between her teeth.

She was positive that she saw his eyes flicker down to her lips that time.

"*Yeah,*" he breathed, a smile forming on his full lips. "I own the bar, don't worry. Where are we going?"

"It's a secret."

On her way to *The Beer Lounge*, Ophelia had ultimately decided that she was going to take him to the pool that all the seniors would sneak into towards the end of the year during her high school years at some fancy five-star hotel. It was strictly off-limits to anyone but the guests, so they would hop the white fence at night to get inside.

"A secret?" James repeated, his eyebrows raising curiously.

Ophelia nodded enthusiastically.

"And to get there, you're going to have to..." she trailed off in a false, suspenseful tone. "Keep up!"

And then she was running, her red Converse scraping against the concrete sidewalk as her blonde hair whipped around her face, peeking over her shoulder to laugh at his stunned expression. The adrenaline pumped through her veins as she ran down the street, mixing with the bundle of nerves in her stomach.

"*Wait!*" he yelled after her. "What?"

"*Run!*" she shouted back, a grin spreading across her face. "Keep up, old man."

For a split second, Ophelia worried that maybe her idea was too childish, something that would weird him out instead of coming off exciting like she had hoped it would. She'd always had a childlike soul at heart, innocent and pure despite having an exhausting childhood. The inability to have the same experiences growing up as all the other kids around her was undoubtedly to blame. But her worries melted away when she heard his deep laugh behind her and the sound of his boots against the pavement as well. She could feel her skin buzzing with excitement as he chased after her, the nerve endings igniting simultaneously in a staggering manner.

The street lamps flooded the quiet streets in a hazy glow, moonlight cascading against her skin as she picked up the pace—bolting toward the hotel at the end of the block. The fence was faintly in her view, making her smile as she threw her head back to look over her shoulder once more. She hadn't expected him to be practically right next to her, matching her pace with ease as he glanced down at her in slight awe.

They approached the white fence; the pool awaiting just beyond it—closed for the night.

Placing her hands on the gate, she looked back at him with wide, exhilarated eyes. "Now, we just have to hop the fence."

His eyes flickered hesitantly to the gate before peeking back down at her.

"It's okay, c'mon."

As she pulled herself to the top of it, she slung her purse over to the other side, giggling as it smacked loudly on the concrete. Swinging her leg over the top, she peered down at James to see him gnawing at the inside of his lip uneasily.

"You're telling me that the big, muscly motorcycle man is scared to sneak in the pool?" she whispered playfully, her chest heaving from running.

He flashed his white teeth at her as he smiled, shaking his head as he walked up to the fence to hop over the top of it as well.

Her heart could've possibly failed at that moment with how hard it was beating against her chest—either from the running or the way he smiled at her. She couldn't quite tell.

Ophelia popped her head up to watch him climb over once her shoes hit the ground, bouncing excitedly on her heels as she grasped his leather jacket, pulling him towards the bright, blue water. The glow from the pool lamp illuminated the area, the ripples in the water's surface reflecting across them as they looked down at it.

Here goes nothing.

Whisking her baggy hoodie over her head, she took in a shaky breath as her white, lacy bra came into full view. Her braid fell to the middle of her back, tickling her skin as she unbuttoned her jeans to kick them off, too. She observed her bra and panties briefly, the way they made her skin appear more tanned than it was, before nervously looking up at James.

Her comfort zone was entirely surpassed, falling to the ground with her clothes as she stood in front of him, vulnerable in a way that she'd never felt before. Butterflies swarmed around in her stomach as she saw his eyes examining her, flickering down every inch of her exposed skin before meeting her gaze. His throat bobbed as he swallowed thickly. Was he appalled? Shocked? Wishing he'd never agreed to chase her down the street a few minutes ago?

"You're s-*swimming*." He cleared his throat. "In that?"

She nodded timidly.

"I can't," James muttered.

"You can't swim?" she squeaked.

"No, I can *swim*," he urged quietly, rubbing his hands together. "I just—"

"You don't want to swim with me," Ophelia finished gently,

crossing her arms over her chest.

Crap. Crap. Crap.

The slight breeze made goosebumps travel across every inch of her bare skin, her body trembling as she rubbed her arms. Flicking her tongue out to wet her dry lips, she pursed them nervously as she stared down at her white-painted toes.

The sound of James whisking off his leather jacket made her peek up at him through her thick lashes, her mouth popping open as her eyes fell on the scarring of his right arm that had been hidden underneath this entire time. The raised, discolored skin cascaded from his shoulder down to his wrist, faint in some places while more prominent in others. She immediately wondered what could've happened to him to cause such tremendous amounts of scarring.

The look on his face told her that he had expected her to be freaked out by it, but instead, Ophelia was amazed.

Stepping hesitantly closer to him, she reached up to trace her fingertips along the old scars, all the way down to his hands. She could feel how tense he was underneath her touch, but with each caress of her fingers, his shoulders relaxed more and more. Her eyebrows pulled together intently as she studied him. Every pale, white, and pink color swirled into one, carefully guiding her finger on the enigma in front of her.

"It's weird, I know."

She shook her head to disagree, her eyes flickering up to meet his as she kept her fingers lingering against his trembling ones.

"I think it's cool," she commented quietly, flashing him a reassuring smile.

"I don't like for people to see it," James said, watching her with curious eyes as she examined him once more.

While she was too busy worrying about him possibly not wanting to even be here with her right now, he was only fretting that she was going to see his scarred arm.

"Why not?" she whispered. "It's just like a freckle or a beauty mark. It's specific to you. It makes you unique."

A breathless laugh fumbled from his lips. "I wish I could see it that way."

"Well, I think it's badass."

A relieved look cascaded across his features as the corners of his lips turned upwards, his eyes glancing down to follow her fingertips as they glided back up his arm. Their chests were still heaving from the run, the silence filling the air as she continued to trace his arm. Not wanting to put any more pressure on him than she already had, Ophelia held back a grin as she encircled her hands around his arm and tugged him backward with her as she crashed into the cold pool water—breaking any trace of tension as they sank beneath it.

Closing her eyes, she relished in the frigidness against her skin before swimming up to the surface. As her head emerged out of the water, warmth spread through her chest to see James flashing her a toothy grin from across the pool. His wet hair was slightly slicked back, a few trails of water dripping down his face and neck.

"Now my clothes are soaked," he chided in a vivacious manner, pulling at his drenched t-shirt, his smile somehow managing to grow wider.

He looked mouth-watering.

"*Oops.*" She shrugged innocently.

Twisting until she was floating on her back, she kicked her feet lightly until she had glided over towards him in the water, his face coming into view as he hovered above her now. Her head brushed against his abdomen as she stared up at him, his eyes searching hers as they basked in the silence.

"So." James swallowed. "What's something vulnerable about you? I think it's only fair that you give me something now that you've seen my arm."

She narrowed her eyes up at him.

"By default. I never *asked* you to show me."

"I didn't have much of a choice since you brought me night swimming," he teased, his lips forming a faint smirk as he glanced down at her.

She could feel the tension flooding back in, and she wondered if he could feel it, too.

"You could've swam in your jacket."

It was his turn to narrow his eyes down at her now. Biting down gently on her lip to suppress the wide smile that had threatened to form along her mouth, she batted her lashes innocently up at him. It was maddening just how much anticipation that eye contact could hold, how immense the pressure could feel when someone as beautiful as him was staring down at her.

"You have to stop looking at me like that," James pleaded quietly, his eyes never wavering from hers.

"Like what?"

Ophelia flipped over again, standing in the shallow end in front of him, the hair pricking on her arms as the cold air washed over her bare skin. She cocked her head sideways as she peered up at him, nibbling at the inside of her lip.

"Like *that*," he groaned softly.

"I can't look at you?" she asked.

He sighed defeatedly, a weak laugh escaping his lips as he leaned back against the siding of the pool. "I'm too old for you, Clark. I'm practically a fossil."

He remembered her last name, too.

"Hmm." Ophelia hummed gently, stepping forward as her hand grazed his underneath the water. "If you think I'm too young, then how come you're focusing on how I'm looking at you? Wouldn't you just…not *care*?"

James pressed his lips together, hiding his smile as best as he could as his eyes averted hers.

"That's what I thought," she told him sweetly.

She could feel his gaze on her as she pushed away, swimming backward as she spread her arms out and stared up at the night sky. Tiny stars speckled the dark atmosphere, and the moon was only a crescent shape tonight. The air was cool against her damp skin that wasn't submerged in the water, making goosebumps prick along her shoulders and neck.

"What's your last name?"

"My last name?" he echoed softly.

She nodded, the water rippling around her. "You know mine. I think it's fair that I know yours, too."

"Benton."

Ophelia snickered. "James Benton."

And then she was suddenly beneath the water, sinking as James dunked her underneath, his laugh echoing in her ears as she broke through the surface to rub her eyes. Her mouth parted as she scoffed animatedly, watching as he climbed from the pool, throwing her a playful look over his shoulder.

"What was that for?" she squeaked, observing him as he picked up his jacket from the concrete.

"You pushed me in."

He smiled as he walked towards the white fence, throwing his jacket over his wet shoulder as he began to climb back over it, his eyes falling on her figure still in the pool.

"Where are you going?" she whispered loudly, swimming to the edge and putting her hands on the concrete, water pooling around her fingers.

"Back to work," he said, his boots hitting the ground on the other side as he hopped down.

Ophelia made a pouting face.

"Don't worry, Clark. You'll see me again."

As she watched his figure disappear from view, she groaned loudly as she realized that she still didn't get his damn number.

CHAPTER THREE

Ophelia was quickly reminded why she never wanted to tell her parents that she was home for the summer as she listened to her mother scold her from the other end of the phone.

The shrill volume of her voice made Ophelia grimace as she twirled her finger around the lid of her coffee that she had been so excited about this morning. Squinting down in annoyance at the etches in the marble of the kitchen counter, her mother droned on and *on*. The condescending manner of her mother's words was one that she was quite used to hearing throughout her childhood, but that never made it any less maddening to listen to.

"You know your father hates it when we find out you're back in town from everyone else but you."

That was her way of inadvertently saying that it was *her* who hated that.

"I thought you guys would be busy with work." She sighed, rolling her eyes as she grabbed her purse and coffee before walking out the door. "I've only been home for a little over a week, anyway."

"I don't know why you didn't just finish another semester over the summer," her mother grumbled in a patronizing tone. "You should be more focused on your studies if you want to make it into medical school, Ophelia."

Pinching the bridge of her nose, she walked down the hallway, jabbing the button for the elevator with her finger in an impatient manner. She could already feel the migraine forming inside of her temples, one that even the caffeine in her hand wouldn't fix by the time her mother was finished babbling about her usual nonsense.

"Thanks for the vote of confidence, Mom."

Her parents would be livid if they knew that she had almost zero interest in the medical career field these days. Ophelia had contemplated switching majors at least three times already—the only thing holding her back was the conversation that would arise with them after deciding something that big. She grew up around her abrasive surgeon parents her entire life. Why would she want to continue the cycle?

Her college.

Her *career* choice.

All of it was them forcing her to follow in their footsteps. If she had normal parents or a life where she was allowed to freely make decisions that made her happy, she would've gone to culinary school instead. Baking was the one thing she loved to do.

"You have big shoes to fill," her mother lectured in a vexed manner. "You can't have surgeons as parents and then barely get by during medical school."

She wondered if it would be too dramatic to throw her phone down the elevator shaft.

"Yep. You don't have to remind me."

Picking at the fuzz from her cardigan, Ophelia stepped from the elevator as it reached the first floor, gnawing at the inside of her lip as she walked through the foyer of Wren's apartment building. Sweat had begun to prick along her forehead and top lip—her body feeling heated from the conversation and the coffee, making her regret her decision to wear the layers during a California summer. She held the phone between her ear and her shoulder as she started to shrug off the cardigan.

"I hope Wren isn't the reason behind your willingness to slack off recently."

And *there* it was.

The only person on the planet who loved and accepted Ophelia for who she was, so of course, her parents despised her best friend. Her entire childhood consisted of both her mother and father constantly yapping about how much of a bad influence she was.

"Not *this* again," Ophelia grumbled in annoyance.

"I thought that the older you were, the more you would finally realize that you could use a much better friend, honey."

The sweet pet name at the end of a rather pompous statement made her want to gag.

Crossly whisking open the front door to the entrance of the building, Ophelia's eyes widened as her coffee cup slipped from her fingers, crashing to the ground and staining the concrete in the precious liquid that she was looking forward to after the dense phone call. Her heart sank inside her chest as her mouth popped open in disappointment.

"You made me drop my coffee," she whined in an exasperated huff, pressing her palm against her forehead as she mourned the loss of her much-needed caffeine. "So frankly, I don't like you very much right now. I'm hanging up."

"Ophelia Clark, don't you dare—"

Click.

Discarding the remnants of her coffee cup into the trash bin outside, Ophelia stuffed her phone into her purse with an aggravated sigh.

Her mother sucked the good out of everything without even having to be in the same vicinity.

"You miserable, *miserable* woman," she hissed under her breath, staring down at the brown stains along the concrete with a small pout. "All I wanted was my coffee—"

"Hi."

Ophelia jumped slightly, snapping her head up as her eyes met the blue ones that she hadn't seen in almost a week. Her full lips parted as she blinked up at James—who donned a cream-colored sweater almost like the one she previously had on. Her heart thumped harshly in surprise at seeing him. The flutters erupted deep in her belly as she observed his rings and necklace that hung low against his chest.

He looked particularly delicious this morning.

"Hello," she squeaked, swallowing the lump that had formed in her throat at the sight of him.

"Rough morning?"

His eyebrow raised curiously as he smirked ever-so-faintly down at her, chewing at the inside of his lip as his eyes flickered to the spilled coffee. His right arm caught her attention. The sleeve was pulled up a quarter length; the sun shining down on the scarring that trailed down his forearm.

Ophelia struggled to hide her smile—perhaps she had more of an impact on him than she originally had thought.

"It's a long story," she commented softly.

"*Hmm*." James hummed gently, licking his lips as he examined her. "You seem to have a lot of those."

She wondered what those lips would feel like on hers.

"Are you free?" she quipped playfully, stepping forward timidly as she peeked up at him. "I could use a wise old man's perspective on it."

James tilted his head sideways as he chuckled at her words, taking his bottom lip between his white teeth as he glanced down at the ground briefly—sending heated tingles down her spine. It was hard to focus when her eyes kept falling on his pink lips, the way his eyes crinkled when he smiled, or his faint innocence when it came to her obvious flirting.

"Of *course*, of course." He nodded enthusiastically, extending out his elbow as he gestured for her to loop her arm through his. "Let's go get some more coffee so you don't have to keep talking to those stains on the ground."

How cute.

She always liked someone who could match her sense of humor, or at least keep up with it.

Grinning sweetly up at him, she stepped towards him and hooked her arm through his, wasting no opportunity to grip his bicep in her fingers. And she was far from disappointed as she felt the large muscles beneath her hand—only making the covey of butterflies dive deeper into her belly and down to her core as she imagined the strength that could emanate from his grip.

"I promise I don't always talk to myself."

"Hmm, that's relieving to hear," he teased gently as they walked down the sidewalk. "Because that was totally a deal-breaker for *me,* you know, the guy with the messed up arm."

"Speaking of," Ophelia countered curiously. "I see that you're not trying to hide it."

He glanced down at his forearm that emerged from the sleeve of his sweater, flexing it faintly as he struggled to hide his smile. His eyes flickered down at her—examining her lips for a brief second before meeting her eyes. She mentally made another tally to the list of how many times she'd caught him looking at her mouth.

"Yeah," James said innocently, nodding his head. "Someone told me that it was badass, so I thought I would try it out, you know?"

The sun had just begun to cascade across the streets of downtown Los Angeles, the early morning breeze giving her goosebumps despite the warmth of his arm intertwined with her own. Although, the chills more than likely had everything to do with their proximity and nothing to do with the wind.

As they rounded the corner of the street, approaching the tiny, local coffee shop where the employees knew her and Wren by name, he reached out to whisk the door open for her as he gestured for her to walk in first.

"Sounds like a pretty smart person, if you ask me," she commented teasingly over her shoulder before stepping inside.

The cafe smelled of coffee beans and freshly cooked danishes, filled with brown booths and dimly lit lamps dangling above all the tables. A few people were reading a book or sipping at their coffee as they entered, the atmosphere just as relaxing as she remembered. She wanted to own a place almost like this one, somewhere she could bake and sell pastries.

"Go sit," James murmured next to her ear, leaning down from behind her, his breath fanning across the back of her neck. "How do you take your coffee?"

Turning to face him, she squinted playfully up at him as she crossed her arms against her chest, attempting to nonchalantly compose her breathing. They were barely even a foot apart now. He was close enough to reach out and touch if she wanted.

"Surprise me," she chirped softly.

Shaking his head jocosely, James faintly rolled his eyes as he smiled down at her. "Fine. Now sit."

The statement was harmless, innocent, even—but she couldn't help but gnaw at the inside of her lip at his demanding tone.

"Yes, *sir*."

She observed him intently as she took a seat at one of the booths, resting her chin in her palm as she ogled at the size of his back while he walked up to the counter to order. It was so wide, and his beefy arms only made him look bigger. It was enough to make her dab at her lip to make sure she wasn't drooling at the sight of him.

Ophelia made it her mission to crack his shell. She wanted

to see everything on the inside. She'd only just scratched the surface, and she couldn't help but want to claw her way in.

A few minutes had passed before he approached the booth she was perched at, setting the coffee down in front of her before he took the seat across from her. Resting his elbows on the table, he flashed her a small smile and his eyebrows raised impatiently, glancing down at the coffee suggestively.

Ophelia brought the brown liquid to her mouth, taking a long sip.

An espresso with a hint of steamed milk.

Impressive.

"You're more observant than I took you for," she commented slyly.

"Well, I'm not very talkative, remember? I have more time to pay attention to detail."

Brushing her waves back over her shoulder, she leaned against the seat, sipping at her coffee once more as she peeked at him over the cup.

His tone was teasing, *slightly* flirtatious.

"Are you teasing me?" she quipped, her lips twitching in the corners.

The back-and-forth banter between them only made her attraction to him grow. The tension was thick now, at least for her. The pressure between her legs was almost humiliating at this point.

"I don't know," he drawled out with a dramatic sigh, leaning back in the seat as well, his eyes unwavering. "Do you like to be teased?"

Ophelia practically choked on her hot coffee, crossing her

legs as the flutters that held her stomach in a vice grip spiraled between them, setting the cup down as she took her bottom lip between her teeth. Clicking her tongue, she leaned forward and rested her elbows on the table once more. As her eyes studied him carefully, he replicated her movements, closing the distance between them as he brought his elbows to the table, too.

"About that long story," she said, reeling the conversation back in before she needed to take a trip to the bathroom just to breathe properly again.

"I'm listening."

He dropped his hands on the table, inches away from her coffee cup.

"I may or may not have relentless, overbearing parents," Ophelia continued, casually bringing her hands down to cradle the cup.

"*Ah*," James acknowledged with a slight nod. "So that's the miserable woman you were talking about."

"You heard all of that?"

"I may or may not have been listening," he said, his fingers stretching out slightly, dangerously close to grazing her own.

Ophelia didn't know what had gotten into this man when he crawled out of bed this morning, but it was exactly what she'd been hoping to see. In a perfect world, she probably would have leaped across the table by now. She was feeding on the tension like she was starving.

"She wants me to be exactly like her. Follow in her exact footsteps," she mumbled, tearing her eyes away from his to watch her finger draw circles on the rim of her cup. "She hates that I'm nothing like her."

"Why do you think she hates that?"

"Because there's never an opportunity where she doesn't find one way or another to express it."

Her voice shook, and she realized just how vulnerable she had sounded.

Yuck.

This was usually the point where she would put up the wall, slam the door shut, and stop any possibility of feelings becoming involved. She hated the way being vulnerable made her sound. It was why she could never make it past the first few dates. It was easier just to agree on being friends with benefits—no feelings attached, no sappy conversations. If it ended, *when* it ended, no one would get hurt because no one cared.

His fingers flexed outwards to faintly caress hers, pulling her from her intrusive train of thought. Her eyes peeked up to meet his curious ones.

Sighing, she leaned back against the seat again, bringing her hands away from the table and away from their tense bubble to rub her jeans as she smiled timidly. She took a few long sips of her coffee as the silence shrouded them.

"Is that what she was doing before you spilled your coffee?"

Her eyes flickered up to him. "Unfortunately."

Despite creating distance between them, his knee found hers, rubbing against it gently as he watched her. He wasn't crowding her or suffocating her with too many questions. He was just letting her know that he was there. It made her heart skip inside her chest.

"I'm sorry," he offered after a few beats.

This man was too good to be true. No doubt about it.

"So," she said, changing the subject. "Feel like walking me back home?"

James examined her, his eyes trailing across her features as his lips formed into a thin line, smiling half-heartedly. The look that flashed in his eyes told her he understood, but he didn't push the topic anymore—which she was thankful for. Instead, he stood up from the booth and extended his hand from her seat. A gentleman, as usual.

Ophelia felt bad for allowing herself to shut down from talking about her feelings, but it was instinctive, like a knee-jerk response. With parents like hers, she wasn't used to opening up to people that actually wanted to know how she felt. So she strayed away from it to avoid it altogether.

Maybe it wasn't the male population, maybe it was *her* that was all wrong.

"If I overstepped, I'm sorry," he apologized slowly as she stood up. "I wasn't trying to pressure—"

"*No*," Ophelia squeaked, glancing up at him as he towered over her. "You didn't do anything wrong. I promise. It's me. It has nothing to do with you."

His eyebrows pulled together worriedly as he chewed at the inside of his lip.

"James, seriously. It's okay," she continued, looping her arm through his once again as they exited the cafe and stepped into the warm sunlight. "Just ignore my *parental* issues."

"If it makes you feel any better," he mumbled. "I know

exactly what you mean."

"You do?"

Her head snapped up to gawk at him as they walked down the sidewalk, her lips parting as she waited for him to respond.

He nodded. "And we don't have to talk about it if you don't want to talk about it."

"Thank you," she whispered, squeezing his arm with her fingers. "And thank you for the coffee."

As they approached the apartment building, she peered at him out of the corner of her eye as they came to a stop, dropping her arm gently as they twisted to face each other now. His face was relaxed again, a slight smile playing along his lips as he reached his hand out between them.

"Friends?"

Her heart lurched in her chest.

It sounded like the perfect storm. Friends could be dangerous territory with the way he made her stomach feel like it was practicing for the Olympics, but friends are all that they could ever be. He was here permanently, while her stay was only temporary.

Placing her palm into his, they shook each other's hands delicately.

"*Friends,*" she agreed.

As their hands lingered and their eyes locked for a few moments, Ophelia thought that *maybe*—it wouldn't be the worst thing in the world if she opened up to him. He made it so easy, sometimes.

That's what friends do, right?

CHAPTER FOUR

"I'M GOING TO START charging your ass for all of these free therapy sessions that you don't listen to." Wren narrowed her eyes down at Ophelia, her hands on her hips.

Ophelia grimaced playfully, peeking up at her through squinted eyes as she pressed her lips together tightly.

"But we agreed to be friends. That's good, right?"

The tightening of her jaw and the pursing of her glossed lips told Ophelia that it was undoubtedly not good at all. Wren was more than likely waiting on some successful *"I went back to his place and we had sex"* story, but she had buried herself in the friend zone instead. It was practically a twenty-foot grave.

Here lies Ophelia Clark—dumb bitch.

"With benefits?" Wren raised one eyebrow.

"Well, we didn't say that."

"Did you happen to get his number this time?"

In her dreams.

"No—"

Wren threw her hands in the air as she spun around on her heel, an exasperated groan leaving her lips as she began to pace back and forth in front of where Ophelia sat perched on the couch. Her motherly stance made it feel as though she was about to give a long lecture on the *dos* and *don'ts* of hooking up with boys at bars.

"You're killing me, Lia," she whined as her head fell back, her fingers reaching up to pinch the bridge of her nose. "He practically fucks you with his eyes and you freak out. No feelings attached, remember? You're here to get laid, not marry the guy."

"I know, I *know*," Ophelia groaned softly. "But then we started talking about my horrid relationship with my parents and it got too *deep*—"

"Are you going to let your mother ruin another thing for you?"

Wren's confrontational approach to life could be somewhat of a harsh one, but she loved her for it. When she reacted this way, it was coming from a good place. She needed someone in her circle to give her some tough love now and again—something her parents could never give her. They chose the no love at all pathway, instead, and *their* words derived from the depths of hell.

Ophelia bounced her feet against the carpet hastily.

"No."

Wren cupped her hand behind her ear as she glanced over at her. "I'm sorry, I couldn't quite hear you."

"*No*," Ophelia said louder.

"No," Wren repeated enthusiastically, walking towards her and grabbing her shoulders to shake her gently. "That witch doesn't get to ruin anything else for you, so put some cute clothes on and let's go. We're going to the bar."

"We?" she squeaked, her thick eyebrows raising. "We're going to the bar?"

"You obviously need your wing woman."

This is why she was her best friend.

"Okay," Ophelia murmured slowly, looking down at her casual attire which consisted of a sweater and some worn mom jeans. "But what's wrong with what I'm wearing?"

Wren seemed as though she was inches away from her wits' end as her eyes rolled, her mouth popping open as she growled under her breath before disappearing into her bedroom without another word. Ophelia could hear her rummaging through her drawers faintly before her red hair flashed in the hallway, walking quickly towards her with a white-colored shirt in her hand.

"Here. I'm going to pretend you didn't just ask me that," she chirped in a softer tone, throwing the shirt in her lap. "Put this on."

Ophelia held the crop top up to her chest, her eyebrows knitting together skeptically at the small cloth that would expose more skin than it would cover. She remembered a time when she wouldn't have ever hesitated to wear something like this, a time where she hardly lacked confidence—but throw a hot, older guy into the mix and all of that seemed to fly completely out of the window.

"Your boobs will look fantastic in that top, and tonight you *need* magnificent-looking boobs."

Ophelia sighed.

She was going to need a lot more than her fantastic boobs to get her through tonight.

Ophelia's feet were already killing her in the cute, white high heels that Wren had insisted that she wear with her jeans and cleavage-heavy crop top as they walked down the sidewalk towards *The Beer Lounge*. The pain pulsated through her heels, throbbing along her ankles towards her calf muscles.

She had never been a heels type of girl, she'd rather throw on a pair of chunky Converse any day.

As they stood in front of the doors, she suddenly felt overly dressed and entirely too self-conscious. Brushing some of her blonde locks behind her ear, Ophelia sucked in a deep breath as she observed her figure in the reflection of the glass. As cute as she appeared, for some reason, she still felt lackluster.

Meanwhile, Wren looked like she walked straight out of a magazine, as usual.

"You came here by yourself before you knew him?" Wren asked sheepishly. "*Willingly?*"

She tried not to giggle at Wren's hesitant expression as she stared up at the sign that flickered faintly. Smacking her friend's shoulder, she shook her head.

"It's not as bad as you think, Wren."

It was undoubtedly not the most pleasant-looking place, just slightly outdated, but nothing that wasn't easily fixable.

Ophelia prided herself on not judging people on what they had or didn't have. She knew not everyone came from money. If it had been up to her, she would've picked any other life than the one she had growing up in a rich household. Money did not buy happiness.

"Tell that to the creepy, flickering sign," she grumbled dubiously, peeking up at the buzzing bar sign once more as she daintily grabbed the door and whisked it open for them to walk inside.

It had been four measly days since Ophelia had seen James, but her heart reacted as if she hadn't seen him in weeks. It thumped against her chest erratically as her eyes fell on him behind the bar, donning a blue t-shirt that squeezed his muscular arms and a pair of jeans. His arm was uncovered once more, piquing her interest and making the corners of her lips twitch faintly.

Who knew that all he needed was a slight confidence boost for him to feel secure in flaunting it around freely?

It was quite cute.

"Holy *shit*."

Ophelia turned to look at Wren, whose jaw was practically on the floor as she observed the hottie behind the bar, struggling to hold back a snicker as her friend's green eyes flickered towards her in awe.

"Shh, Wren." She giggled quietly. "I know."

"You said he was hot, Lia, but for fuck's sake. You didn't tell me he was—"

"Ophelia?"

A deep voice made both of their heads snap up to see

James, hands perched against the bar counter, with a white rag thrown over his shoulder as his eyes examined the two of them hesitantly. The corner of his mouth turned upwards slightly as the girls approached him, Ophelia sending him a tiny wave before she ducked her head shyly, brushing her hair behind her ear as she gulped.

"Hello," she greeted.

She felt Wren jab her with her bony elbow, clearing her throat nonchalantly as they stood in front of him at the bar.

"This is Wren, the friend I've been staying with," Ophelia continued, peeking up at him briefly before glancing over at her friend. "Wren, this is James."

"It's nice to meet you."

His eyes had fallen on Wren for a moment as he spoke, only to immediately flicker back to Ophelia as they trailed across her features, examining her outfit. She watched as they glimpsed ever-so-faintly at her chest, her stomach doing somersaults as he gnawed gently at the inside of his lips.

She made a mental note to thank Wren later.

"Likewise," Wren responded, hopping onto one of the bar stools. "A beer for me and a—"

"Shot of tequila," he finished for her, his eyes falling on Ophelia once more. "Coming right up."

Wren raised her eyebrows curiously at Ophelia as she took the stool next to her, pursing her lips suggestively as she flicked her hair back over her shoulder.

"He is *so* into you," she whispered under her breath. "And I was right about the shirt."

"What's your big plan of action then, miss wing woman?"

Wren sighed.

As James brought over the glass of beer and shot of tequila, setting it down in front of them, Wren peeked at Ophelia out of the corner of her eye. Before she could even begin to question what exactly it was that she was cooking up in her brilliant mind, Wren innocently reached for her beer, only to knock over the glass and send the bread-smelling liquid all over Ophelia. It drenched the white crop top and her lap as a gasp escaped her lips.

Ophelia twisted her head to gape at Wren, her hands hovering in the air as she blinked slowly in shock at her friend.

"*Oops*," Wren squeaked artlessly, batting her long eyelashes up at James, who looked just as confused as Ophelia had felt. "Do you have an extra shirt? Or maybe something in the back to help Lia clean up? I'm such a klutz."

Ophelia could feel her cheeks heating up—probably from the mixture of humiliation and inability to control her laughter at the situation before her.

"Uh, yeah." He nodded quickly, looking over at Ophelia with a friendly smile. "C'mon, let's get you cleaned up."

Nodding faintly, she smiled through tight lips as she hopped down from the stool, nudging Wren with her arm as she glared at her.

"I *hate* you."

"You love me," Wren cooed hushedly. "Now go work your magic, while I work mine."

Following Wren's eyes, Ophelia caught sight of Sean at the opposite end of the bar. His dark eyes were having a hard time avoiding Wren as well. She made another mental note to ask

Wren a million questions later about that. Rolling her eyes, she let out a drastic sigh as she left her friend alone to get her flirt on as she followed James through the door that led to the back of the bar. The music sounded muffled now as they kept walking, the quietness seeping in its place as she kept her eyes on his back.

It was hard not to focus on how tall he was, towering over her tiny height, as she observed him from behind.

"I'm sorry about Wren," Ophelia murmured after a few moments. "She can be a bit...*forward*."

James laughed.

They approached a small, low-lit office near the back, scattered with boxes of paperwork that read *final notice* in bright red letters—making her heart lurch with sympathy inside of her chest. The boxes were dusty. A thick layer had formed on top of every exposed surface.

She wondered if those were for the bar or where he lived.

"No, it's okay," he assured her gently, shuffling around in the gym bag that was sitting on top of the faded desk inside the office. "It's funny. I thought that *you* were forward when I met you."

"*Me*? I—"

Her words halted inside of her throat as James suddenly turned around, whisking his t-shirt from his body, revealing his chiseled abdomen beneath. She choked on the breath she had tried to inhale as she observed how defined his torso was. Her eyes darted from his tattoos to his broad chest down to his waistline before she gulped. Her neck felt hot as the blush traveled from her cheeks down to her chest.

"Here, you can wear this."

Her lips popped open at his words, her eyes darting from his outstretched hand to his muscles, to his eyes, and back again.

Hot wasn't even the correct word for him.

"No, I'm okay," she mumbled shakily, still taken aback at the sight of how ridiculously fit he looked. "It'll dry. You keep it."

Running his tongue along his bottom lip, he turned to grab his black leather jacket from his bag, throwing it over her shoulders and pulling her towards him by the collar. Butterflies swarmed inside her stomach at their proximity. They fluttered up through her chest, constricting her lungs and making it hard to breathe. She could almost feel his breath fanning across her exposed skin. She never thought she'd be this close to his bare torso, but here she was, close enough to see every indention and detail.

The air mixed with the dampness of the shirt made her nipples harden beneath the fabric.

"You know," he said, hesitating slightly. "White fabric is see-through when it gets wet."

Holy—

Goosebumps traveled down her arms, the hairs prickling as she blinked up at him through her long lashes, her heart malfunctioning inside of her chest.

"Now who's being forward?"

His lips twitched at her words.

He seemed as though he was about to speak, his eyebrows knitting together as his mouth opened more to prepare himself, but the moment was too soon interrupted by Sean.

"We got some assholes beating each other up out here," Sean said, his lips forming a thin line as his eyes darted between the pair and then to James' shirtless figure with a slight eyebrow raise. "Breaking our tables and shit."

James dropped his head as he squeezed his eyes shut.

"Shit. Okay, I'm coming."

Ophelia chewed at the inside of her lip as she peeked up at him, her fingers pulling at the leather jacket to take it off. "Wait, here—"

He shook his head, his eyes lighting up as they took in her appearance. Grabbing his t-shirt to whisk back on, he said, "No, keep it. It looks better on you, anyway."

Their gaze lingered for a few moments before he walked around her, brushing her shoulder with his own, disappearing back up front before either one of them could say another word. She was frozen in place for a few seconds, still comprehending what had just happened.

Friends, my ass.

Taking her bottom lip between her teeth, Ophelia tore a piece of paper from the stack of boxes near his desk and jotted down her phone number so Wren wouldn't strangle her to death for not making some sort of move this time.

At the bottom of the note, she signed,

Since we're being forward.

CHAPTER FIVE

UNKNOWN: *Hello pretty girl.*

Ophelia bit down on her bottom lip to hide her smile as her eyes examined the text message that popped up on her screen.

Pounding rain trickled down the windowpane in the living room where she sat perched on the couch, legs crossed underneath her as she stared down at her phone with a cheesy grin forming on her face. It was likely the first bit of rain that Los Angeles had seen all year, covering every inch of the city in tiny droplets and saturating the dying grass that had needed a day like today.

OPHELIA: *Still being forward, I see.*

Ophelia stuck her thumb between her teeth, nibbling on it softly as she pressed the blue arrow to respond.

JAMES: *Yep—forward and wondering if you felt like coming down to the bar right now?*

OPHELIA: *Sean is probably sick of me distracting you while on the job.*

As much as Ophelia wanted to throw nearly all of her coherent thoughts that she had left in her mind out of the window and tackle the man—she needed to at least try and pretend she wouldn't fall on her knees at his feet if he had asked her to. The whole *"friends being forward with each other"* thing only made the tension ten times as strong, anyway.

And she wanted the tension to feel as thick as honey.

JAMES: *Sean isn't here, actually. This rain has us closed down for business today because the ceiling is leaking, so I thought maybe I would ask if you wanted to come help me out.*

Her and James alone? In his bar? With all of this rain?

She would gladly make a deal with the devil for this type of opportunity.

Ophelia plopped down on her stomach as she whisked her feet into the air before typing back. It was pathetic how giddy his text messages made her feel.

OPHELIA: *I suppose I could since we're friends and all.*

JAMES: *Try not to wear white this time. You know, since it's raining and all.*

She could feel her cheeks heating up as she jumped up from

the couch, kicked off her pajama pants, and grabbed a pair of jeans from the guest bedroom. Her hair fell in her face as she hurriedly swapped her raggedy t-shirt for a rain jacket. Struggling to maintain her balance, she quickly pulled on her favorite pair of chunky, pink Converse before she responded.

OPHELIA: *Yes, sir.*

The rain had only begun to fall even harder as Ophelia made her way down to the foyer of the apartment building to wait on the Uber she had called for while still in the elevator. She watched it pour from the gray sky as she peered out of the giant windows, crossing her arms in front of her chest as she paced back and forth excitedly. She needed to exude any ounce of elation before arriving so that she could continue her composed facade around him. Although, with the way her heart thudded against her chest in anticipation, the feat seemed nearly impossible.

The suspense only doubled in size as her ride whisked her away to *The Beer Lounge*—butterflies swarming maddeningly inside of her stomach with every minute she watched the scenery flash by in the backseat. The feelings of being nervous and exhilarated blended after a while, the line becoming rather blurry as the seconds ticked by. Her hands grew clammy as she rubbed them together.

She couldn't remember the last time she had felt this anxious about spending alone time with a guy, or if she ever had.

As the car came to a halt in front of the bar, Ophelia stared through the misty window up at the flickering sign, sucking in a deep breath.

The downpour of rain dampened her hair and smacked against her face as she stepped out of the Uber, running up to the entrance of the bar. Her shoes sloshed in the puddles on the sidewalk.

As she whisked the door open and stepped inside, Ophelia's jaw dropped at the partially flooded floors of the bar. The water that drenched her shoes outside was nothing compared to this. Buckets were scattered across the floor and tables, attempting to catch more water that was pouring through the ceiling.

"Yeah, it's kind of worse than I made it seem over text."

Ophelia lifted her head to see James walking from around the bar, his boots splashing through the water as he approached her with his hands inside his leather jacket pockets. His eyes fell on her simultaneously, trailing down her attire and back up again as the corner of his lip twitched.

As her eyes fell on the gold chain around his neck, she couldn't help but notice the black outline of what looked like a fresh tattoo popping out of the collar of his t-shirt next to the ones she'd noticed that first night at the bar. The very muscular torso that she saw a few days ago with a brand new tattoo on it. The collected facade was going to be much harder than she originally anticipated.

"You kind of failed to mention that the place was flooded," she teased softly, her eyebrows cinching together sympathetically.

His nose scrunched slightly as his lips formed into a thin line, dropping his head playfully as he squeezed his eyes shut.

"I'm hoping it's salvageable, but I'm not sure how much water damage there is."

Her heart lurched inside of her chest for him—her mind flickering back to the final notices that she had seen in his office the other day. Putting two and two together only told her that he wouldn't have the money for damages. Ophelia felt sad just thinking about the possibility of James having to shut down his bar.

Reaching her hand up to squeeze his shoulder gently, she gave him a reassuring smile.

"Well, c'mon, I'm here to help," she reminded him. "Show me what I can do."

"I have these giant brooms that I've been using to sweep some of the water outside," he explained. "Luckily, there's also a drain in the back that's helped some."

She nodded understandingly. "Then let's get to sweeping, mister."

And that was what they did for a while. Ophelia swept as much water out of the front door as she could, despite the water that seemed to only slosh right back inside, while James swept water towards the drain in the back of the building near his office. The only sound that could be heard was the rain pelting against the roof and the water that was splashing into the buckets. One bucket had already started to spill over, replacing any water she was desperately trying to push outside.

With a tired sigh, Ophelia propped her broom against the counter as she tiptoed through the water toward the back to get James. Pushing through the door, she peeked into the room to see him wiping his forehead with the back of his hand as he groaned under his breath.

As she walked slowly through the water, her eyes caught sight of another room to her right—a tiny cot resting inside that had a pillow and a blanket laying on top of it.

Did he *live* here?

"That's, *uh*—"

James tried to explain, but he ultimately fell silent as reached up to rub the back of his neck.

"Do you sleep here?" Ophelia asked in a small voice, peeking up at his humiliated expression through her lashes.

"I, um, yeah," he sighed.

Her stomach churned as his face fell just slightly. His throat bobbed as he swallowed thickly, his eyes not quite lifting to meet her own. He was undoubtedly embarrassed, although he had no reason to be, especially not with her.

"I'm so sorry that this happened," she said in a small voice, exhaling gently. "I know this must be frustrating."

As Ophelia observed the sad, puppy-dog expression that was plastered across his features, she stood up on her tiptoes and flung her arms around his neck. Squeezing him tightly, she pressed her face into the crevice of his warm neck as she breathed him in.

His smell was intoxicating. Vanilla, sandalwood, and a hint of leather.

It made her head spin.

James seemed stunned at first. His hands hovered by his sides as she enveloped her arms around him—something clicking inside of his mind as he pressed them lightly against her back. Pulling her closer to him, he buried his face into her hair as his shoulders relaxed.

The whirl of flutters inside of her stomach was overwhelming now, threatening to absorb her oxygen as the breath halted inside of her lungs. Ophelia wondered if he could feel her heart hammering against her chest, reverberating through her as she pressed against him.

"You don't have to be embarrassed with me, James. I would never judge you."

She could hear him take a shaky, deep breath. His hands gripped her rain jacket as they continued to embrace each other, his chest vibrating against her own as his heart pumped erratically.

She loosened her grip after a few moments, falling back down on her heels as she looked up at him. Her hands lingered on his neck as her fingers grazed the necklace dangling around it.

James' blue eyes searched hers as they stared at each other, their faces mere inches apart.

He was so close that she could see the freckle on the right-hand side of his forehead, the crinkle next to his eyes, and his elongated nose that sat perfectly symmetrical in the middle of his face. She stored these characteristics in her memory, etching them there for safekeeping.

"*Friends,*" he muttered, almost too faint to even hear.

"What?"

"We're friends," he said louder this time, flicking his tongue out to wet his bottom lip.

"Yes," she whispered.

"*Just* friends."

"Mhm." Ophelia hummed quietly, sliding her hands down his neck towards his chest to pull away.

It was a pitiful hum—one that sounded as though she were trying to convince herself more than just him.

James grasped both of her hands with his own before she could step backward, his cold fingers making goosebumps rise along her skin.

"Then you should probably tell me that I shouldn't kiss you right now."

The flutters spiraled down to her core at his words, her lips parting in awe as she watched his eyes flicker down to them hungrily. His eyebrows knitted together faintly as his eyes glanced back up to meet hers. A need wavered inside of them that she hadn't seen before.

He shouldn't kiss her. It would complicate things. Tacking on the benefits always complicated friendships. They could never truly be anything more, but now that the words had left his lips, she couldn't think about anything *but* kissing him.

"Why shouldn't you?" she blurted out softly.

Shit.

"*Ophelia,*" he panted weakly.

His eyes were practically begging her to tell him not to. And that was somehow the hottest thing she had ever seen in her entire life.

So hot that her brain threatened to shut off entirely, her feet arching to stand back up on her tiptoes to press her lips against his when suddenly a weak part of the ceiling broke off and collapsed to the ground with an immense amount of water following it. Perhaps it was the universe reminding her that it was a terrible, *terrible* idea.

James pulled her away from it almost immediately, pushing her behind him, both of their chests heaving now as they watched the water pour through the open hole in the ceiling.

"Shit," he muttered.

"You can't stay here, James." Ophelia grasped his forearm. "There's not much we can do with it still raining like this."

"Yeah," he whispered, glancing around at the water on the ground that had risen by a couple of inches at least.

This man couldn't catch a break.

"Hey." She tugged his arm until he was facing her once more, cocking her head sideways as she peered up at him. "Come sleep at the apartment tonight. We can come back tomorrow and assess the damage."

He looked hesitantly down at her.

"I don't know, that's too much to ask—"

"*James*," she said sweetly.

"I can go stay with Sean, you really don't have to help me like this."

Her hand glided down his arm to grasp his, squeezing reassuringly as she tugged him towards her, pressing her chin against his arm as she blinked up at him.

"James, come stay with me," Ophelia demanded with a playful pout. "Wren is staying with her brother and won't be home until tomorrow, anyway. It'll be fine."

He peeked down at her, his lips turning upwards.

"Okay, I'll stay with you."

CHAPTER SIX

Ophelia observed James from her bedroom doorway as he fluffed the pillow on the couch and grabbed the blanket that was draped over the back. The dim light from the nearby lamp cascaded across his figure, casting a glow on his features as he began to whisk his shirt over his head. His muscular torso came into view, revealing a fresh tattoo.

It was a beautiful piece of a girl just along his collarbone, trailing across his chest. Her hair fell in front of her face, partially hiding her eyes that held a prominent story inside of them. A sad one, at that. Even the space between her brows was cinched faintly.

It was the realest-looking tattoo Ophelia had ever seen. The shading and detail were astonishing. But who was she? She must have been someone special to him.

"Who's the girl?" Ophelia asked softly, pushing from the door frame as she walked into the living room.

His blue eyes flickered up to look at her before glancing down at his chest, a faint smile dancing along his bearded lips.

"She's my sister," he murmured.

She trailed her fingers along the back of the couch as she

rounded it, her eyes observing the tattoo once more as she stood in front of him now.

"She's beautiful."

James' eyes studied her intently as she reached her hand up, caressing the artwork with her pointer finger, tracing along his warm skin as she examined the tattoo further. His chest heaved slowly as she outlined the ink with her finger, and his eyebrows pulled together meekly.

"Yeah, she passed away a few years back," he whispered, gnawing at the inside of his mouth.

Her eyes left the tattoo to peer up at him forlornly, blinking slowly as her hand fell.

"Oh," Ophelia murmured. "I'm sorry, James."

He stepped back hesitantly, reaching up to rub his neckline—his gold necklace moving slightly against his skin as he did so.

That damn necklace.

"It's okay."

She could sense his ambivalence, examining the way his body language changed and the way his eyes stared down at the floor. Ophelia was no stranger to feeling closed off from others. If anything, she might even be the queen of emotional damage. She completely understood the reclusion.

Not wanting to press the issue any further, she stepped back simultaneously, brushing her waves behind her ears.

"Where did you get your necklace?" Ophelia swallowed thickly. "I noticed that you wear it a lot."

He fiddled with the chain. "It was my sister's."

So much for not pressing the issue.

She nodded. "I like it."

James held onto the pendant as he lifted his head to look at her. His lips parted as if to say something, but nothing came out. Instead, they clamped shut once more. But his eyes spoke everything that his mouth couldn't; it was a sore subject. The day had already been hard enough for him, so she could only imagine how overwhelmed he must be feeling.

"Well, get some rest," she said gently, taking her bottom lip between her teeth. "Everything will be okay, you know."

"Yeah," he breathed.

Retreating around the couch, Ophelia threw her hand up to send him a small wave, her lips forming into a thin line.

"Ophelia?"

She stopped immediately. "Yes?"

"Thank you for this." He sucked in a shaky breath.

Turning to face him once more, her eyebrows knitted sympathetically. "You don't have to thank me, James. I want to help you."

Dropping his head, he nodded as he stared down at the floor.

She could see the turmoil in his features; could practically hear the thoughts swirling around in his head as he fidgeted with his fingers.

"*Hey*," she murmured, stepping closer until her thighs hit the back of the couch. "I hope you know that you can talk to me. About anything."

He remained quiet for a few beats. It was obvious that he was either embarrassed or uncomfortable about the entire situation. And she couldn't blame him. It had been a strenuous day.

"I know. I'm just exhausted."

Ophelia nodded just as he lifted his head to smile half-heartedly at her. She wouldn't press the issue any further tonight, not when he needed to sleep the stressful day off. It was the least she could do when he so graciously was respectful enough not to press her for any information over coffee the other day. She understood the hesitancy in having these kinds of conversations.

"I'll let you get some sleep," she said softly. "Goodnight."

He paused for a few seconds as his eyes studied her.

"Goodnight, Ophelia."

Staring up at the ceiling, her feet crossed and her hands resting on her stomach, Ophelia huffed loudly as she blew a strand of her hair from her view.

She racked her brain for hours last night, overthinking how the night had ended with James, as she tossed and turned further and further away from sleep. It wasn't like her to care so much about something like this, but she couldn't help herself.

She was losing her mind over this man, and she hadn't even kissed him.

The tension grew with every conversation. Every glance

between them. It was almost suffocating at this point. The timing was never right, though. There were always things getting in the way of the possibility of even *thinking* about kissing him. Like her feelings, for example. Here she was, practically the poster girl for not wanting any strings attached, allowing her heart to start creating tiny strings.

They hadn't had much of an opportunity to talk things over this morning because he needed to get back to the bar to assess the damage. He slipped out early after a small cup of coffee, looking like he hadn't caught a wink of sleep, either. As much as Ophelia wanted to ask to tag along, or ask him to stay, she didn't. This was important to him, now wasn't the time for her *feelings*.

"Am I fucking dreaming? Or did I *actually* see bartender guy leaving the building while I was coming in?" Wren's voice echoed in the living room.

Ophelia let her head fall to the side to see Wren standing in her bedroom doorway, her eyes wide with excitement as she intertwined her fingers eagerly. She was even hopping from one foot to the other with a little too much enthusiasm.

"Don't get too excited, Wren." She sighed. "Nothing happened."

Wren's arms fell to her sides as her face dropped in disappointment. "I need a drink."

"Make me one, too," Ophelia called out solemnly, sticking her lip out into a pout.

Wren stopped in her tracks, grabbing the doorframe, as she looked back towards Ophelia with knitted brows. Her head tilted sideways rather sympathetically as a sigh left her lips.

"That bad, huh?"

Ophelia nodded with a wince.

"Spilling my beer on you didn't work?" Wren whined playfully.

"I got his number," Ophelia said with a shrug, sitting up from her position on the bed as she placed her chin in her palm. "But he has a lot going on right now."

Wren raised her eyebrow doubtfully.

"Seriously, his bar flooded yesterday, and the roof was practically falling in on us."

Just thinking back on it made Ophelia feel sheepish again. The sinking feeling settled back into her stomach. It was bad enough that he couldn't pay for his expenses, but now the bar was going downhill. It was like a rotten cherry on top of the already rotten cake. Not to mention, he *lived* there.

James deserved better.

"And that explains him being here last night *how*?" she questioned in a teasing manner.

"He sleeps there, Wren." Ophelia exhaled defeatedly, standing up from the bed and running her fingers through her hair. "You should've seen it. There was no way he could stay there last night. I just wish there was something that I could do for him."

Wren's eyes widened cautiously as she approached Ophelia, putting her hands on her shoulders as she clicked her tongue.

"Lia, do you have feelings for this guy?"

"What? *No.*" Ophelia rolled her eyes, swatting at her friend. "He's just a good guy. He doesn't deserve any of this to happen to him."

During her overthinking last night, she reflected on all the factors that could be working against the possibility of their friendship tacking on the benefits title. James either wasn't interested in her at all, or he was interested but too worried about their obvious age difference. What if he just didn't want to get involved with a college girl? Could she even blame him?

"Good, because a relationship would be too messy." Wren breathed a sigh of relief, swiping at her forehead with the back of her hand. "Especially when you have to go back to Georgia after the summer is over with. It's best to stick with the no strings attached scenario, friend."

"I know, and I will," Ophelia chirped in a happier tone. "But that doesn't mean I can't worry about him. That's what *friends* do."

"Uh-*huh*."

"I'm serious, Wren," she pressed. "It's just a summer fling. That's all."

"Right," Wren drawled out slowly, putting her hands on her hips as her eyes narrowed. "This sounds a lot like the time when you found a stray cat and hid it in your basement because you wanted to take care of it without your parents knowing when we were eight."

Ophelia remembered that cat fondly—a stray little tabby that she found on her way to school one morning, meowing and wandering around without its mother. There was no possible way she could've just left it behind. It was alone. It needed her. She took it straight home and gave it food and water for a week before her parents found out about it. Her mother, being the wretched witch that she was, dropped it off at a shelter.

Okay, so maybe Wren was a teeny bit right? Maybe she wasn't cut out for a friends-with-benefits kind of thing, after all.

Ophelia groaned miserably.

"I'm joking. Kind of," Wren snickered, flicking her hair back over her shoulder before crossing her arms over her chest. "You're just lucky I'm your best friend, because I have a brilliant plan."

Her ears perked up at that one.

"Oh?" Ophelia squeaked.

Wren Michaels—the master schemer.

"Yep, one that will earn your stray some money and allow him to see you all soaped up in a bikini."

"He's not a stray. Be *nice,*" Ophelia scolded as she sent Wren an annoyed look. "But go on."

Wren began to pace back and forth in deep thought as she usually did when she was coming up with some diabolical plan. Her fingers intertwined determinedly in front of her as her eyebrows knitted together arduously, her white-painted toes padding against the floor furiously as she marched around.

"You and me, in the cutest bikinis that we own, washing cars. I can tell Paul to bring a bunch of his college buddies to start us off. It's perfect."

Paul was Wren's twin brother, which was ironic considering they were the complete opposite of each other. Wren was brutally honest where it counted, never afraid to tell someone how she felt, while Paul was the biggest softie she'd ever met in her life.

"A car wash?" Her voice was skeptical.

"We can't fix his financial problems." Wren shrugged. "But it's the thought that counts."

"And how does that help me get out of the friend zone with James?" Ophelia questioned. "He's already seen me in my bra and panties. How is this any different?"

Wren stopped suddenly, a mischievous smile forming along her full lips as she batted her eyelashes innocently.

"Because." She grinned wildly. "College boys fawning after *the* Ophelia Clark in a hot bikini while she washes their cars? If that doesn't make him jealous, I don't know what will."

Ophelia sighed.

"I hope you're right about this."

"I am so right about this, Lia," Wren chirped happily, hopping on her heels as she whisked out her cell phone. "I'm going to call Paul. *You*—shave, moisturize, do what you need to do."

"Oh, you get to grill me on James, but I don't get anything about what happened with Sean the other night?" she teased gently.

"When I have more *juicy* details to give you." Wren looked up from her phone, wiggling her eyebrows playfully. "You'll get an earful, babe. I promise."

Ophelia shook her head at her friend, laughing as Wren practically ran out of the room to call her brother before she snuck over to the dresser to sort through her stash of bathing suits that she brought with her for the summer. If she never amounted to anything in her life, she would at least have a kick-ass bikini selection. She had more than enough to choose from.

As she dug through the pile, she pulled out her phone to send James a text.

OPHELIA: *How's the bar looking?*

JAMES: *It's a fucking disaster.*

Slinging her cheeky white bikini onto the bed, Ophelia jutted her bottom lip out sympathetically as she read his message.

Poor Jamie.

OPHELIA: *Breathe. Don't freak out. Me and Wren are coming to the rescue—we're going to wash cars to earn you some money.*

JAMES: *You really don't have to do that, Ophelia.*

OPHELIA: *What? Scared to see me in a bikini washing a car?*

Ophelia tossed her phone on the bed as she changed into her bathing suit, throwing a pair of frayed denim shorts on top as she slung her hair up into a clip. Scrutinizing her reflection in the mirror, she sighed as she pursed her lips at herself.

This would have to do.

Her phone screen lit up with another message, one that acted as a domino effect for the swarm of jitters growing inside of her stomach.

JAMES: *Scared I'm going to like it too much.*

CHAPTER SEVEN

THE SUN RADIATED DOWN on Ophelia's tanned skin, the heat of the California summer at an all-time high, as she and Wren prepared for the car wash set up in the empty lot across the street from *The Beer Lounge*.

Being the organized queen that she was, Wren had an entire setup prepped for Paul and his friend's arrival—cute signs to signal to others that were interested, buckets, towels, the whole shebang. She had even bribed Sean to perch at the foldable table and be in charge of all the cash.

Although, it probably didn't take much convincing on his part—the pair were very obviously flirtatious with one another. Ophelia had noticed the stolen glances. Very long stolen glances. It was rather cute, and she made a mental note to hound her friend endlessly about it later until she spilled the beans.

"White again, hmm?"

Ophelia glanced up, her hand hovering above her eyes as she squinted from the sun beaming down to see James peering down at her with a slight smirk dancing along his lips.

Even though the heat was almost suffocating, the temperature reaching up into the nineties, he still donned a long sleeve shirt and jeans. It was the first time he had hidden his arm since the night at the pool. He must've felt uncomfortable with all the strangers that would be popping in and out today.

"Yep." She laughed softly, looking down at her bikini as she put her hands on her hips. "Good thing it's meant to get wet, huh?"

His eyes studied her for a moment.

Before he could say anything else, Paul pulled into the empty paved lot, waving toward them with a goofy grin plastered on his face. His curly blonde hair glistened in the sun, and his blue eyes lit up as they fell on Ophelia. They hadn't seen each other since the last summer.

Paul had always been a friend to Ophelia, too.

He was like the older brother that she never had. Growing up with Wren, he would often join in on their sleepovers—stealing all the popcorn and making fun of the rom-com movies they would watch—but he was also the teddy bear type. She couldn't even count on both of her hands all the times he was right there along with Wren every time she showed up at their house after a fight with her parents.

"*Clark!*"

His voice bellowed happily as he climbed out of his car, throwing his hands up in the air as he shot Ophelia a wide smile.

"Well, hello to you, too." Wren rolled her eyes as she turned back to chat with Sean.

"Ah, shut up." Paul snorted, waving her off as he rounded the car. "I just saw you last night, dork."

Running up to Ophelia, he swooped her up in his arms, slinging her over his muscular shoulder as he twirled her around with a snicker.

"Put me down, you butthead." Ophelia groaned as she swatted his back, her waves cascading messily as she hung upside down.

Phase one of making James jealous—*check*.

Before Paul set her back down on her feet, she had caught the smallest glimpse of James' bewildered expression through her hair. She had to hold back a giggle as his jaw clenched slightly. His entire body had tensed up, and his nostrils flared irritably before quickly glancing away.

Now we're talking.

"Jeez, short stuff, you get prettier every time I see you."

Ophelia rolled her eyes.

"Yeah, yeah. Paul, this is James." She introduced them with a smile, motioning to James, who seemed reluctant to look at them again. "James, this is Wren's brother, Paul."

"Hey man," Paul greeted warmly, sticking his hand out towards James.

"Hello."

James' tone was clipped, firm. As cold as his voice sounded, he still returned the favor, reaching his hand out to shake Paul's outstretched one. The shake lasted a fraction of a second before both of their hands dropped to their sides.

Yikes.

"Listen, Pauline, where are your buddies?" Wren questioned with a raised eyebrow, thankfully interrupting the tense atmosphere. "We need to get this party started."

"They're coming, *Mom*."

As they continued to throw verbal jabs at each other, Ophelia turned back to James with a sheepish grin, observing the way his eyes were scrutinizing her with a look she couldn't quite decipher.

"He's bringing friends, huh?"

Ophelia gnawed at the inside of her cheek to keep the grin from spreading across her lips at his tone. It was like someone had peed in his cornflakes; the annoyance written all over his beautiful features. His jaw muscles tightened, his brow furrowed deeply, and he fidgeted with the rings on his fingers.

"Yeah, to get us started," she responded innocently. "Are you okay?"

James hummed quietly in response as more cars began to pull into the lot. Turning to walk over to Sean, who was still sitting behind the table without another glance or word, he left Ophelia standing there with her mouth parted dumbly.

The plan may have been working a little too much.

"He is *so* jealous of Paul. It's written all over his face," Wren mumbled into her ear as she came to stand next to her, a bucket in one hand and a sponge in the other. "This is perfect."

Ophelia sighed as she peeked over at James once more, examining the way his lips were pursed as he chewed at the inside of his mouth, the way his arms were crossed in front of his burly chest, and the way his eyes were scrutinizing all the college boys climbing out of their cars.

"He looks pissed, Wren."

"That's exactly what we want him to be, Lia." She wiggled

her eyebrows. "He'll either throw a punch at the first guy who looks at you a little too long or he'll drag you away. Calling it now."

Or what if he didn't want anything to do with the situation at all? *Or* her?

"What if this was a mistake?" Ophelia whispered reluctantly under her breath. "What if this all comes off too…childish or something?"

"Have confidence in yourself, Ophelia," Wren urged in a softer tone, sending her a reassuring wink. "What if this isn't a mistake? What if it all goes smoothly because it was meant to? What *if*—this guy is actually waiting to tear your clothes off? *Gasp*."

"Shush."

Ophelia jutted Wren's rib cage with her elbow as Paul led a group of guys over to them, stifling a giggle as Wren stuck her tongue out at her briefly before sending the batch an innocent smile.

Almost immediately, Ophelia could feel curious eyes on her.

As cute as some of the college boys were, she held zero interest when it came to them at all. She had dealt with her fair share of guys her age, and quite frankly, she didn't have the motivation to even try with them anymore. There weren't many who didn't suck. At least none that she found.

"Let's give them a show, hmm?"

Wren shot Ophelia a tiny smirk as she placed the bucket on the ground and grabbed the water hose as she began to spray one of the vehicles. Water showered the red paint in tiny droplets, soaking the pavement beneath their feet.

As Ophelia knelt down to submerge the sponge into the soapy water from the bucket, Wren pointed the hose in her direction, drenching her white bikini and frayed shorts with a laugh.

Ophelia's mouth dropped open in awe as she blinked slowly up at her friend, her hands frozen in mid-air as the water trickled down her skin.

"Bitch," she hissed as she stood up, her lips curving upwards as she glared at Wren.

"*Oops.*"

Ophelia lunged towards her friend, reaching out to steal the hose from her hands as a snicker escaped her lips. A pair of arms wrapped around her waist, pulling her backward as they lifted her into the air.

"Spray her again," Paul demanded with a goofy grin, pinning Ophelia to his torso as Wren showered the pair in water with a mischievous smile dancing along her lips.

"I hate you both!" Ophelia squealed as the cold water drenched her once more. Her hands raised to block her face as she giggled uncontrollably.

The frigid water felt good against her warm skin, trickling down in small beads as her hair pricked along every inch of her exposed exterior.

"That's what you get for calling me a butthead," Paul teased.

With the sudsy sponge still in her hand, Ophelia smashed it directly into his face with a snort, wiggling free as his lock around her waist loosened. The grimace on his face made her laugh as she ran around the other side of the car before he could snatch her up again.

She could hear the echoes of everyone laughing, making her head snap up to peer over at James—who was very much not laughing at all. His eyes were focused solely on her, his jaw flexing tightly as he ground his molars together. His fingers rubbed his chin irritably before glancing away.

Phase two of making James jealous—*check*.

"You're going to regret that, Clark," Paul called out, wiping the soap from his face as he narrowed his eyes at her from over the top of the car.

As he ran around the vehicle, Ophelia squealed as she darted the other way, quickly bounding over towards James—who still stood next to the table where Sean was sitting. Grasping his arm, she sprung behind him to hide, her chest heaving as she struggled to catch her breath. Peeking up at him, she took her bottom lip between her teeth to hide her meek smile. A small peace offering.

"Can I borrow you for a second?" James blurted out swiftly, just before Paul could come running over to swoop her up. "I need to, uh, grab a table inside."

"Sure," Ophelia said, smiling sweetly up at him.

He was almost too fast to keep up with as she stumbled behind him, peeking over her shoulder back at Wren—who was giving her a big thumbs up as they crossed the street. She gnawed at the inside of her lips as she studied his muscular back, listening to the sound of his boots against the pavement as they made their way toward the bar.

The silence was deafening.

"James?" she murmured.

"Hmm?"

"Are you alright?" she asked in a worried tone, following closely behind him as he whisked open the entrance door, holding it open for her to walk inside. "You seem upset—"

The energy shift was almost immediate as they stepped through the door, his cross demeanor changing into something completely different as his fingers encircled Ophelia's arm.

"Come here," James breathed, pulling her around the corner, and pressing her against the wall as he leaned down to smash his lips against hers.

Warm tingles rippled down her spine, fluttering through her core like wildfire as a muffled whimper escaped her lips. His hands entangled in her messy waves, pulling her deeper into himself as he devoured her curvaceous lips. A low groan rumbled through his chest as he pressed his abdomen against her, pinning her tightly against the wall. He inhaled her sweet, heady scent as his lips moved against hers feverishly like he was *starving*.

Ophelia tentatively tried to keep up with his movements. her hands rested on his chest, gliding down every ripple of muscle as she arched her back. She desperately needed to feel closer to him, although it was thoroughly impossible. Her skin was buzzing as a heated blush cascaded from her cheeks down her neck. His mouth molded with hers like he had been dying to taste her.

"*Shit*," he hissed, breaking the kiss as he pressed his forehead against hers. "I should've asked you if that was even okay—"

Ophelia knotted her fingers in his thick hair, tugging him back down as she crashed her lips into his, lifting her leg to hook around his waist.

"Just kiss me," she panted, guiding his lips down to her neck as she leaned her head back against the wall, grinding her hips against him.

"Fuck," he groaned.

His lips peppered kisses down her neck as his beard tickled her skin. His hands gripped her waist pressingly. Closing her eyes, Ophelia's lips parted ardently as the flutters multiplied, sucking all of her oxygen from her lungs as they overwhelmed her chest. Every kiss that he pressed against her skin ignited every single nerve ending inside of her.

"What about—" he paused, his tongue flicking out of his lips to taste her collarbone before pressing another kiss to her skin. "Being friends?"

Her head was spinning maddeningly.

"Friends," she moaned softly, leaning into his kisses as he trailed back up her neck. "With benefits. Definitely the benefits."

He groaned in response; the sound erupting from the back of his throat as his lips found hers once more. His hand reached down to grip her thigh that was wrapped around him still, digging into her skin as he kissed her forcefully.

Breaking the kiss once more, his brow furrowed as his chest heaved heavily, and his lips parted.

"I'm *old*."

Her fingers reached up to grip his chin, forcing him to look down at her. "I don't think so."

"No?"

"It's just for the summer," Ophelia cooed tantalizingly, glancing up at him with sincere eyes. "I'll go back to Georgia in six weeks, and we can pretend it never happened."

He swallowed. "If we're going to do this, I need you to promise me something."

"Anything."

"No more games." His voice was insistent. His eyes were soft. "No more shows to make me jealous."

Ophelia cocked her head up at him. "I promise."

"If we're doing this, you're *mine*."

The words were like music to her ears.

She was liking this more than she expected. He was laying it all out on the table; he was too grown for antics. The possessive nature of his tone sent heated shivers up her spine.

"Yes, *sir*." Her lips twitched in the corners.

James pressed his lips to her forehead, sighing. She could feel his breath fanning across her skin.

"We should get back out there before everyone wonders what happened to us."

Ophelia nodded, slightly disappointed, her swollen lips pouting.

Running his thumb across her protruding bottom lip, James smiled faintly. His pupils were dilated as he studied her, showcasing just how cerulean his eyes were.

"And Ophelia?"

"Yes?" she whispered faintly.

"I don't want to pretend this never happened."

CHAPTER EIGHT

OPHELIA: *Are you working?*

Ophelia pressed the blue arrow to send the text to James, who she hadn't seen since the day of the car wash.

Which was five days ago.

Five *excruciatingly* long days to daydream about his full, bearded lips against hers again. It was damn near lethal how overwhelmed she would get with goosebumps at the mere thought of kissing him. The swarm of flutters in her stomach felt as though it was nearly swallowing her whole.

And she had only kissed him.

JAMES: *No, the floor people are almost done replacing the wood at the bar, so we won't actually open again until tomorrow.*

After their secret make-out fiasco, they had made quite a bit of money from washing cars. The line kept coming—they were baking in the sun for hours, washing what felt like every car in Los Angeles. Using what they made from working away all day, coupled with the amount that Sean threw into the mix to help his friend, James could replace the flooring from all the water damage that had occurred from the rain.

OPHELIA: *Wanna come pick me up?*

Twisting her hair into a loose braid, Ophelia could feel the anticipation of his response building inside of her stomach. She anxiously watched her phone screen as she waited for it to light up.

JAMES: *Hmm, say I do. What do you have in mind, pretty girl?*

She'd be lying if she said the nickname didn't make her insides feel as though they were doing cartwheels. That was all her body seemed to do these days.

Sticking her thumb between her teeth, biting it gently as she smiled softly, Ophelia quickly typed back.

OPHELIA: *Guess you'll have to show up to find out.*

JAMES: *Getting on my bike as we speak.*

As Ophelia bounced happily on her heels, three loud knocks sounded from the front door, making her head snap up curiously. Blowing her blonde hair from her face in a huff, she waltzed towards the door, whisking it open.

The last face that she had expected to see was that of her mom, who had her signature grimace imprinted on her features. Her beady, blue eyes scrutinized Ophelia quickly, and her arms crossed in front of her chest as her lips pursed in vexation.

"Mother," Ophelia greeted.

"Well, don't look so disappointed to see me, Ophelia."

Sighing, Ophelia dropped her hand from the door, walking towards the kitchen as her mother followed closely behind her. Her nude heels clicked on the linoleum floor.

She was the spitting image of her mother. They could practically pass as twins. Their eyes were the same shade of blue, and their hair was the same shade of blonde. Her mother was just the older version of Ophelia. The only difference was the added frown lines and wrinkles next to her eyes.

"I thought witches only traveled on brooms," Ophelia muttered. "Where is yours?"

Her mother narrowed her eyes.

"I wouldn't have to show up here if you bothered to answer your phone when I called."

"I can't help that my phone thinks you're a spam call and immediately sends you to voicemail." She shrugged innocently.

"I know it's summer, but that doesn't mean it's party time, Ophelia." Her mother scoffed faintly, shaking her head in disapproval. "I'm here because I have an internship waiting for you at the hospital."

There was always a catch to her mother randomly showing up unannounced. She could never show up because she wanted to see her daughter, ask her how things were going, or catch up on the things happening in her life. It was always because she still wanted to try to control her entire existence.

"What are you talking about?"

"I want you to come study under me for the rest of the summer," her mother chirped in a happier tone, her nose turning upwards. "You need to be prepared for medical school. There's no time to waste."

Ding ding *ding*.

And there it was.

Ophelia groaned loudly, rolling her eyes as she turned to open the fridge, grabbing the bag of grapes on the middle shelf before twisting around again to face her mother. Leaning against the marble counter, she popped one in her mouth.

"Ophelia—"

"I would rather chew my arm off than follow you around a hospital for five weeks."

Her mother scowled. "Will you stop being so dramatic? It's time to grow up. This is your *career* that we are talking about."

More knocks resonated from the door, and for a moment, she had forgotten that James was already on his way. It was nearly impossible to think clearly with this wretched woman in her face, but relief washed throughout her body with the reassurance that he was outside of the apartment.

"Hold that thought, will you?" She held a finger up at her mother, rushing towards the door to fling it open.

James stood on the other side—donning a button-up underneath his black leather jacket, and a pair of suede boots instead of his usual black boots that he wore. It was different for him, but he was still achingly gorgeous, nonetheless. The man could make a trash bag look good. His eyes brightened at the sight of her, and his lips twitched upwards as he smiled faintly down at her.

"Hi, come in," she blurted out, grasping his arm and tugging him inside, eager to diminish the horrendous conversation with her mother as soon as humanly possible.

"Hello."

"James, this is Julie," Ophelia spoke quickly. "My mother."

His eyebrows raised perplexedly as his eyes flickered towards Julie, who was still in the kitchen with her arms crossed irritably in front of her, as he nodded slowly. "*Oh*, nice to meet you, Mrs. Clark."

"If you don't mind." Her mother sneered with a factitious smile. "I'd like to continue this conversation with my daughter. Alone."

"I mind." Ophelia butted in, still holding onto his arm as she spoke. "He was invited here. You were not."

Julie's piercing eyes flickered down to her hands wrapped around his forearm. Her tongue pressed against her cheek as she uncrossed her arms, placing her hands on her hips condescendingly.

"Don't tell me this is the reason you won't take the internship." Her mother chuckled in disbelief. "Oh, Ophelia. You can't be this stupid."

She could feel James staring down at her now, probably in shock that her mother was openly saying this in front of a stranger, but this was nothing new to Ophelia. Her mother loved to attempt to embarrass her in front of others by talking down towards her, or by lecturing her. The woman was a blood-sucking beast.

"Mother, *please*."

"Men only want one thing from a young girl like you, and once he gets it, you'll be thrown out like bad leftovers."

"*Mom.*"

"I think that you should leave," James said coolly.

Ophelia's head snapped up to gawk at him, her lips parting in awe as she blinked up at him through her lashes.

That was hot.

"*Excuse* me?" Julie retorted incredulously.

"You can be rude, but I can't?" he countered calmly.

Her mother glowered at both of them for a few seconds, her lips parted in bewilderment before she shook her head. Walking towards the door, she held her hands defensively in the air. As she stepped out of the apartment, she turned on her heel to give Ophelia one last look. "I give it a week until he breaks your heart, sending you running back to your father and me. Until then, I'll be waiting for my apology."

Ophelia hurried to swiftly close the door before her mother could say anything else, pressing her forehead against the wood as she sucked in a deep breath.

Turning around exhaustedly, she pinched the bridge of her nose. "I'm so sorry. I had no idea she was coming over."

James was a lot closer than she had expected him to be, standing only a few inches away from her now, his head tilting to the side sympathetically as his eyes studied her.

"Are you okay?" he asked softly.

Ophelia peeked up at him with a playful pout. "Yeah, I'm fine now."

"*Ophelia.*"

It amazed her how he could just sense that she wasn't okay deep down—she couldn't recall the last time she had been okay. Her mother had been like this for as long as she could remember. Perhaps she was permanently never going to be okay again.

Eternal mommy issues.

She shrugged, scrunching her nose faintly.

James reached his hand up gingerly, tracing his finger along her crinkled nose until she relaxed again. "Do you want to talk about it?"

Ophelia shook her head, observing his face as he hovered over her now. And just like that, just by the proximity alone, the tension was back. His fingers then brushed a few strands of hair from her face, tucking them behind her ear, lingering as his thumb caressed her cheek lightly.

"Whenever you're ready then," he murmured tentatively.

She leaned into his touch as she flashed him a thankful smile.

"Want me to take your mind off of it?"

Holy *shit*.

She would sign her soul away right now if he asked her to.

"Depends," she mumbled, her chest heaving shakily the longer his eyes examined her.

"On?" he countered.

She pretended to nonchalantly reach up to adjust the collar of his leather jacket. "Does it involve your lips on me?"

Scooping her up in his arms like she weighed nothing at all, a low chuckle rumbled through his chest before his lips connected with hers. Gripping her thighs to hoist her up, he walked them over to the couch. His mouth moved heatedly against hers as her fingers tangled in his hair.

A whimper escaped her lips, reverberating against his as he crashed on top of her as they slammed into the couch. His abdomen pressed deeply against her as his lips molded with hers, and his hands glided up the sides of her body as they grasped her crimson cheeks to kiss her more vigorously.

Her hands grasped his leather jacket, sliding it down his forearms before desperately unbuttoning his shirt partially, flinging it down over his shoulders to expose his muscly chest underneath. Breaking the kiss, she trailed her fingers along his chest tattoo, pausing as she came across a new tattoo right below his shoulder on his bicep. It was a floral piece that only accentuated every dip and crevice of his physique.

"Another tattoo?" she panted, her head falling back as his lips pressed against her neck.

"*Mmm.*" He paused, kissing her neck once more. "Perks of having a friend who does my tattoos for free."

His clothes were disheveled, his hair a mess from her hands, and his eyes were wild with hunger. His arms wrapped around her waist as he pulled her closer, leaving sloppy kisses against her skin as his lips trailed down her chest.

Ophelia felt her nipples prick beneath her exposed bra, arching her back into him, needing more.

And then the front door flew open—Wren waltzing inside, throwing them a dramatically raised eyebrow as she fought back a smile.

Of course.

"*Whoa*, can I watch?" she teased, throwing her stuff on the counter as she walked into her bedroom.

Ophelia sighed hopelessly as she giggled, holding James' head that rested against her chest. His body shook as he laughed quietly, too. Their chests heaved in sync as they pressed against each other, still entangled from their heated kiss.

"I have to go check on the guys working on the floor, anyway," James reassured her gently, lifting his head from her chest to press his lips against hers. "How about I pick you up tomorrow night after I get off work?"

"Hmm." Ophelia pondered playfully. "What are we going to do?"

"Anything you want."

She groaned as he climbed off the couch, adjusting her shirt so that her bra wasn't showing anymore as she sulked flippantly up at him.

"Don't worry," he murmured with a gentle smile, rubbing his thumb along her cheek. "I plan on kissing a lot more of you tomorrow."

CHAPTER NINE

Brushing through her messy waves, Ophelia sighed as she observed her reflection in the mirror. Her phone buzzed with a text message as she threw on her favorite brown jacket.

JAMES: *Get your cute ass down here.*

Giggling quietly, she threw on her shoes before quickly rushing out of the front door, her purse smacking against her side as she hurried towards the elevator eagerly.

They had come to the agreement that they would drive to the beach once he got off work. Ophelia had always enjoyed walking on the beach at night. It was quiet. All the commotion from the day disappeared as the waves crashed against the sand. It was the one thing she had truly missed about California when she moved away for college.

It was just before midnight; the moonlight cascading through the large foyer windows into the dimly lit lobby as she made her way towards the entrance. She could already see James perched on his motorcycle out front. The butterflies in her stomach fluttered with anticipation as she fought back a smile.

His head twisted to look over at her as she pushed through the glass doors, his lips curving upwards as his eyes trailed over her. His hair was disheveled from the wind, and his beard accentuated his jawline and full lips. It immediately made her wish he was reddening her skin with his scruff as he kissed her everywhere like he had promised.

His leather jacket squeezed his arms, as did his jeans with his legs, drawing her attention to his brawny thighs. He was burly in all the right places. It was almost distracting.

If Ophelia had to choose a way to go, it would be death by getting crushed between them.

"Hey, pretty girl."

Ophelia smirked as she approached him, her eyes flickering up at him through her thick lashes. "I have a cute ass, huh?"

James chuckled softly, his lips twisting as he gnawed at them gently. His hands enveloped her waist as he pulled her closer to him. His fingers gripped her in a way that screamed how eager he was to have them on her again.

"I don't *know*," he murmured mischievously, his hands traveling down until they were stuffed into the back pockets of her jeans. "I think I need to feel it one more time. Just to be sure."

"Hmm." She nodded slowly, swinging her leg over the top of him as she slid into his lap, her eyes never wavering from his. "If you must."

His eyes flickered down to her mouth. His hands slid out of her pockets and traveled down her thighs, hoisting them up around his waist as his tongue ran along his bottom lip.

"I have been thinking about those lips *all* fucking day."

The words made her want to clench her legs together as the flutters spiraled deeper into her core, but she fought against the urge since they were currently latched around his waist.

"Well." Ophelia clicked her tongue. "The sooner you get to the beach—"

The motorcycle suddenly revved back to life, making a squeak escape her lips. Her arms wrapped around his neck as she jumped, and her face brushed against his beard as she leaned into him.

"Hold on." He chuckled, positioning his hands on the handlebars.

"You're going to drive with me sitting in your lap?" Ophelia asked with a cheeky grin, tightening her arms around him. "Am I rubbing off on you?"

She could feel a laugh reverberating through his chest as she pressed herself against him, her hair ruffling in the wind as he began to zoom down the street. The possibility of any police pulling them over for driving like this was exhilarating. Made adrenaline pump through her veins and shivers shoot down her spine as she pressed her lips against the warmth of his neck.

Ophelia smiled coyly as he leaned into her touch, crooking his neck faintly as she trailed kisses up to his ear, taking his earlobe gently between her teeth.

She heard a groan escape his lips.

Mission accomplished.

"Are you trying to make me crash this God damn bike?" he growled.

She could feel him hardening underneath her, only enticing her even more now as she ran her fingers through his thick hair—gripping it firmly as she planted sloppy kisses back down his neck.

His hand released the handlebar suddenly, gripping her waist *hard*.

"Stop *teasing* me."

His voice was low, needy.

"Or what?" she challenged boldly.

Ophelia had been craving to see this side of him. As much as she was attracted to the sweetness of his voice, his kindness, his softness—she always wondered if there was a darker side. Someone who would tell her what to do. To provoke her or be more dominant.

"Or you're going to be the first girl I've ever bent over this motorcycle."

Her cheeks flushed a deep crimson at his blatant words. Despite hearing such crudeness before, she was shocked that they came from him.

"Is that supposed to make me want to stop?" she mumbled, taking her lip between her teeth as she ran her nose along his jawline slowly.

"*Ophelia.*"

She laughed timidly as she pressed her face into his neck, surrendering for now as they glided down the open highway, hair whipping around wildly. The cold night air made goosebumps rise along her tanned skin as she listened to the roar of the bike.

The beach was only about a half hour away during this time of night; no traffic blocked their path as they whizzed down the asphalt roads toward the coast.

The air gradually continued to feel cooler the closer they got to the ocean. She could smell the salt in the air just faintly, reminding her of summer with Wren and Paul as a teenager. They had always spent a lot of their free time at the beach, playing volleyball, or attempting to surf.

Georgia wasn't nearly the same.

Some days, she wondered if it was even worth it.

Venice Beach resembled a ghost town as they pulled into an empty parking lot. There were no cars or people to be seen anywhere as James pulled into a spot closest to the walkway that led into the sand. She could already hear the waves crashing against the shore as the motorcycle shut off, her lips twitching with a grin as she reveled in the sound.

Leaning back slightly, James peered at Ophelia in awe, observing her as she closed her eyes—breathing in the piquant air with a faint smile.

"You haven't been here in a while," he presumed softly.

Ophelia opened her eyes slowly, shaking her head as she slid from his lap, bouncing on her heels next to his perched figure on the motorcycle as she combed her fingers through her tangled hair. "Not since last summer."

"Did you miss it?"

"So much," she breathed.

"Then let's go."

Hopping off the bike, he extended his hand out for her to take, which she didn't hesitate to grasp as she practically dragged him towards the beach. Before they began to trudge through the sand, they kicked off their shoes, her Converse in one hand while his hand entangled with the other.

The sand under her feet was cool, and soft, as they walked out onto the beach. Their fingers intertwined as she tugged him along with her.

Her eyes fell on one of the vacant lifeguard towers halfway to the water, pursing her lips cheekily as she glanced back at him over her shoulder.

"What was it you said about kissing a lot more of me?" Ophelia teased, gesturing towards the tower, before slipping her hand from his and taking off towards it—kicking sand everywhere as she ran.

Arms enveloped her waist just before she could reach the faded blue ramp, twirling her around as she giggled, before plopping her back down in the sand again. Her head snapped up to peek up at James, who was smiling widely down at her, as she tugged her bottom lip between her teeth.

"You're quite the tease today," he scolded playfully, his hand reaching up to caress his thumb along her lip, pulling it from her teeth lightly.

"That's too bad, huh?" she quipped, looking around them with a small shrug. "There's no bike to bend me over out here."

And then suddenly he was scooping her up again, throwing her over his shoulder as he carried her up the ramp and inside the lifeguard tower as he gripped onto her inner thigh. Ophelia could feel the dampness seeping through her panties from his touch, her mind running to wild places as she imagined what his fingers would feel like between her legs.

As they entered the dark tower, the moonlight entering the

single window on the side, James set her back down on her feet as his lips collided with her own. The small tingles in her core felt like they were swarming her entire body as he kissed her feverishly, his hands grasping her face as he leaned deeper into her.

Her hands rested on his forearms as his lips devoured hers, her heartbeat quickening as he let go of her face to tug the zipper of her jacket down, brushing it off of her shoulders until it had fallen to the wooden floor.

"You're beautiful." He broke away from her lips to observe the black bra she had worn underneath her jacket as his fingers caressed her collarbone, her chest, and her stomach.

Ophelia could feel her heart hammering against her chest as she blinked up at him, her swollen lips still parted as she reached up to pull him back down to her, smashing her lips against his. A groan reverberated through his mouth as his tongue darted between her lips, tasting her as his fingers dug into her waist.

There was a tiny, tattered loveseat against the wall in the corner of the tower, just big enough for him to hoist her up in his grip and place her down on as he hovered over her now. Her legs splayed out as he pressed his abdomen between them.

His lips left hers as he kissed down her neck, nipping and lapping at her warm skin as he traveled down to her chest, towards her navel, achingly slow. Her stomach twitched with every touch of his lips, squirming slightly beneath him as the pressure inside of her core continued to build from his kisses alone.

His skilled fingers unzipped her jeans, yanking them impatiently down her legs as his mouth found her hip bone, nipping it tentatively as her eyebrows knitted from the contact.

"I have wanted to do this since the night you walked into my bar, pretty girl." His breath fanned across her inner thigh, making goosebumps rise along her exposed skin.

A needy sigh left her lips as she stared down at his blue eyes that peered up at her, his lips leaving a trail of kisses along her panty line.

He looked fucking delicious from this angle.

His hand gripped her thigh, pushing her legs open wider as he hovered just above her. She could feel her clit throbbing in a syncopated rhythm with her heartbeat. She wanted to practically beg him to touch her. It took everything inside of her not to whine out for him as she ardently watched him observe her damp panties.

"*Fuck*," he commented in a pant. "You're already this wet for me?"

"Mhm." Ophelia hummed fiercely, biting her lip as his eyes flicked back up to hers with a newfound desire in them.

Staring up at her unwaveringly, his finger slid underneath her panties, pushing them to the side as he pressed his mouth against her clit. His tongue flicked between her folds as he tasted her, and his thumb rubbed circles against her most sensitive spot.

Ophelia jerked underneath him, her head falling back as she moaned softly.

"*Yes*," she whined.

His beard tickled her skin, turning it tomato red as it rubbed against her roughly. His hands pried her legs open every time they would begin to squeeze around him with every flick of his tongue.

"You taste just as sweet as you look."

"Fuck, James," she groaned fervently.

She could feel the pressure building more at his words, even more so after his mouth connected with her again, his finger sliding inside of her slowly.

Pumping his finger harder, his tongue lapped and flicked across her swollen clit; his small moans vibrating against her through his lips.

"I can feel you tightening around my finger already," he panted. "You gonna come for me?"

Ophelia nodded frantically, biting down harshly on her lip. The coil tightened more with each thrust of his finger inside of her.

Her orgasm bubbled over the moment he added another finger, curling them upwards. Her breath halted in her throat as her climax reached its peak, her eyes fluttering closed as he quickened the pace at which his tongue was pressing against her clit.

Her head was spinning madly. She felt intoxicated by the way he was making her feel.

Her back arched as it washed over her, a loud moan escaping her plump lips as her fingers knotted in his hair, her juices dripping down his hand as he finger fucked her.

The best orgasm of her life.

From his fucking fingers.

"Good girl," he coaxed softly, pulling his drenched fingers

from her as she relaxed, sliding them into his mouth as his eyes squeezed shut. "Mmm, *so* sweet."

Lifting her head to gaze at him through her euphoric daze, her lips twitched with a smile as her chest heaved, her hands loosening from his hair as she trailed a finger down his nose lightly.

He, too, was beautiful.

His lips were swollen from his handiwork, his eyes were heavy-lidded as he peered up at her, and his beard was still glistening from her.

"What about you?" she asked, her voice small.

"This night was all for you," he noted with a grin, leaning his head against her inner thigh.

"What a gentleman."

He continued to smile up at her from between her legs, and she couldn't help herself as she reached down to cup his bearded cheek. Rubbing her thumb across his cheekbone gently, she watched as he practically melted into her palm.

"Always to you."

She could feel her cheeks heating up under his gaze. Ducking her head feebly, she pressed her face tentatively against her shoulder as she peeked at him.

James sighed, sitting up as he observed her still sprawled out along the small couch, his head shaking as he licked his lips.

"I'm fucked."

"Huh?" she squeaked, propping up on her elbows as she frowned up at him.

He hesitated weakly.

"Now that I've gotten a taste." He paused. "I don't know how I'll ever be able to stop."

CHAPTER TEN

James' bar looked almost brand new since the last time Ophelia had been inside—the floors were dark wood now, looking much better than the faded woodwork that it once was. Even the booths were updated to a modern, dark green. The holes in the ceiling were patched as well, in case there was ever a day when Los Angeles decided to be glum again.

The facelift would have never been this vast if some of the regulars hadn't generously pitched in to fix the place. The car wash money was only enough to replace the old wooden floor. They didn't want the bar to eventually end up closing due to repairs that couldn't be mended.

It was heartwarming to see the reflection of how James ran his bar in his patrons. They loved it almost as much as he did. So much so that one of his regulars was still hanging out twenty minutes past closing time.

"Listen, man, I'm so glad you didn't have to close this place." The drunken older man slurred. "Woulda been a *real* bitch, ya' know?"

James' eyes flickered towards Ophelia, who sat perched at his bar, his lips twitching with a smile as he glanced back over at his intoxicated customer. Flicking his white rag over his shoulder, he let out a sigh as his tongue darted out to wet his bottom lip.

"I've got this," Sean muttered as he rounded the corner, patting James' shoulder. "Joe, I called you a cab, man. Let me walk you outside."

Incoherent mumbling came from the man next to her as he hopped off of the bar stool, the metal squeaking from the weight shift, as Sean exited from behind the bar to lead the inebriated Joe out to his awaiting cab.

Finally.

"I'll catch you two later," Sean called out, sending a smirk over his shoulder.

"Say hello to Wren for me," Ophelia shot back, giggling softly as he waved his hand dismissively before they disappeared out of the entrance.

Wren had divulged in great detail about the long nights that she had spent with Sean after the car wash. They had actually exchanged numbers the day that Ophelia had left hers for James. The pair seemed to be hitting it off well, considering it was the first time she'd seen Wren blush while talking about a guy before. While Ophelia couldn't be happier for her, she also wanted to gouge her ears out with a fork rather than hear the dirty *deets* of her best friend's sex life.

James was staring at her with a faint smile as she turned to look back at him now, resting her chin in the palm of her hand.

"Sorry about Joe." He chuckled. "He's a bit of a talker—"

Reaching her hand out to grasp his dark t-shirt, Ophelia stood up on the bar stool's footrest and tugged him across the counter towards her, smashing her lips against his before he could even finish his sentence. A needy groan erupted from the back of his throat as his hands found a home in her blonde waves, brushing her hair from her face as he cradled her head.

It was safe to say that she was pining for him like he was essential for her lungs to create oxygen. As dangerous as her growing addiction may have been, it had reached untameable heights. She was beyond the point of fighting it anymore.

"*Fuck*, Ophelia," he panted faintly, breaking from their heated kiss as he pressed his forehead against hers.

"Are you going to show me your newly renovated bedroom or—"

As the breathless words were leaving her lips, the door to the bar swung open, interrupting their growing tension as a woman walked through the entrance. Her bright green eyes scrutinized the entangled pair with a faint smirk, her long, black hair falling down her shoulders in perfect waves. Her hand immediately went to her hip, making Ophelia examine the silky black dress that made her jealous of the woman's long legs, as she clicked her tongue crassly.

"I hate to interrupt," the long-legged goddess said coolly, her green eyes focusing on James now. "But I would like to speak with my husband."

Her what?

She could hear the brakes screeching inside of her mind.

Ophelia choked on her saliva that she was in the middle of gulping as she stumbled down from the footrest of the bar stool, her hand catching the wooden counter-top to steady herself as she swayed slightly, her wide eyes leaving the woman to gawk at James.

She could hear a faint ringing in her ears as her heart hammered harshly against her chest, her stomach churning so deeply that she could practically taste the bile rising in her throat.

"Ophelia, it's not what you—"

"You're *married*?" she hissed, her eyebrows knitting tightly together.

His eyes narrowed at the woman before flickering back to hers, softening as soon as their gazes connected. His head tilted sideways somberly. His hands twitched as if he wanted to reach out to her, but he swallowed thickly as he kept his hands glued to the top of the bar.

"Just stay here," he pleaded quietly, quickly shuffling from behind the bar as his hand hovered over her lower back. "Just *wait* here. Please, don't leave."

Ophelia's lips parted in complete shock as she stared up at him, watching as his lips formed into a thin line before he guided the woman back outside from where she entered, leaving her standing alone in the empty bar with her very loud thoughts. Her hands started to shake from the adrenaline that had begun to course through her veins, making her anxiously cross her arms over her chest.

Why did these things always happen to her?

Was every guy really the same?

As she paced back and forth, she gritted her teeth to keep the tears that were welling up in the corners of her eyes from trickling down her cheeks.

She heard the door open once more, making her look over to see James rubbing his forehead as he approached her hesitantly. Her pacing stopped abruptly as she flung her hands aimlessly in the air.

"Is she your wife?" Ophelia questioned fervently. "You had a wife and didn't say anything? You just let this whole thing continue?"

"Ophelia, I'm so—"

"You're just like every other guy I've ever been with," she snapped, shaking her head as she put her face in her hands, pacing again. "I'm *always* the side girl, always. Do I not deserve to be the main—"

"*Ophelia.*"

"You—" She stopped suddenly, pointing her shaky finger at him before stepping towards him to jab it against his chest. "*How* could you? Why did you even—*fuck*, James! I don't even know what to say to you right now."

James grasped her face in his large hands, making her stop unexpectedly as her chest heaved with trembling breaths, his thumbs swiping across her cheekbones sweetly.

"She's my *ex*-wife, Clark," he urged in a small voice, his eyebrows pulling together. "We're not married anymore and we haven't been in a long time."

An exasperated sigh blew from her lips in a loud huff as she dropped her gaze, gnawing at the inside of her lips as she stared down at her white shoes.

"You're shaking," he commented softly.

"Yeah, well."

"Pretty girl," James murmured, tugging her face back up to

meet his eyes. "You're not the side girl. The only girl that is *ever* on my mind is you."

With words like that, how was she ever supposed to stick with just friends with benefits? How was she supposed to not like him any more than she already did? How?

Summer fling.

It's just a summer fling.

"What did she want?" Ophelia asked quietly, blinking slowly up at him, her frown still apparent on her features.

"She likes to come around every so often just to cause problems," he explained, dropping his hands to his sides. "I'm really sorry. I should've just told you about her from the start."

She shook her head, sucking in a deep breath as she brushed her hair behind her ears. "No, it's okay. It's not like I'm sharing all of my baggage with you. I shouldn't expect you to share yours with me."

"And if I want to share it with you?"

Ophelia ran her fingers through her hair as she started to pace again, taking her bottom lip between her teeth.

"Do you think we've become–" She paused, searching for the right word, groaning loudly. "I don't know, too *attached*?"

"Do you?"

She peeked over at him to see him gazing at her, his jaw clenched, his mind running wild behind his eyes.

"There's not supposed to be feelings," Ophelia urged softly, taking her thumb between her teeth as she frowned up at him. "And here I am, practically having a stroke at the possibility of you being married."

She was going back to Georgia in barely five weeks. It would be unfair to pursue anything more than what they had in such a short amount of time, especially when she wasn't here to stay. Feelings would only make it more complicated than it needed to be.

"Is that such a bad thing?" he asked weakly, rubbing his beard with his hand.

"I'm *leaving* in a couple of weeks, James."

"And?" he countered.

She groaned tentatively, putting her face in her hands once more.

"So I'm not allowed to like you because you're not staying?" he continued. "You're going to have to give me a better reason than that, Ophelia, because I'm already there."

Her heart lurched at his words, his confession leaving his bearded lips, as she lifted her head to look up at him through her damp lashes. The stupid traitorous tears had come back, threatening to bubble over now as she struggled to compose her ragged breathing.

"But you can't," she argued feebly.

"Give me a *reason*," he urged. "Not an excuse."

"Because—" Ophelia hesitated, shrugging weakly, licking her dry lips. "Because I am leaving."

It was deeper than that—she knew that. He knew it too by the look on his face, his eyes begging her to say something more, pleading with her to open up. Even if she tried to explain why it wouldn't work, it would only open the floodgates of her tears. The emotional damage would follow her around, haunting her everywhere she went.

Maybe she was permanently damaged.

Damaged goods.

"You know that's not good enough."

"Because I'm going back to college for something I don't even want to do. My parents would never let me live it down if I gave up on medical school. And because I'm very much the opposite of the woman that just walked in here—is that what you wanted to hear? How I'm just not good enough for anyone, ever?"

The stupid tears had trickled down her cheeks as the words fumbled out of her mouth like word vomit, making her turn around to face the other direction so he wouldn't see her so vulnerable. She wanted to kick herself for allowing this to happen, allowing herself to get too overwhelmed. To cry in front of him.

"Ophelia—"

"I should go," she mumbled, wiping her face with the back of her hand.

She wished she could snap her fingers and disappear, vanishing from this humiliating moment.

"Ophelia, she *is* the complete opposite of you, but that's what I like about you," James practically growled, grasping her arm to twist her around to face him again. "Our marriage was so toxic and unhealthy, but being around you isn't like that at all. I've never felt more at ease."

Ophelia sniffed, staring down at her shoes again.

"Stop focusing so much on the *what-ifs* and just let things be what they're supposed to be," he murmured, his hands finding her face again. "Go with the flow and just enjoy this with me, yeah?"

"I do enjoy this with you," she squeaked. "I'm just scared of what's going to happen when our five weeks are up. When the summer is over."

"We'll find out when we get there."

He pulled her into his chest as his arms enveloped her shoulders, his chin resting on top of her head as he hugged her gently. Rubbing her back comfortingly as her arms encircled his waist. It was nearly impossible *not* to melt into his embrace as she inhaled his familiar scent.

For the first time in a long time, the overbearing weight that sat on her shoulders had lifted.

CHAPTER ELEVEN

Wren appeared in the living room, her eyes taking in Ophelia's unkempt appearance with a raised eyebrow as her hands fell on her hips. Her mouth popped open to say something sarcastic, but as she observed the way Ophelia blinked up at her tiredly, her face softened.

"What happened?"

After coming home last night, Ophelia had crashed on the couch, tossing and turning for hours as she racked through her overbearing thoughts. She didn't even have the energy to crawl into the bed in the guest bedroom.

The black-haired woman kept flickering through her mind. How striking she had been compared to Ophelia, and how completely different they were. James' ex-wife was more his age, beautiful, and confident about it, too.

How could he ever be attracted to Ophelia?

Her hair was platinum blonde, the polar opposite of the woman's raven-colored hair. And her eyes were blue, not bright, emerald *green*. The woman was a model—Ophelia didn't even feel close to existing on the same pedestal.

Doubts had taken the place of hopefulness that she had

previously held for their friendship. And Ophelia hated that she cared so much.

"It's nothing," Ophelia responded meekly, shaking her head a little too long.

Wren pursed her glossed lips for a moment, crossing her arms over her chest as she walked over towards where she sat perched on the couch, plopping down next to her.

"It doesn't look like nothing."

Ophelia peeked up at her friend, her eyebrows pulling together as she struggled to muster up the right words. Were there right words for their situation?

"It's dumb," she squeaked. "Because I shouldn't even care to begin with."

Wren wrapped her arm around Ophelia's shoulder, tugging her into a one-armed hug as she rubbed the sleeve of her sweater gently, pressing her cheek against her head. "But you do care, babe."

"I do care," Ophelia repeated in a whine, staring down at her hands that were entangled in her lap. "*Shit*, Wren, I can't do this. I can't start to feel this way about him. It's not fair to me or him. It just wouldn't work."

Georgia was over two-thousand miles away—resting on the complete opposite side of the country. She had so much school left ahead of her, and tackling medical school would be stressful on its own. What would even be the point of dragging someone else into that with her? She couldn't just leave school, and he couldn't just leave his bar.

It was unfair.

Perhaps this was her fault for pursuing him in the first

place. She should've never stepped foot into that bar that night. She should've sucked it up and went out with the momma's boy, anyway. James was far deeper into this than she was. She could feel it—she could *see* it every time she looked into his eyes.

"You're catching feelings."

"No—"

"You *poor* girl." Wren sighed dramatically, rolling her eyes in a teasing manner. "You're falling for the hot bartender guy who is smitten with you. Your life must be so hard."

"I'm serious, brat." Ophelia jabbed her elbow into Wren's ribs as she stuck her bottom lip out into a pout. "We said no feelings."

"Gah, the dick must seriously be good."

Ophelia took her bottom lip between her teeth as she winced playfully, glancing at her friend out of the corner of her eye.

Wren's eyes widened as her jaw dropped, flying up from the couch as she pointed a finger in Ophelia's direction accusingly, her head cocking sideways.

"You haven't slept with him?" she asked incredulously. "*Ophelia*! You haven't even had sex?"

Ophelia smiled weakly up at her. "Well, no, not fully—"

"You're catching feelings before you've even seen his—" She paused, shaking her head in disbelief as her jaw dropped open again. "*Lia*."

Flinging her hands in the air, Ophelia fell back into the couch cushion, pouting fiercely as she stared up at the white, speckled ceiling. "I know."

"I thought for sure you might be dick-whipped."

"I'm an idiot," Ophelia grumbled, grabbing one of the fluffy couch pillows and squeezing it in her lap. "His ex-wife came into the bar last night. He was *married*, Wren, to a fucking goddess."

"I need a drink." Wren groaned, palming her forehead. "It's too early for this."

"How am I ever supposed to compete with something like that?"

Perhaps she needed a drink, too.

"Ophelia—"

"He was married to the complete opposite of me, Wren," Ophelia continued, her chest heaving as she spoke her thoughts out loud. "He loved her, lived with her, and married her. I'm not her, not even close. How could I ever expect to believe that he's into me?"

Wren whisked the pillow from her lap, throwing it into her face as she scolded her gently. "Your parental issues are showing, Ophelia. Stop doubting yourself so much and please listen to me when I tell you that you are *so* deserving of love. And if James is willing to give that to you, well—let him."

Love.

Did she even really know what love was? She had never received it as a child, or at least, not the kind that she was supposed to get. All Ophelia knew how to do was constantly work to be good enough for those around her, but always somehow falling short. No matter what she did, she never felt wanted.

"Wouldn't it be easier if I just stop seeing him altogether?" she asked shakily. Even the thought of breaking it off made her stomach churn. "Before it gets any deeper than it is. Save us both the hassle."

Wren flicked her tongue out to wet her lips as they formed a thin, contrite line.

"Well, it's a little late for that, because the boys are coming over for a movie tonight."

Ophelia gulped.

"They're coming *here*? Tonight?"

"I'm afraid so." Wren frowned apologetically. "So get your ass in the shower and put on something cute. You look like hell."

"Back up." Ophelia squinted jocosely at her friend, holding a single finger up as she pushed up from the couch. "We're having a *double* movie date night?"

Wren shrugged nonchalantly as she nodded. "Yeah, it's not a big deal, right? We're all just friends hanging out."

"Uh-*huh*."

Ophelia's eyes narrowed as her hands rested on her hips.

"Don't look at me like that." Wren rolled her eyes, turning to walk into the kitchen as she tried to escape her glare. "I know what you're thinking. It's *not* a big deal."

"You and Sean hook up a few times and now you're having romantic movie nights together." Ophelia snickered. "Which is way out of Wren Michaels's character, so I would say it's not *not* a big deal."

"Lia—"

"You've got it just as bad as me, babe."

Wren threw her hands aggravatedly in the air as she huffed, her hair puffing out in front of her face as she waved Ophelia off. "Shut up and get ready before I launch the first thing I can find at you. Which—oh, would you look at that? It just so happens to be a frying pan."

Ophelia laughed as she flung her hands up in defeat, rushing into the guest bedroom before she could be used as target practice. The doom that had bubbled in her stomach all night subsided at the thought of her best friend going through the same turmoil as her. She wouldn't be alone in the fight against the growing feelings that were making it hard to think these days. Her heart was caught in a vice grip of roots that had James' name all over them.

And as it usually did, her heartbeat thudded harshly against her chest at the thought of seeing his face again.

Ophelia jutted her bottom lip out as she examined herself in the bathroom mirror, flicking a couple of strands of her hair from her face as she sighed faintly.

Her hoodie fit loosely on her petite body, followed by her pajama shorts. She had changed clothes at least a dozen times, contemplating whether she should dress up or dress comfy. Ultimately, she decided to go with the latter.

It was just a movie night.

"You look beautiful."

Ophelia jumped slightly, her hand coming up to her chest as she gripped the edge of the counter, a soft laugh escaping her lips as her eyes fell on James. He perched in the doorway, donning his hoodie and sweats, looking ravishingly cozy.

"You scared me," she hissed playfully.

"Wren sent me to come look for you," he said with a sweet smile, pushing from the doorframe as he walked towards her steadily.

He looked so good in gray sweatpants.

"You found me," Ophelia murmured, her neck craning to look up at him now as he hovered over her, his eyes searching hers.

His hands snaked underneath her hoodie, finding her hips as he pulled her towards him. His lips pressed against her forehead as he hummed quietly. It was silent for a few moments as she buried her face into his chest, melting into his hug, and inhaling his warm scent that she had gotten so used to.

It was easier to hug than to talk.

Which is what they would eventually need to do.

"Are you okay?" James asked in a hushed voice.

Ophelia nodded, unmoving, as she intertwined her clammy hands in between his chest and her own. She knew that if she spoke, he would undoubtedly catch onto her white lie, knowing that she wasn't nearly okay at all.

"*Ophelia.*"

"I'm okay," she urged softly.

"What are you thinking about?" he pressed further, pushing her away partially, his finger tilting her chin upwards so their eyes would meet once more.

"Nothing," she fibbed, blinking slowly up at him. "Really."

A deep sigh left his lips as his hands brushed her hair back, his fingers combing through her messy waves, pressing her against the bathroom counter as he examined her tentatively.

"I know you're thinking about last night." His thumbs rubbed her temples as he held her face in his palms. "And I want you to stop. I'm here with *you*. Don't let my bad decisions from the past worry you so much like this. Be present with me."

She didn't deserve all of his kindness. At least, she didn't feel like she did. But maybe that was the daddy and mommy issues talking again.

James was such a sweet soul, he radiated a warm aura every time he was near. It was almost contagious. She'd never felt so comforted and safe with someone before. It was another one of the things that she enjoyed so much about him.

"Are you guys coming or what?" Wren called out from the living room.

"Smile," James ordered tenderly, his hands dropping from her face as his fingers encased her own.

Ophelia smiled up at him, sucking in a deep breath as she reached up onto her tip-toes to plant a kiss on his scruffy cheek.

"That's my pretty girl."

She had to hold in her audible moan at his words; the butterflies spiraled to her core as he pulled her out of the bathroom, leading her into the living room as he held her hand.

"Please, man. Back me up here," Sean pleaded as they entered the room, his dark eyes falling on James. "Please vote no to a chick flick."

Ophelia giggled as she grabbed a soft blanket from the bin next to the couch, taking a spot on the sofa as she flicked a piece of fresh popcorn between her lips from the bowl that Wren had just prepared.

"What's wrong with chick flicks?" James teased.

Wren nudged Ophelia secretively as she leaned over towards her, pretending to eat from the popcorn herself, as her eyebrows raised in surprise.

"Big dick energy," she whispered under her breath as the boys began to bicker back and forth.

Ophelia snickered quietly, putting a finger up to her lips to silence her friend as she rolled her eyes playfully. Hiding under the blanket, she took a moment to observe just how delicious James looked standing there, his back towards her.

Fuck.

This is why she could never think straight.

"Ophelia," Sean urged, narrowing his eyes pleadingly at her. "*Ophelia*, you know you want to watch an action movie."

"I don't know." Ophelia shrugged nonchalantly. "I think you're just scared you're going to cry if you watch a chick flick."

That earned a laugh from James as he held his hand to his

chest, his nose scrunching as he sat in the empty spot next to her, throwing the blanket over him as he fought back a smile.

"Oh, he would definitely cry," Wren teased, tossing some popcorn at Sean as he threw his hands in the air. "He's a big softie."

It warmed Ophelia's heart to watch her best friend with Sean. The way their eyes connected, and the way their body language shifted when they were around each other. It was like watching a pair of magnets. She was almost envious of them, even. It seemed so easy for the pair to just be together. There was no way that Wren could deny her feelings after tonight, not after watching them firsthand.

And then the lights were turned off—the only glow cascaded from the TV screen as Wren started the sappy romance, turning towards Sean as she curled up into him on the other side of the couch.

As Ophelia watched the opening credits, her heart lurched inside of her chest as James' hand rested on her knee, rubbing circles against her warm skin with his thumb.

Her body was pressed against his side, her knees curled up as she leaned them on his lap. Their figures cascaded in the warm blanket. She fought every urge to look over at him, the sexual tension growing vast as his thumb caressed her, goosebumps pricking her skin.

What was oxygen again? Because she was barely getting any as she struggled to compose her breathing. Thankfully, the movie was loud enough so no one could hear her shaky breaths.

She shuddered involuntarily as his hand crept further up

her leg, resting in the middle of her thigh as his fingers gripped her now, the atmosphere immediately changing as she peeked over at him in the darkness.

James brought a single finger up to his lips, his eyes observing her as a smirk danced along his features, signaling for her to be quiet.

It took every ounce of strength in her body not to clench her legs together needily as he brushed his hand upwards again, tickling her inner thigh and sending electric ripples straight to her core.

"Can I?" he whispered ever so softly in her ear, making her tremble beneath his hand as it twitched, asking for permission to touch her.

She bit down on her lip, nodding faintly as she peered over at him for a fraction of a second, before directing her attention to the TV.

Ophelia could feel herself soaking through her panties as they clung to her skin.

His fingers trailed up her thigh, whisking her shorts to the side as they found her soaked underwear, rubbing up and down slowly before sneaking beneath the lace fabric. She inhaled sharply at the sensation of his fingers against her, chewing at the inside of her lip as her eyebrows knitted together.

"Always *so* wet," his voice murmured for only her ears, making her clench around nothing as he rubbed circles against her clit.

Ophelia had never been so turned on in her life. She wanted to scream.

There was something incredibly hot about him touching her like this as they were sitting on the couch next to their friends, who were completely oblivious to what was happening beneath the covers.

Her hand gripped his arm firmly as she tried not to squirm underneath his skilled fingers, her tongue darting out to wet her dry lips.

"If we were alone," he drew out slowly. "*Ahh*, the things I would do to you."

Sweet Jesus.

Was she sweating? She was definitely sweating.

He gently pushed one finger inside of her, making her hips buck weakly, pumping it in and out as he curled it upwards. She could feel her juices leaking into his palm, but fuck, she couldn't help how turned on he made her feel.

"I want to bend you over this couch and fuck you so bad, baby."

Tears pricked the corners of her eyes as she held back a sob, her pussy pulsing around his fingers at the pet name. Her grip on his arm tightened so hard that her knuckles paled.

"I want you screaming my name."

She pulled the cover up to her face with her free hand, covering her crimson cheeks as she bit her lip so harshly that she could draw blood. He pushed another finger inside of her, filling her up, making her yearn for the feeling of him fucking her.

Thank God the couch was quite large, with a whole cushion between them and the canoodling pair at the other end.

"Turn towards me," James said under his breath, his voice

raspy. "*Slowly*. Come here."

Ophelia did as she was told, turning her body gently towards him, holding her breath to abstain from gasping as he shoved his thigh between her legs. Whisking his fingers from her, his hands slid underneath her hoodie, his thumbs finding her hardened peaks as his jaw clenched.

"Ride me," he ordered lowly, only so she could hear.

She gazed up at him innocently, taking her lip between her teeth as she nodded feebly, steadily bucking her hips as she ground her throbbing cunt against his massive thigh.

She'd never done this before.

"That's it." His lips brushed her ear, making her shiver. "Just like that, not too fast."

The words leaving his lips were enough to make her reach her climax now, his deep voice hot in her ear, making her want to fuck him right there—not caring who witnessed it. She shuddered softly as she rubbed against him, the sensation of his hands on her breasts making her cinch her eyebrows.

Wren and Sean laughed at something on the screen, making her freeze, as they continued to share popcorn like nothing was happening a few feet away.

Her heart was hammering in her chest, her neck warm as beads of sweat formed along her skin. Her hands gripped his hoodie under the blanket.

"Such a fucking good girl," he cooed, nipping her earlobe as he spoke. "Riding my thigh. Look at you."

Ophelia had never wanted to moan so badly in her entire life. She could feel the immense pressure between her legs now as her orgasm reached her, so close but so far, especially with the slow pace at which she had to buck against him. His hands slid down from her breasts, holding her waist, guiding her at an achingly slow pace as she thrust against his thigh.

"*More*," she mewled in his ear, begging for more words, more filth from his mouth.

"I can't wait to bury my dick inside of you," James whined hushedly. "Feel how tight you are. How wet."

The squeezing pressure in her core reached its climax, her orgasm washing over her, taking her breath away as she buried her face into his neck—nipping at his skin to keep from letting out the string of moans that were built inside of her chest. It took everything she had not to make a sound, twitch too hard, or move too much. As she came down from her high, James chuckled softly, holding her against him as he pressed a kiss to her temple.

"Feel better?" he asked.

Ophelia grinned.

"*Much*."

CHAPTER TWELVE

JAMES: *Want to go to San Francisco?*

Ophelia beamed down at her phone screen, her thick eyebrows knitting together in confusion as her fingers swiftly flicked across the keyboard as she typed back a response.

OPHELIA: *Wait, what? When?*

JAMES: *Today?*

San Francisco was at least a six-hour drive from Los Angeles, and that was if the traffic wasn't horrendous. And judging by the late afternoon time on the clock in Wren's kitchen—it was going to be an eight-hour drive *max*.

The thought of being stuck in a car with James for eight hours straight excited her *and* scared her. A lot of conversations could happen during that time.

OPHELIA: *What's the occasion, mister?*

Not that Ophelia needed an occasion to want to be around

him. There were only four weeks left of her summer before it was back to Georgia and fall classes, which she was trying hard to push to the back of her mind these days.

JAMES: *Just thought it would be better if I fucked you for the first time in a nice hotel overlooking the Golden Gate City.*

Snickering loudly, Ophelia clamped her hand over her mouth as her stomach practically dropped down into her butt, the butterflies erupting as her eyes scanned over his text one more time.

Where do I sign up? She thought.

OPHELIA: *Awfully bold of you, Mr. Benton.*

JAMES: *You haven't seen bold yet, pretty girl.*

Ophelia had already started to throw clothes into a small suitcase as they messaged back and forth, purposely making sure she packed her cutest lingerie sets.

OPHELIA: *How long should I plan to pack for?*

JAMES: *All weekend.*

An entire weekend away with James. If that thought wasn't enough to make her whisk her belongings into the suitcase as fast as she possibly could, she didn't know what else was. Her chest was heaving with excitement by the time she was done packing, brushing her messy hair behind her ears as she stared down at her handiwork before zipping the luggage closed.

Her eyebrows cinched tightly as a round of knocks resonated from the front door.

Throwing on her shoes, Ophelia stumbled into the hallway, teetering on each foot as she hurried to whisk open the door. Her hopes were answered as she met James' blue eyes with her own, crinkling in the corners as he smiled down at her. She must have looked crazy. Her heart was pounding against her chest so fast that she was sure it would burst through at any second.

His leather jacket was switched out for a brown dress coat, donning a pair of dark denim jeans and dress boots to match. His beard looked fuller than she remembered, accentuating his lips and angular jawline that she was constantly thinking about.

"Were you texting me from outside?" she teased, her eyes narrowing playfully up at him.

"Hmm, *no*, what gave you that impression?"

His voice was light, a hint of amusement lacing his words as he spoke.

Ophelia hummed as her fingers found his, holding his hand faintly. "What if I had said no? Would you have gone home?"

Stepping into the doorway slowly, he tugged on her hand, pulling her flush against him. "I knew you weren't going to say no."

She wondered if he could feel how harshly her heart was beating against her chest.

"You don't know that," Ophelia countered sweetly, blinking up at him through her lashes. "Maybe I had a hot date tonight."

"Yeah." He paused, his lips pecking hers. "With *me*. Now get your suitcase. We're hitting the road, Clark."

The kiss was so domesticated like he had been doing it for years, as though it was instinct to give her quick kisses. Did he even have to think about it? Was it just natural? Did he think too much about it? Or was she the only person who would think that much into it?

Her heart screamed for him inside of her chest, begging for more kisses, long kisses. Hot kisses. But her head told her that it was bad enough that he was giving her docile kisses at all.

Friends with benefits.

The line was so far beyond blurry that she wasn't even sure that there was a line. But it sure felt too damn good to care, sometimes.

Ophelia tried to keep her mind from being preoccupied with those thoughts as they made their way down to the front lobby. James tugged her suitcase along behind him as his eyes kept peeking to the side to glance at her, darting away every time she would lift her gaze to meet his.

Her lips twitched with a smile.

Sean gave James the keys to his black, luxury SUV for the weekend, not in much need of it since he was planning on having Wren over at his apartment for a few days. It made Ophelia's heart swell with happiness seeing her best friend so smitten with someone. They were practically created for one another, like two puzzle pieces that were meant to fit together. They *could* be together.

She was jealous.

Opening up the passenger door for her to climb inside, James reached his hand out to help her as she crawled into the lifted vehicle, sending him a sweet smile before watching him walk around the car to hop into the opposite side.

"Why San Francisco?"

Her voice was soft as she pondered out loud.

Pulling away from Wren's apartment complex, James swallowed thickly before responding. "That's where my sister lived."

The beautiful girl from the tattoo. From the way he reacted as he spoke of her and the decision to get an entire tattoo of her, it was obvious that the pair had been close. It made her heart lurch in her chest to think about how he had lost his sister.

Wren was her soul sister—she couldn't even bear the thought of losing her.

Ophelia stared quietly out of the window for a while, allowing him some space in case the question had brought up any bad memories.

"Have you ever been?" he asked after a few beats of long silence.

"No."

"You'll love it. I used to drive up almost every week just to see her before everything happened," he explained, his hand reaching up to rub his chin. "It's beautiful."

"What was her name?" Ophelia questioned gently, peeking over at him timidly as she did so, gauging his reaction to her words.

"Brianna," James murmured.

She noticed the way he readjusted his position in the leather seat, his hand gripping the steering wheel harder. His jaw muscles clenched so tightly that she could see it through his thick beard.

Reaching over to place her hand on top of his white knuckles, stroking her thumb across them, she sucked in a deep breath.

"Hey, I'm sorry if that was too much. We don't have to talk about that if you don't want to," Ophelia reassured him.

He relaxed under her touch, his shoulders sagging as the tension in his body went away, his eyes quietly thanking her as he peered over at her thoughtfully.

"I have an idea," she chirped excitedly when he didn't say anything, her hand dropping from his as she patted his knee jocosely. "Let's ask each other questions. Like speed dating, you know? A question for a question, if you will."

James laughed, making relief wash through her as a smile spread across his lips.

"If you're trying to get to know me, Clark, just say so."

Ophelia rolled her eyes flippantly as she sat back in her seat, tapping her chin as she thought of the perfect question to hit him with.

"When is your birthday?" she asked.

"January 10th," he replied swiftly. "When is yours?"

"*May* 10th."

He hummed, seemingly pleased with that answer.

"What's your favorite color?" Ophelia questioned even

quicker now.

His head turned to look at her, his lips curving slightly. "Blue."

"What kind of blue?"

"Whatever kind your eyes are."

Ophelia flushed as she gave him a pointed look.

"What's *your* favorite color?" he continued with a smirk.

"Depends on the day. Today? It's probably like a pastel yellow." She huffed, crossing her arms as she pouted. "You know, you're supposed to ask your own questions, not just repeat mine."

"What do you actually want to go to school for?"

The question took her by surprise, her eyes widening as she stared over at him now, blinking dumbly as she attempted to gather her words. No one had ever asked her that before. Telling people that she wasted her time becoming a surgeon when all she wanted was to bake seemed humiliating, but if she lied, he would be able to tell right away. Somehow, he always knew.

Diving right in.

"What if I don't know the answer to your question?" Ophelia mumbled tentatively, gnawing at her lip.

"Does that count as a question?" he countered playfully, his eyes darting over towards her briefly before falling back on the road.

She sighed, intertwining her fingers in her lap. "I'll have to get back to you on that one."

"That's fair."

"How long were you married?"

Since we're asking serious questions.

His tongue flicked out to wet his lips, *slowly*, before he swallowed. She had surprised him with her brazen question, just as he had surprised her with his own. She secretly enjoyed watching him squirm a bit, mentally reminding herself it was a smidge of payback for not telling her to begin with.

"Five years," James said after a while.

"Five *years*?" She choked.

Five years was a long time to be with someone. To live with someone. To sleep in the same bed next to someone. Wake up to that person every day.

"I've been divorced for two," he added, his voice gentle now.

Ophelia took a deep breath as she stared at the highway ahead of them, her eyes focusing on the white line drawn on the pavement as she gathered her bearings. She hadn't even realized that her hand was gripping the leather seat.

"What was your longest relationship?" he continued coolly.

"I've never actually been in one."

She sounded small, far away, and mentally maybe she was. Her mind was still reeling at the fact that he had been with someone for who knows how long before they decided to get married, and then five years on top of that. And now she had to dwell on the sad fact that she'd never been committed to someone like he had.

"*Never?*" James shot back incredulously.

Ophelia nodded, keeping her gaze forward. "It's hard to be in a relationship when you're always the side girl. The rebound. The second option."

The truth was, she had never been the priority for anyone in her entire life, not even for her parents. Every guy she had ever seen potential with secretly had a girlfriend, had their priorities set elsewhere, or they were too emotionally scarred for a relationship—and now, perhaps, she was, too.

"Ophelia."

His voice brought her back.

"Hmm?" she asked.

"I know how difficult it must be for you to have parents that love their job more than their own daughter," he said softly, his hand creeping over to squeeze her thigh faintly. "And having boys who don't know their head from their ass. I'm sorry that no one has ever prioritized you the way that you deserve."

Her eyes welled with tears, stinging slightly, as she bit back the sob that formed inside of her chest. No one had ever said that to her before, not even close—she didn't know people even thought that way aside from the men in fictional movies. But he wasn't done.

"And I know that it's intimidating for you to hear that I was married to someone," he whispered, his eyes flickering over to meet hers briefly before they were forced to glance back at the road, but his hand squeezed her again for reassurance. "But you have to remember that I'm older than you are. I've lived more life than you have. Marrying her was a mistake from the start. I knew it was, but I did it anyway. I learned from that lesson and realized I didn't want to make mistakes like that anymore. Waste time that I don't have."

She blinked back the tears that threatened to trickle down her cheeks, turning to stare out of the window so he wouldn't see as she listened to him speak.

"Doing this—whatever the definition of this is—is not a mistake to me."

She twisted to look at him, her chest heaving shakily. "You don't think so?"

"I know that it's not." He sounded certain.

She knew she couldn't respond. Her sob was in her throat now, fighting violently to be set free. Instead, she unbuckled her seat belt and crawled over to the middle seat as she buried herself into his side. Melting into him, the warmth of his body, she hid her face in the crevice of his neck. His arm wrapped around her, pulling her in closer, rubbing her thigh as she pulled her legs up to her chest.

They sat like this for a while, in silence.

It was like he knew that she couldn't talk without crying. An unspoken acknowledgment was confirmed every time his hand squeezed her reassuringly or his cheek pressed more firmly to the top of her head.

That's when it hit her—*hard*. It felt like the wind was knocked out of her. Her chest heaved like there was a ton of weight pressing down on it, crushing her.

James Benton was either going to be the greatest love of her life or the greatest heartbreak.

And from where she sat, either one seemed like a good place to be.

CHAPTER THIRTEEN

THE SENSATION OF JAMES grazing his finger along Ophelia's cheek made her stir awake, blinking slowly through slits as she sat up straight.

She had passed out against him earlier, slumped down practically in his lap as she slept. She could feel the indentations that the seam of his jeans had made against her skin. Even her hair was ruffled from her slumber. It was dark outside now, the only light coming from the dash screen inside the car. It illuminated the pair as they sat silently in the leather seats.

"How long have I been sleeping?" She groaned raspily, stretching her arms out sleepily as she glanced out of the windshield. "Where are we?"

Moonlight cascaded across the empty parking lot they were in, reflecting off of the waves that crashed against the shoreline in front of them. Her eyes scanned a beach she didn't recognize.

"A beach in San Francisco," James said softly. "I didn't want to wake you."

"We're already here?"

"You passed out, and you looked cozy." He chuckled, his

eyes flickering up to meet hers. "So I figured you needed the rest."

Brushing her messy hair behind her ears, Ophelia glanced back out to the beach, listening as the water crashed against the sand. "Why are we at the beach?"

"Because you like the beach."

She couldn't quite explain it, simply because she didn't understand it much herself, but something was stirring inside of her. Every time he spoke, every time he looked at her, every time he moved—she craved more of him. It was like a rush of electricity through her veins when he touched her. And she wanted to feel it everywhere, all at once.

"Want to go swimming?" she asked in a playful whisper, her eyebrows raising excitedly as she smiled over him now.

He looked hesitant.

"The water is probably freezing, Ophelia."

She giggled at his perplexed expression, leaning over as she placed her hand on his thigh for leverage. "Mmm, *yeah*, but we'll have each other for warmth."

James chewed at the inside of his lip, his eyes darting down to her mouth as he sucked in a deep breath. Glancing back up to meet her eyes, she noticed the uncertainty in his.

"*Swim* with me," she whispered.

"But our clothes." His voice wavered.

"Will be safe and dry on the beach."

His lips parted as the realization of what she was saying sunk in, the corners of his mouth twitching as he fought back a smile. Pushing open the car door, he climbed out, turning back towards her with a small nose scrunch.

"Well, lead the way, pretty girl."

Climbing over the seat to hop out after him, Ophelia shot him a smile as she grabbed his hand, tugging him along behind her as she trekked towards the sand. The wind was chilly, nipping at her cheeks as they approached the water, her hair whipping around her face.

A few feet away from the crashing waves, she released his hand, twirling around to face him as her fingers gripped the hem of her sweatshirt—whipping it over her head as it dropped to the sand. His eyes immediately fell on her bralette; his lips parting as he examined her as though it were the first time.

"Jesus, Ophelia," he muttered.

"What?"

Unzipping her jeans slowly, she waited on his answer, walking backward gradually until she pushed the denim down her legs and kicked them off along with her shoes. The air was freezing against her skin, making her hair prick with every gust of wind. Her nipples hardened in response.

"Just—*you*," James stuttered, flinging his coat from his arms impatiently as he followed her now.

The ocean nipped at her heels as the water glided up the sand; the rigidness making her flinch as goosebumps trailed across every inch of her exposed skin.

Ophelia observed as he tugged his shirt over his head, exposing his bare, tattooed chest that glistened in the moonlight. He looked absolutely delicious. Her mouth felt dry as he approached her now, unbuttoning his jeans.

His hair was disheveled from removing his clothes, and she

had to fight the urge to run her fingers through it. He breathed heavily as he stared at her, his hands shaky as he removed his pants.

She loved when he was vulnerable. It made her feel like liquid, just like the icy water that rushed past her feet.

Ophelia hadn't seen him like this before, in just his tight boxer briefs, squeezing him around his large thighs and chiseled waist. She wanted to touch him everywhere, feel every detail of him underneath her fingertips.

He stepped closer, his hands reaching up to tug her bra straps down her shoulders, pressing a kiss to her skin as he did so. The feeling of his beard scratching against her made her shudder.

"You're beautiful," he murmured, reaching around to unclasp her bra, pulling it from her body as his eyes trailed down her chest.

Ophelia pressed herself against him, his warmth spreading across her cold skin like a flame, as her hands rested on his burly chest.

"Touch me." Her voice trembled.

James groaned as his hands cupped her ass, his lips parting as he pulled her tightly against him, and his fingers slid beneath the waistline of her panties. She could feel how hard he was underneath his boxers, making her cheeks flush a deep crimson color.

"Take these off."

Taking her lip between her teeth, Ophelia shook her head, grasping his shoulders as she shoved him urgently down to his knees—his eyes at level with her navel.

"You take them off," she ordered, her fingers finally tangling in his hair.

Yanking them down her legs now, he gazed up at her as he trailed kisses across her waistline, his fingers lingering on her legs as he caressed them lightly.

"You're killing me," he said in a strained voice.

Seeing how desperate he was getting for her only encouraged her more. Pushing away from him, twirling around to face the ocean now, she flicked her head over her shoulder as she observed the way his eyes raked over her body. The water was beyond ice cold as she stepped into it, but she was determined not to let it show.

She was knee-deep before his jaw had finally clamped shut, his boxer briefs disappearing from his body as he hurried in after her, hissing from the temperature of the water.

"Shit, *shit*," he panted. "This is fucking freezing."

Reaching her hand out to him, she wiggled her fingers as a smile crept onto her full lips.

"Come here."

Ophelia wanted to laugh at how quickly he grasped her fingers, tugging her to him as he pulled her flush against his chest, their waists fully submerged in the water. Everywhere his body touched hers felt warm; her skin hummed from the contact.

"You feel good," he breathed through a smile, wrapping his arms around her as he buried his face into her neck for warmth.

Her hands rested on his back, gliding down softly until they fell on his hips. She could hear the way his breath hitched in her ear, making the butterflies come alive in her stomach.

"Do I?" Ophelia questioned innocently.

He swallowed thickly, humming in response.

And then she felt it. Despite how piercing the water was, she could feel his hard length brush against her inner thigh. And she was a lot shorter than he was, so that meant that he was hu—

"Jesus fucking Christ," James whined, his beard scratching her neck as he spoke. "If making me hard in this cold water doesn't tell you the effect you have on me, I don't know what does."

"*Hmm.*" She sighed deeply, trailing her fingers around his waist, down his happy trail. "I make you hard, James?"

Bucking his hips against her, he grunted faintly.

Her hand stopped just above his dick now, pulling her head back to look up into his eyes that were begging for her. "Can I touch you?"

The words made him shiver, his head bobbing up and down eagerly. His lips parted in awe as her fingers encircled him. He was fucking huge. She didn't have to see it, she could feel it.

James' eyes closed as she started to stroke him steadily, taking her time, feeling every inch of him—imprinting it in her mind as she reached up to grasp the back of his neck with her other hand.

"*Fuck.*"

Ophelia grinned.

Stroking him faster, her fingers entangled in his dark hair, making his eyebrows cinch together.

"Do my fingers feel good, baby?" she asked with a whimper, falling in love with the way he shuddered beneath her.

His eyes flashed open at her words, and his lips smashed into hers almost immediately. Their teeth clashed slightly as he devoured her mouth.

He bucked against her hand, his fingers digging into her waist as his chest heaved shakily.

"Fuck, Ophelia, I'm already close."

His breath fanned across her cheeks, and her neck, as he broke away from her lips. Flicking her wrist now as she twisted her fingers around him, she listened to him moan, relishing in the sound.

"I wish you were inside of me," Ophelia murmured into his ear, nipping his earlobe.

A guttural moan escaped his lips as he twitched inside of her hand, his hips pressing against her as a wave knocked against them—swaying them close to shore as he came, holding her so tightly that she was sure she might've bruised.

His head rested on her shoulder as he came down from his high, pressing kisses softly to her skin.

"Clark?"

His voice was weak.

"Hmm?" Her eyes closed as he continued to pepper kisses along her collarbone.

"This doesn't feel like friends with benefits."

She peered up at him now, her head tilting sideways as she reached up to place her hand against his scruffy cheek, running her fingers through his beard.

"I know." She smiled softly.

She had broken her own rule, no feelings. As she stared up at him, held his face in her palm, listening to his heavy breathing from what she did—all she was *doing* was feeling. She felt him everywhere, all at once. He was in her veins like he belonged there.

Ophelia had never felt like that with any of the other guys she had been with. She ultimately got bored with their antics or got the ick.

There was no ick when it came to James.

"We should get back to the car," he mumbled, kissing her shoulder once more. "Get the heat on before we catch a cold."

She nodded in agreement, pressing her forehead to his chest briefly before they waded out of the water together, hurrying to put their clothes back on before the chilly air could penetrate their bones.

It was there again. The unspoken.

Words didn't need to be said about how they felt. All they had to do was look at each other and they knew.

And the unspoken, for her, was that she liked him *way* too much to be fine when she left at the end of the summer. She was quite positive that it was going to sting like a deep cut through her soul.

And there were still four weeks left.

CHAPTER FOURTEEN

By the time they had arrived at the hotel last night, Ophelia and James were past the point of exhaustion, so tired and still cold from their skinny-dipping escapade that they immediately collapsed on the giant California king and passed out.

As Ophelia slowly opened her eyes, a smile flashed across her lips as she glanced over at James, who was still knocked out.

His hair was ruffled against the pillows, his lips in a sleepy pout as he snoozed away, and his arm entangled around her leg. He was warm against her, as he usually was, making the soft bed feel even more cozy.

How had she already slept in the same bed as this man without having sex first?

As the thought flickered through her mind, it was as though he could hear it, his eyes fluttering open in a sleepy manner. His cheeks lifted as his eyes fell on her, his hand squeezing her thigh as he shifted quietly in the bed. Stretching out with a small yawn, he hummed contently.

"Good morning," she cooed.

"Mmm." He hummed raspily, tugging her towards him by her legs. "*Yes,* it is."

A giggle escaped her lips as she quickly tried to crawl away from him, her hands prying him from her as she went to climb from the bed. "I have to brush my teeth!"

"*No.*"

James pulled her against him, making her fall back onto his chest as his arms enveloped her waist. Burying his face into her waves, he pressed a kiss to her shoulder.

"Stay." He sighed.

The word should've been simple. But she knew it was deeper than that. He knew it was deeper than that. It meant stay here past four weeks, *stay*.

They both were quiet for a while, his arms remaining around her, his face in her neck. She rested her head back on his shoulder, staring up at the speckled ceiling as she struggled to compose her nervous breathing.

"I should get up and take a shower," Ophelia murmured, trailing her fingers along his arm. "Get ready for whatever you have planned for us today."

"Shower with me," he pleaded in a soft tone.

The urgency in his voice tore her heart in two, making it quickly set in that he was far deeper into this than she was. He had fallen down the black hole with no hopes of climbing out again. If she hadn't been fighting it so much, she'd be jumping in head first, right behind him.

Twisting around in his arms so that her chest was pressed against his, she peered down at him, her hair cascading down around them. Licking her lips, she trailed her finger along his collarbone, and the ink imprinted into his skin.

"Can I ask you something?" she pressed gently.

He nodded slowly, his neck craning to allow her fingers free rein.

"When you said that this doesn't feel like friends with benefits," she murmured, her eyebrows cinching as she spoke. "What did you mean? What does it feel like?"

Ophelia wondered mostly because she wanted him to describe how she was feeling. She wanted him to give it a name, a description, a meaning. She couldn't put words to something she had never felt before in her entire life. Perhaps she just wanted vocal confirmation that he felt the same.

"It feels like I'm not ready for you to go back to Georgia."

She sighed, closing her eyes.

The confirmation didn't feel as good as she expected, it only made her more anxious. Should they have stopped this before it got too far? Should they have never started to begin with?

"What does it feel like to you?" he asked.

"I don't know," she mumbled truthfully, her eyes falling to her hands on his chest. "I've never felt this way before."

"Do you *want* to go back to Georgia?"

The question made her head reel with overwhelming thoughts, a groan escaping her lips as she pulled away from him now, sitting up in the bed as she faced the other way. She wasn't sure why she naturally felt the need to avoid this conversation, but it made her stomach churn uneasily to have it.

"I have to go back," she whispered. "I've put so much time into it already. My parents have spent so much money on college. A lot is riding on this."

"Is it what you want, Ophelia?" James questioned firmly

now, the bed shifting underneath them as he sat up, too.

"It's more than just what I want, James," she said, standing up as she faced him, her arms crossing over her chest. "I wish it could be that simple, but it's not."

"But it can be that simple." His thick eyebrows knitted together as he stared at her, his chest heaving from their conversation. "Why are you so set on making your parents happy, but not yourself?"

Ophelia pinched the bridge of her nose as she walked towards the bathroom. "*Don't*. We can't have this conversation right now."

She wanted to step away and create distance before things got too heated to the point where one of them was saying something that they didn't mean. And that's exactly what would happen if they continued this way.

The situation with her parents was more complicated than anyone knew, even Wren. Ophelia didn't want anyone to worry about her, didn't want anyone to think she couldn't handle herself or her parents—but they had paid for her college expenses, and they were going to pay for medical school, as well. None of this would happen if they weren't so keen on her following in their footsteps.

She couldn't afford college on her own.

She couldn't afford to go to college for something she wanted to do on her own.

It wasn't ideal, but it's what things were. They had this giant leverage over her head and there was nothing that she could do about it.

Turning on the water for the shower in the bathroom,

Ophelia pressed her forehead against the wall as she waited for it to warm up.

"*No*," James' voice called out from behind her, making her squeeze her eyes closed. "You don't get to just walk away. You need to talk to me."

"There's nothing to say, James," Ophelia snapped gently, twirling around as her hands flew in the air. "That's just how things are. We decided what this was from the beginning. I don't know what to say."

His jaw clenched.

"*We* didn't decide this," he said, his finger pointing at the both of them. "You did."

She scoffed. "You didn't refuse, you know. You could have said no."

"Because you had me so wrapped around your finger since the night I met you that I would have agreed to anything just to be around you, Ophelia."

There were only inches between them as they glared at each other now. Her nostrils flared irritably as she fumed up at him with a pout, the shower steaming behind her as she sucked in a deep breath.

"Then why couldn't you just stick with it?" she asked loudly, blinking up at him. "Why didn't you just keep your feelings out of it?"

"It's not like I had a choice." James huffed, his eyes staring down at her in disbelief. "With you batting your eyelashes and biting your fucking lip and—"

"Don't blame this on me."

"Shut *up*."

As a gasp escaped her lips at his words, it was quickly muffled as he smashed his lips against hers, his beard scratching her skin as he devoured her heatedly. His hand grasped her face, tangled in her hair, and tugged her forcefully to him as his tongue dipped between her lips.

A moan rumbled through his chest as he tasted her, pushing her back up against the wall that she was previously resting her forehead against, yanking her sweater over her head before clashing his teeth with hers as he kissed her with desperate hunger.

His touch was angry. And it only made the butterflies in her stomach feel like a flame igniting, spreading throughout her body with so much heat that she could hardly breathe.

Pressing his abdomen against her, pinning her to the wall, he grasped her hands and shoved them above her head—peppering sloppy kisses down her neck, her collarbone, and the valley between her breasts. Her nipples hardened from his touch, and her legs clenched together as her panties dampened.

She could feel how hard he was through his jeans, pressing against her inner thigh as he encased her nipple in his mouth, making her pant softly. His beard was a stark contrast to the gentleness of his lips as he suckled her.

"I—"

Suck.

"Am going to—"

Kiss.

"Fuck you against this shower wall."

She shuddered underneath him, arching her back as she bit

her lip, wanting his lips everywhere.

Dropping her hands, he kissed down her stomach, his fingers unbuttoning her jeans as he tugged them down her legs impatiently. Crouched down in front of her, his eyes flickered up to gaze at her before he slid his fingers beneath her panties, feeling how wet she'd already gotten for him.

"*Please*," she whined, the word escaping her lips before she even had a chance to stop it.

Sliding her panties down her thighs, his lips pressed against her clit, his tongue flicking between her folds as her hips bucked against his face. His beard rubbed her in all the right places as he lapped at her.

Ophelia leaned her head against the wall as she sighed softly, her fingers tangling in his messy hair, as he tasted what he did to her. In moments like these, she didn't even remember what Georgia was.

Fuck Georgia.

His lips left her as he stood, the disappointment almost settling in, but it disappeared the moment he whisked his shirt from his body. Her lip tugged between her teeth as she watched him undress, fully able to see him now in the light of the bathroom, the drool threatening to drip from her lips.

Feeling how huge he was, that was one thing. But seeing it now? Another thing entirely.

"Come here," James breathed. The softness in his voice was back, just faintly as he whisked open the shower door to pull her inside with him.

His hands were still angry, and she loved it. The hot water showered over them, making her inhale sharply from the initial sting, only having little time to recover before his hands were holding her face again.

She was engulfed in his lips and water as he pressed her back against the wall, inhaling her as a groan left his mouth. The sound reverberated against her, making her arch into him needily. His hand twisted her around, shoving her against the wall, pulling her hips towards him as his knee shifted her legs further apart.

She couldn't tell if it was water dripping down her legs or *her*.

"Fuck." He growled, his teeth sinking into her shoulder. "I have to grab a condom."

He turned to leave the shower, his length grazing her thigh before her fingers linked around his wrist to stop him. Looking over her shoulder, she shook her head tentatively.

"I'm on the pill."

She wanted him now. No more waiting. Not even a second.

"I'm clean," he breathed.

Her thumb rubbed his wrist gently as her tongue wet her bottom lip. "So am I."

With a moan, he had his hands on her again, teasing her entrance with the tip of his cock as he grabbed her shoulder for leverage.

"I wanted to fuck you, *hard*," he mumbled lowly. "But now I think I want to go really slow. Make you *feel* me. Make you regret ever saying you wanted to be just friends."

Before she could reply, he pushed himself inside of her gently, easing in second by second. Her hands pressed against the wall firmly as her mouth popped open, a whimper escaping her lips as he stretched her out. He didn't stop until he was buried inside of her, pausing as she adjusted to his size, both of them panting heavily from the sensation of her already clenching around him.

"You okay, Lia?" James said gently next to her ear, his chest leaning against her back as he pressed into her.

Lia.

He'd never called her that before.

"More," she rasped weakly. "I need more."

Pulling out of her almost fully, neither one of them was prepared for the feeling of him slamming back into her, harder this time. They moaned in sync, his hands squeezing her skin as he pressed his forehead to her back.

"Holy shit," he breathed. "You feel so good. So fucking good."

Ophelia impatiently rocked her hips against him, needing the friction, needing the sensation of him moving inside of her. She could feel his length twitch at her movements.

"Please, Jamie," she panted. "I need you, I need this."

It was like those words lit a match, something inside of him bursting into flames as he whined softly, thrusting into her now.

Over.

And over.

And *over*.

Her cheek and breasts were pressed into the wall as his hands gripped her wet hair, pounding into her so hard—but she didn't care. She needed more. Water splashed everywhere as their skin collided continuously, clapping together so loudly that she was sure the entire hotel could hear it.

"Jesus fucking Christ, baby," James groaned, his voice cracking.

As she moaned in response, he suddenly pulled out of her. Before she could protest, he turned her around to face him as he whisked her up into his arms, hoisting her legs around his waist as he climbed out of the shower and walked into the bedroom.

Water trickled down her skin as she kissed his neck, trailing them down to his collarbone as he threw her wet body onto the bed, not hesitating as he slid himself between her legs.

"I wanna look at you while I fuck you," he admitted with a moan, guiding his dick inside of her once more. "Want you to look at me while you're coming and then tell me you still want to be friends."

Ophelia whimpered as he thrust into her, her arms enveloping his neck as her eyes flickered down to watch him slam into her. Her mouth popped open from the pressure building inside her core.

"James," she mewled, practically melting into a puddle of mush as he held onto her, his impressive speed making him pant in her ear. "I could never just be friends with you."

The feeling of him pulling completely out of her, only to slam into her to the hilt each time, was making her head spin. Stars speckled her vision as her climax rose, the pressure becoming almost unbearable now.

"That's my girl." He sighed, the relief washing over his words as they trickled from his mouth, the butterflies erupting in her stomach. "*My* girl. Come for me, yeah? Come on my cock."

Her legs wrapped around his waist as she bit into his shoulder. As her eyes squeezed shut, her toes curled, her body shook, and the coil snapped. James wasn't far behind her, gripping the sheets next to her head as he slammed into her for the last time. A whine left his lips that could've sent her straight into orbit.

As they came down from their highs, the butterflies only seemed to grow inside her stomach as she replayed his words over and over inside her head.

His girl.

CHAPTER FIFTEEN

Ophelia rested her chin on James' shoulder, peeking up at his focused features as he drove. Her finger trailed along his scarred arm that was hidden beneath his jacket. His eyes were trained on the pavement of the road as his hand rested on the steering wheel, the other on her thigh.

Her body was still tired from the escapades earlier that day, but she loved it. She relished in the soreness that proved he had been all over her.

After breakfast in bed, and a stroll around the city to see the sights, now they were on the way to—well, she wasn't really sure.

It was a surprise.

Somewhere he liked to go and wanted to show her. It made her chest squeeze warmly to know that he wanted to let her in on a special spot, a place that he would go for himself. He was opening up even more to her, even though she didn't feel like she deserved it. Especially after throwing those harsh words at him earlier. The thought of what happened afterward made a blush creep into her cheeks.

"I've never asked you before." She licked her lips hesitantly. "But, what happened to your arm?"

She wanted to squeeze her eyes shut and cross her fingers in hopes that it wasn't a touchy subject for him. She didn't want to ruin him taking her to his special place, but she was curious.

Ophelia could feel his body tense underneath her for a moment, her fears realized as he sucked in a deep breath. Leaning forward to press a reassuring kiss to his neck, she watched as he relaxed.

"A car accident."

He looked like he wanted to say more, so she stayed quiet, blinking up at him as her eyebrows pulled together sympathetically.

His fingers tapped against her leg now, his anxiety apparent as he swallowed thickly.

"I wasn't wearing a seatbelt." He sounded regretful, his voice low as he spoke. "Went through the windshield."

"The *windshield?*"

Ophelia picked her head up from his shoulder, her eyes wide in shock at his words, as her hands still held him comfortingly. She couldn't imagine what it must have been like to experience something so scary, so life-threatening. Her chest hurt at the thought of him being scared at that moment. She didn't want to think about it at all. In pain or on the verge of life or death, was not a picture she wanted to paint in her mind of him.

James cleared his throat.

"Yeah, that's the day Brianna died."

Her face fell; her heart thudded against her chest as her lips parted.

"My arm was shredded from the glass, and the skin was past the point of saving," he continued quietly. "I had an open fracture in my forearm. They were going to amputate, but they chose to do skin grafts to try and save it."

Ophelia gulped, her throat dry from the cottony wad of saliva stuck in the middle of it.

"Brianna was driving. Had her seatbelt on—did everything she was supposed to do." James paused, biting the inside of his cheek. "The other car just came out of nowhere. Hit the front corner where she sat. It killed her on impact, but yet *me*, the idiot who didn't wear his seatbelt and got thrown through the windshield, I lived."

Tears pricked the corners of her eyes as she listened to him speak, watching the hurt wash over his features as his fingers tightened around the steering wheel. She blinked them away quickly. Pressing her forehead against his shoulder, Ophelia wrapped her hands around his arm, caressing him with her thumbs gently.

"I'm so sorry, James."

"All I can remember is waking up in so much *pain*. But it could never amount to what I felt when the paramedics arrived and announced her dead on the scene."

Ophelia swallowed as her eyes stung with tears. She never got to experience what having siblings was like; Wren and Paul were the closest people that she had to the real thing. The thought of something ever happening to one of them made her stomach churn, so she couldn't begin to imagine what James had gone through that day.

It was quiet for a few beats before he cleared his throat. "I always wished that it was me instead of her that night. I hated myself because I was the living reminder that my sister was dead."

Lifting her head, she perched her chin on his shoulder. Words didn't feel good enough at that moment; there weren't words that she could say to make anything better or take the grief that he felt away. So, instead, she ran her fingers through the hair at the nape of his neck. Massaging his scalp with her fingertips in a way that she hoped was comforting.

"I guess I didn't get off as much as I think I did," he whispered, a faint chuckle slipping from his lips as he tried to lighten the mood. "I'm probably the only person on the planet with a disgusting, scarred arm."

All this time, she thought he was ashamed of his arm. Embarrassed by it. It never occurred to her that he hated looking at it because it reminded him of the worst day of his life.

"There's nothing wrong with your arm," she scolded gently.

James' lips twitched as he took a second to look down at her, his eyes darting across her features in admiration before settling back on the pavement ahead of them. His hand traveled up her thigh, searching for hers, as he linked his fingers with her own.

"You're the first person to make me see it in a different light."

"I am?"

He nodded. "Ever since you said it was badass."

"It *is* badass." Ophelia giggled, pressing her face into his shoulder as she hid her crimson cheeks. "It really completes your whole... bartender, motorcycle man ensemble."

A laugh escaped his bearded lips. A loud one, one she hadn't heard before—and it was beautiful. She would never get tired of hearing it. She would die happily if it was the last sound she ever heard. As much as she didn't want to brush over this moment, if laughing it off made him feel better, then she'd listen to him laugh all night.

"You really think that?" he asked as he smiled down at her.

She nodded with a sweet smile to mirror his own.

"It's not a, uh–" He hesitated, clearing his throat. "Turn off?"

"Did I seem turned off to you a few hours ago?"

The mention of what occurred earlier that day made the lightest shade of red flash across his cheeks. Not at all resembling the dominant man who shoved her against the shower wall. His blush made her stomach somersault.

She made James Benton blush.

"We're almost there," he said after a few moments.

The last place she expected him to pull up to was a cemetery. As they drove through black metal gates, she examined all the different headstones as they passed them by, knowing exactly why they were there. Her first reaction was to panic. He didn't have to bring her here. Somewhere so insanely personal to him, to his relationship with his sister—someone Ophelia had never even gotten to meet.

Looking up at him anxiously, her bottom lip pursed as she gnawed at it from the inside. She hadn't even realized she was squeezing his arm as hard as she was until his eyes flashed down at her tense fingers.

"She's here," Ophelia mumbled weakly.

"Yes."

"*James.*"

She stared at him apprehensively, releasing his arm as she slid back over to the passenger seat.

"What's wrong, Ophelia?" James asked softly, his eyebrows knitting.

"You didn't have to bring me here. It's so personal," she said as she looked around the graveyard nervously. "I'm intruding. I'm intruding on your time with your sister—"

"Gemma doesn't even know where Brianna is buried, do you know that? My own ex-wife never even bothered to visit her grave."

Ophelia stopped. "She didn't come to her funeral?"

"She was too busy fucking one of my best friends."

Her mouth fell open at that one, the dismay written across her face as she blinked over at him in bewilderment. She didn't know what to say. What words were right at this moment? Pulling herself together, Ophelia climbed over the middle of the seat to wrap her arms around his neck, burying her face into him as she hugged him tightly.

"I don't know what to say," she mumbled against his neck. "This must be a lot for you. You didn't have to tell me these things *or* bring me here."

His hands rubbed her lower back.

"I wanted to."

Pulling away partially, her hands went to his cheeks, her thumbs rubbing them gently as she peered into his eyes—searching them for any ounce of hesitation. There was none.

"Okay," she breathed.

"C'mon," James urged, taking her hand in his. "I want her to meet you."

Her heart grew in her chest, swelled with every step they took as they walked through the cemetery, every second that his hand held hers.

He wanted her to meet Brianna.

Ophelia felt herself staring at James as they approached the small headstone that read *Brianna Benton*, examining every twitch in his expression to make sure he was okay. He was stoic, however; his features were careful not to give anything away as the pair stood in front of her grave, hand in hand. It was quiet for a while as he stared down at the headstone.

"Hey, Bri."

Who knew two simple words could hold so much emotion? So much weight?

She could feel the pressure in her chest, the sob that grew inside of it as she listened to his voice. What was wrong with her? Why were tears building in her eyes? If anyone needed to be crying, it was him. Yet she could hardly contain the tremble of her chin.

"I know it's been a while since I last visited." He sighed, his shoulders shaky. "And I know the look that you're probably giving me right now because there isn't an excuse good enough for not coming to see you."

His fingers squeezed hers.

Another long pause.

"I brought you someone. I think you would like her, no—I

know you would like her." James laughed softly, looking down at Ophelia with a faint smile. "This is Ophelia. *My* Ophelia."

That was the last straw. The crack in the dam. A domino effect towards the tears that trickled down her warm cheeks.

She stared down at Brianna's name; the water blurring her vision as she blinked the tears away, and her nostrils flared as she attempted to hold back the sob that continued to amplify inside of her.

"And you know what she means to me if I brought her to see you."

Each word was like a seed being planted in her heart, roots growing, intertwining around her veins—squeezing. Ophelia was a blubbering mess now, silently crying next to him as he talked to his sister about her. Saying things she'd never heard before in her life, at least not about her. Is this what it felt like for someone to care?

Not just when they needed her for something, or because they wanted her to do something for them, but genuinely caring about *Ophelia Clark*?

"I miss you," he whispered.

The roots kept growing.

And *growing*.

They had her heart in a vice grip.

He was spreading like wildfire inside of her, and for the first time in her life, she was relentlessly willing to let the flames swallow her whole.

CHAPTER SIXTEEN

Whisking open the door to Wren's apartment, the last thing Ophelia expected to see was Wren and Sean entangled together half naked on the couch. Her hand flew in front of her eyes as she let out a tiny *oop*.

James collided with her back as she froze in the doorway, a grunt escaping his lips as he gently knocked into her. "*Whoa*, what—"

"My eyes," she squeaked.

"*Oh*, oh God." James pieced it together as he stepped around her, turning away from the spectacle as well.

Wren and Sean's snickers floated around the room, as did the sound of them shuffling to put their clothes back on like two kids who just got in trouble. Peeking through her fingers, as mortified as Ophelia was, she was also happy.

Wren was glowing more than usual. Her porcelain skin radiated as she beamed, flashing her bright teeth as she smiled. Her green eyes were a few shades lighter than she remembered, flickering between Sean and the pair in the doorway with a faint blush creeping onto her cheeks.

"That's what you get for not knocking first," Wren scolded playfully, her hair pulled back in a low, messy ponytail.

"Noted."

"How was your weekend?" She pranced happily after Ophelia as she tugged her suitcase into the other room, clasping her hands together patiently.

Ophelia chuckled as she waited until they were in the safety of the bedroom, peeking out of the doorway slightly to see James and Sean preoccupied with each other. Swiping the back of her hand against her forehead, she sighed.

"Feelings—caught."

Wren's mouth formed an "O" shape as her eyes grew wide, tugging Ophelia from the boys' view as she squeezed her arm. "You like him?"

"A lot." She nodded weakly.

"You're not just dick-whipped?"

"No."

Wren squeaked excitedly, clamping her hand over her mouth as she bounced on her heels. "So you *did* have sex. Ah, finally!"

Ophelia shushed her friend. "What happened to you? Where's my *don't catch feelings* lecture, hmm?"

Wren sucked in a deep breath, puffing the air out of her lips in a *whoosh*, her red strands of hair flying forward around her cheeks.

"Lia, I think I'm the last person to lecture you on that anymore," she admitted gently, wrinkling her nose. "I'm afraid we are in the same boat."

The confirmation that she and Sean were getting serious made Ophelia grin from ear to ear, swooping her friend in for a hug as she rested her chin on her shoulder. If Wren—the queen of one-night stands and no strings attached—could have feelings for someone, then there may be hope for Ophelia yet.

"You guys seem happy." She squeezed her tighter before letting go. "He makes you blush, Wren. I don't think I've ever seen you blush. I've practically known you my whole life."

"Yeah, I guess he proved that I don't *really* have an ice heart."

"Could've fooled me," Ophelia teased.

"I hate to spoil the good moment, brat." Her hands rested on Ophelia's arms as her teasing look eased into something more sympathetic. "But your mom showed up while you were gone this weekend, spewing about cutting you off and not paying for your next term."

Of course, she did.

Two steps forward, five steps back.

Ophelia groaned, her face falling in her hands as she began to pace back and forth.

"She also said that you better not be with that *grown* man she caught you with the other week."

Before expletives could fumble from her lips, her phone started ringing, and her mother's face popped up on the screen.

"Speaking of the wicked witch," Ophelia grumbled.

Wren tiptoed out of the room with a grimace, sending her a half-hearted thumbs up as she disappeared, already knowing how this conversation was going to go. Bringing the phone up to her ear, Ophelia smacked her tongue against her teeth.

"Hello, Mother."

"Where have you been, Ophelia?" Her shrill voice boomed into Ophelia's ear. "I came to see you and Wren said you were gone for the weekend? Off with that man, I presume."

"I don't see how that is your business." Ophelia sighed, rolling her eyes. "What did you want?"

"Your father and I are very disappointed in you for not accepting this internship. All because of someone who is old enough to *be* your father."

No matter what, her parents had always felt the need to involve themselves in every aspect of her life. She wasn't allowed to have any personal space, privacy, or anything. To have that, they would have to lose just an ounce of control over her—which was the end of the world.

"Well, that's where you're wrong, Julie." She clicked her tongue. "I actually just didn't want to be stuck with you for the rest of the summer."

Her mother was silent for a while, and for a tiny second, she thought she had stunned her enough to render her speechless.

One could dream.

"Bring him to dinner tomorrow tonight."

Now Ophelia was the speechless one.

"I'm sorry, what?"

"Bring him to dinner tomorrow night," she repeated in annoyance. "Or you're cut off."

This wasn't the first time that she had held the fact that they had paid for her college over her head. It was the third. Yet here she was—willing to do whatever they asked so that she wouldn't have to quit school. Perhaps it was instinct by now. She had been doing it all her life. How could she know any different?

"*Fine.*"

Ophelia hung up on her mother abruptly, her chest heaving as she flung her phone on the bed, brushing her hair behind her ears.

A knock on the doorframe made her head turn slowly, her lips twitching tiredly as she observed James peeking in. His eyes filled with concern as they looked her over.

"Wren said I should come to check on you," he said quietly as he walked inside, his hands immediately finding her shoulders. "Are you okay?"

Ophelia's posture drooped as she pressed her forehead against his burly chest. "No—my mother wants us to have dinner with them tomorrow."

His hands rubbed her back gently.

"And are we?" he asked.

Ophelia pouted, tilting her head to peek up at him through her lashes, having an inkling that he wouldn't like her response. Or the reasoning behind it.

"She threatened to cut me off if we didn't show."

His eyebrows raised, his lips pursing as he chewed at them from the inside. She could already see the gears turning inside of his head; it was always apparent in his cerulean eyes.

"Do you really think that it's worth all of this?" James questioned carefully, his voice small. "The hold that they have over you. Your career choice. I mean, is this what you want?"

"*James—*"

"I'll go with you." His hands left her back, all traces of

comfort disappearing from his demeanor. "I know. You don't want to talk about it. It's fine. I'll go with you tomorrow night."

"I wasn't trying to upset you," she mumbled softly, her arms crossing over her chest.

"I'm not upset."

"Then what do you call this?" Ophelia whispered, her hand reaching up to smooth out the frown line on his forehead as he blinked down at her.

It was back within two seconds as he frowned down at her, appearing almost sympathetic, as he ran his fingers through his hair with a sigh.

"It's called caring about you, Ophelia. I only say these things because I care about you."

Ophelia's hands encircled her arms as she hugged herself tightly, her gaze falling to her feet. Her eyes focused on the dirt speckle on her white shoes as her brow furrowed.

"I'm sorry," she said tentatively.

She heard him groan before she felt his arms wrapping around her shoulders; her face pressing against his chest, and her shoulders relaxed as she melted into him like honey.

"Don't apologize," he whispered gently, pressing a kiss to her forehead. "We will go to dinner tomorrow night and everything will be okay."

"They're going to try to eat you alive. That's far from okay."

"I'm not worried about me," James mumbled into her hair as he nuzzled his face into her neck. "I can handle myself. I don't know if I can handle them treating you like shit in front of me, though."

Her heart lurched inside of her chest at the thought of him getting angry over how her parents treated her. Her stomach flipped excitedly. It was a foreign feeling, but one that she yearned for.

"Hey, guys." Sean interrupted with a knock against the frame. "I'm heading home, just wanted to see if you needed a ride, Jam? Before I took the car."

His lips formed an apologetic thin line as he looked down at Ophelia. After a beat, he nodded. "Yeah, I'll be out in a sec."

His arms let go of her as his hands trailed down her arms until his fingers intertwined with hers. Bringing them to his lips, he pressed a kiss to her knuckles.

"Tomorrow?"

She forced a smile. "Tomorrow."

It would be the first time they had been apart all weekend, and for some reason, it didn't settle right in her stomach. She felt empty as soon as he walked towards the bedroom door to leave.

She missed him. Before he was even gone.

She wanted to tell him to wait. Wanted to shout that she cared about him, too. But her feet stuck to the floor, and her voice lodged in her dry throat as she watched him disappear with one last smile over his shoulder. Perhaps it was for the best.

If tomorrow went the way she had expected then there wasn't a point in telling him that she cared. There was a chance that the entire thing could go up in flames the moment they stepped foot into her parent's house.

Her phone dinged, pulling her from her destructive

thought process, making her frown as she scrambled to retrieve it from the bed.

JAMES: *I miss you already, pretty girl.*

CHAPTER SEVENTEEN

Tearing the gray clip from her hair, Ophelia let out a frustrated huff, slamming her palms down on the sink as she glared at herself in the mirror.

No matter how many times she twisted her blonde waves up into the hair clip, it didn't look right. There was hair sticking out, or a strand out of place, and it was just wrong. But nothing would feel right when she was supposed to show up at her parent's house with James in half an hour.

Attempting to put the clip in for the fourth time, she growled when it still didn't work.

"*Damn* it," she whined, throwing the clip into the sink, rubbing her palm across her clammy forehead.

A pair of hands squeezed her shoulders, rubbing them gently as she glanced up at her reflection to see James peering at her. Reaching around her to grab the clip, he swirled her hair up into the claws in two seconds. Her annoyance grew as she stared at his perfect handiwork.

"How did you do that?"

"You look beautiful," James said, ignoring her huff tone, his deep voice already soothing her nerves.

"I'm stressed," she corrected snappily, immediately feeling

bad for it as she shoved the silver hoops into her ears. "Sorry."

His hands found her hips, gently shoving them forward as he pinned her against the sink. "Want me to help you unwind?"

His beard scratched her neck as he peppered it with kisses, his fingers digging into her waist through her jeans.

"There isn't enough time." Ophelia sighed, her eyes closing as she leaned into his touch. "We need to leave soon."

"Are you doubting my ability to make you come faster than you ever have in your life?"

Her chest heaved as she inhaled sharply. Her eyes flashed open to see her crimson cheeks in response to his brazen words, taking her bottom lip between her teeth.

"And if I am?"

His lips trailed up her neck until they rested just below her ear. "I suppose I'll have to prove you wrong. I'll even do it with my fingers alone. Just to show you how much you underestimate me."

She could only hum in response, unable to find her voice as his hands slid down to the button of her jeans, flicking it open as his eyes stared at her unwaveringly in the reflection of the mirror.

Her eyes left his as they flickered down to his hand that disappeared in the front of her jeans, and her breath halted in her throat as she impatiently waited on his fingers to make contact with her throbbing core. Once they did, her back arched into him, and a groan rumbled through his chest.

"If we had time," he murmured against her neck, suckling the skin softly as his fingers drew circles against her clit. "I'd have these pants around your ankles while I fucked you over this sink."

As he slid one finger inside of her, his thumb worked her most sensitive spot, the silver ring he wore digging into her skin deliciously. Pumping into her, his other hand glided up her body as he grabbed her breast. The pressure elicited a moan from her full lips.

"*James,*" Ophelia mewled, bucking her hips in sync with his finger.

"That's it, baby," he cooed, adding another finger, his jaw slack as he stared at her in the mirror. "Say my name again. It sounds good coming from your lips."

If there was one thing this man knew how to do, it was say all the right things that made her head spin. She loved how filthy his mouth could get.

"*Fuck*, Jamie."

His fingers curled inside of her, making her gasp as her eyebrows cinched together. The sensation made her fingers grip the marble bathroom counter. She could feel how much she was soaking him, how she clenched tighter around him with every thrust.

She leaned back against his shoulder, her eyes fluttering closed as the pressure between her legs continued to build.

And suddenly his hand left her breast, gripping her chin as he forced her head back down. Flicking open her eyes, she watched the smirk dance along his lips. With his fingers still holding her chin firmly, he slammed into her now, earning a small whimper as she withered in his grasp.

"Look at you." Pressing his lips to her cheek, his eyes still hooked on her reflection in the mirror. "Look at how fucking pretty you are when I'm making you feel good."

This made her pulsate even more; her core felt like it was swelling into her chest, stealing her oxygen as she licked her dry lips. Jerking under his touch, she reached up to grip his arm; her knuckles paling from how hard she was squeezing.

"I'm c-close, *God*, I'm going to come."

"I wonder how He feels about you calling out His name when it's *me* fucking you with my fingers?" he rasped against her cheek.

And that was all it took for her to unravel, her orgasm washing over her, consuming her as she twitched in his hold. The stress released from her body as her euphoric high took over, drenching his fingers as he continued to pump them in and out of her over-sensitive pussy.

"Good girl," James praised, pulling his hand from her jeans as she struggled to catch her breath. "Feel better?"

Her eyes narrowed into playful slits.

"Let's go, mister."

Every time the nerves would creep back in, James would take her hand, placing a reassuring kiss against her knuckles until the worry seeped away again. They were only minutes away from her parent's house now, using Sean's SUV again because she did not want to hear what her parents would have to say about them arriving on James' motorcycle.

Her mother would probably have a stroke.

James chuckled softly, pulling her from her thoughts.

"What?" she asked curiously, peeking over at him with a faint smile.

"I'm just thinking."

"Tell me," Ophelia urged, tugging on their intertwined hands. "I want to know."

A mischievous grin flickered across his lips as his eyes met hers briefly before focusing back on the road. "It's just funny. I'm about to shake your father's hand with the same hand that was just inside of your pants."

"James!"

They both erupted in a fit of laughter. His nose scrunched as his hand released hers, holding his stomach as he struggled to compose himself.

"What? It'll make me feel better when they piss me off by being rude to you. I'll just remember that your dad shook the hand that made you co—"

"*Stop*," she squeaked, clamping her hand over her mouth as she blushed tremendously. "You're bad."

It felt good to laugh this hard with James. The roots that intertwined her veins constricted, tightening so hard that she could hardly breathe.

The smile on Ophelia's face faltered slightly as they pulled into the driveway of her parent's vast, three-story house, and her eyes immediately flickered up to the last window on the right where her old bedroom resided. She couldn't even count how many times she had stared out of that window, wishing to be anywhere but there.

"Are you ready?"

She glanced over to see James studying her softly.

She nodded. "As ready as I'll ever be."

He hopped out of the car, opened the door for her, and took her hand, leading them towards the front door without looking nervous, whatsoever. She wished she could remain as stoic as he did. It made her want to stick her tongue out at him.

As she lifted her hand to knock on the white door, she withdrew her other hand from his. Not because she didn't want to hold his hand. Not because she was embarrassed by him. But because it would save both of them from what was about to come; make it a little easier. There was no warm welcome that was to happen if her parents opened the door to see them holding hands.

Ophelia could sense the change in the atmosphere as she took her hand away, already feeling sick to her stomach for having to do so, but she kept her face forward. She was unable to look him in the eye and see his disappointment as she prepared herself to get enough grief from her parents in about two seconds.

She wasn't nervous for herself; she was nervous because she had no idea what kind of shit show James was going to witness tonight. The shit show she had been dealt her entire life.

The door whisked open; her father standing on the other side, his dark hair speckled with strands of gray. His brown eyes narrowed the second they landed on them standing there.

Ophelia didn't look anything like her father. His hair was black, his eyes were dark brown—he was the complete opposite of her.

"Hey, Dad."

"Ophelia," he greeted warily, glancing toward James with a painful expression.

Here we go.

"It's nice to meet you, Mr. Clark," James said, reaching his hand out. "I'm James."

The sinking feeling in her stomach transformed into a black hole when her father stared down at his hand, leaving it hanging in the air before his lips formed a thin line.

"Come in."

He turned to walk away, leaving the door open for them to come inside.

"Well, this should be interesting," James muttered with a low chuckle as his hand hovered over her lower back, guiding her in the doorway toward the wide foyer.

"I'm sorry," Ophelia apologized under her breath as they followed her father into the kitchen.

She hadn't expected much from this dinner, not even good food. With their jobs, they were never home, so their cooking skills were slim to none. Ramen noodles and microwavable meals were her best friend in high school. As they stepped into the kitchen, she wondered what monstrosity her mother had put together for tonight.

"Glad to see you showed up," Julie chirped with a false

sense of happiness from behind the large island in the middle of the kitchen. "Dinner is almost ready."

"What are you cooking?"

"Spaghetti Carbonara."

Ophelia was already suspicious, eyeing the steaming pot in front of her mother as she led James to the wooden dining room table where her father was already perched, sipping on dark wine.

"Do you want wine?" Ophelia leaned over toward James as she spoke, peeking at him through her lashes. "I can pour us some."

He squeezed her thigh underneath the table, sending her a thin-lipped smile.

"I can do it."

She watched as he stood from the table, entering the kitchen like he knew his way around, still seemingly *not* nervous at all.

"A little *old* for your taste, don't you think?" her father muttered across from her, looking at her over the top of his wine glass.

She pursed her lips innocently. "What's the matter, Daddy? Scared someone's going to take your title?"

Sputtering from her words, the dark red liquid splattered across the white cashmere tablecloth as he struggled to maintain his composure. She bit back a smile as she watched him squirm uncomfortably.

"Honey?" Julie called from the kitchen.

"It's nothing." He recovered quickly. "Just went down the wrong pipe."

"You got wine all over my brand new table linens, Martin," her mother scolded with a shrill whine as she brought the pot of pasta over to the table, setting it down before throwing her hands in the air exasperatedly.

Ophelia ignored their bickering as she turned to examine James, who was pouring their wine into two glasses. His eyes flickered up to see the pair arguing before glancing at her—sending her a reassuring wink.

He would've been proud of her comment.

She made a mental note to tell him about it later.

It wasn't until everyone was seated, made their plates, and began to dig into the food that her mother decided to throw her first jab of the night.

"So, Ophelia, how much longer do you plan to slack off for?"

Taking a deep breath, Ophelia licked her lips. "What are you referring to? I haven't been slacking off. It's summertime."

"The internship," she pressed crossly.

"I told you I wasn't interested," Ophelia said casually, twisting her fork around in her pasta. "That doesn't mean I'm slacking off. I'm allowed to enjoy my summer just like everyone else."

"People who want to get into medical school and become a surgeon don't take summers off."

"We raised you better than this," her father jutted in, his words dancing along the lines of sounding extremely condescending.

That sentence alone made her want to burst out laughing.

Her parents had never raised her. That would entail them having to be home. Which they never were. Long hours at the hospital equaled a lot of alone time spent watching reruns of her favorite shows or staying over at Wren's house. Ophelia had ultimately raised herself.

She felt James squeezing her knee underneath the table, making her relax. It was sweet, the way he kept silently reassuring her that he was there if she needed him.

Her father seemed peeved that she didn't respond as quickly as he would have liked, irritably directing his attention to James, shooting daggers at him from across the table with his dark eyes.

"Tell me, *James*," Martin said. "How old are you?"

"Thirty-four."

Her parents shared a disapproving look.

"And you don't feel that it's wrong?" He grimaced in James' direction. "Fooling around with someone thirteen years younger than you?"

Ophelia took a long sip of her wine, hoping the buzz would help her not rip her parent's heads off tonight. What she hadn't realized was that James was going to do that well enough for her.

"Doesn't feel wrong at all, *sir*," James replied, stuffing a bite of pasta into his mouth.

Ophelia stifled a grin.

"What could you possibly want with our daughter? She's young, in college, and has a future ahead of her. Why bother interfering with that at all?" Julie scoffed with a laugh, flicking her hair over her shoulder.

"I'm not the one interfering with her future."

Her father looked like he was ready to spit wine across the table again.

Ophelia, however, clamped her thighs together because the fact that he could hold his own with her parents was strangely the hottest thing she'd ever witnessed in her life. All she could think about amidst the chaos was his face between her legs, scratching the itch that she was developing as she gawked at him in admiration.

Julie huffed in annoyance. "You're distracting her. And when the summer is over, you'll be nothing more than just the summer fling."

James hummed, his lips twitching with a smile.

"Is something humorous to you?"

"That's enough," Ophelia snapped, glaring at her mother. "I'm not going to sit here and let you belittle him like this. Just stop."

"Don't tell me you have feelings for this poor excuse of a man," her father growled, pounding his fist against the table, making everyone flinch. "What man preys on young women?"

"Oh for fuck's sake, Dad." Ophelia rolled her eyes, setting down her fork. "He's not preying on me."

"Watch your mouth."

She fumed as she stared at her father, her nostrils flaring as she gripped James' hand under the table. Her chest heaved as she shook her head in disbelief.

"This dinner is over." Ophelia clicked her tongue, grabbing her wine glass and downing the rest in one swig.

Standing from the table, Ophelia grabbed James' arm and pulled him up with her, keeping her arm looped through his. She didn't care what they thought of it anymore. Had she really let them treat her like this her entire life? Why did it take someone else sitting here taking the brunt of it for her to open her eyes?

"Sit down," Martin ordered.

"Don't tell her what to do," James cut in, his voice far from gentle now. "She's a grown woman."

"She won't even remember your name when she goes back to Georgia." Her father chuckled darkly, running his tongue along his teeth in vexation.

"She sure remembered it before we came over here when I had her practically falling apart in the palm of my hand."

Before Ophelia could even register what had just happened, her father was coming across the table, his fist connecting with James' jaw.

CHAPTER EIGHTEEN

Ophelia's first reaction to her father swinging his fist directly into James' jaw was rage. A rush of heat coursed through her veins.

But as she stepped forward, ready to scream every expletive that she possibly knew at him, her body froze as James gripped her father by his neck. The room grew quiet, the only sound coming from Martin's lips as he sputtered.

"*Don't.*"

He gritted his teeth.

"Do that."

His chest heaved.

"Again."

Ophelia knew the severity of the situation. She knew it was a big deal that her dad punched James. She knew that it was a big deal that James had a vice grip around his throat. Normal people would probably notice those things. But all she could focus on was how extremely fucking hot James looked while he was angry.

If no one else were here, she wouldn't waste any time climbing him like a tree.

James shoved her father away suddenly, pulling her from

her distracting thoughts, readjusting his leather jacket as he shook his head in disbelief.

"Don't you dare go near our daughter again, do you hear me?" Martin growled as he rubbed his neck where James' fingers once were. "This is the last time you'll ever see—"

"You need to stop worrying about me and focus on the relationship with your daughter, Mr. Clark. All you're doing is pushing her further away and you don't even care," James grumbled, pressing his finger to his lip that had started to bleed. "She deserves a hell of a lot more than the shit you two throw at her all the time."

Taking her bottom lip in between her teeth, Ophelia stared at James in awe, her clammy hands messing with the hem of her sweater as she watched him with adoration. No one had ever stood up for her, ever, and it only made her want to jump him more. That and—well, he was strangely attractive with a busted lip and a grimace etched into his features.

If her panties weren't damp already, they were now.

You're going to hell.

She watched as James approached her gently; the grimace washing away as his eyes trailed over her face. His hand lifted as his finger caressed her cheek, licking the blood from his lip as his brow furrowed.

"You okay?" he asked softly. "You wanna go?"

Ophelia nodded a little too quickly, staring up at him through her lashes, utterly speechless.

"*Ophelia Clark*, you will not go with this man," Julie snapped, holding onto her father as if he wasn't the one who initiated getting choked out to begin with. "He is obviously dangerous—"

"Oh, shove it, Mother."

Taking James' hand in hers, Ophelia pulled him behind her as she walked out of the dining room, into the foyer, and out of the front door without another word from anyone. She didn't stop her determined trek until they were at the car again, climbing inside.

She would undoubtedly be hearing about this again through texts, calls, or random show-ups at Wren's apartment—threatening to cut her off if they hadn't already by the end of today, but she didn't care.

She only wanted him.

As they sat inside the SUV, a few seconds passed before James twisted in his seat to look at her, his eyes filled with regret as he rubbed the back of his neck.

"Ophelia, I'm so sorry."

"Pull down your pants."

He practically choked on his saliva as his eyebrows shot up. "Huh?"

Ophelia kicked off her shoes, unbuttoning her jeans simultaneously, as she peeked over at him. "I said pull down your *pants*."

His eyes flickered down to her jeans that were sliding down her legs, his jaw slack.

"That guy in there?" she continued, tugging her pants from her ankles impatiently. "I can't wait until we get back to the apartment, James. I need that guy now."

"In your parent's driveway?" he rasped.

She was aching between her legs. Pushing her thighs together was not going to hold her off. It was like an itch that needed scratching. It was all she could focus on. Her core screamed for him, clenching around nothing as she thought about being on top of him. She felt nearly feral just looking at him now—his eyes filling with excitement, his lips parting as his chest heaved just from watching her undress, and his mouth still bleeding.

"If you don't want to," she murmured cheekily, sliding her fingers under the waistband of her panties. "I'll just do it myself."

His pants were pulled down to his knees in mere seconds as he reached over to tug her desperately into his lap, his fingers gripping her thighs, her waist, her ass. His lips pressed kisses against her neck as her fingers threaded into his hair.

"I like it when you tell me what to do," he mumbled against her skin, rolling her hips against him to satisfy his ache, too.

She could feel how hard he was already, which only turned her on more if that was even possible. She felt like she was going to combust at any second. Her body was buzzing all over. Ophelia could hardly form a sentence as she bucked against him, the friction between them feeling too good to stop as she let her head fall backward, her back arching with every kiss against her neck. Grasping his hand, she guided it up her body until it was around her neck, staring hazily down at him as she did so.

"*Choke* me," she panted. "Choke me while you fuck me."

James growled as he pushed her back against the steering wheel by her throat, his other hand practically ripping her panties off as he yanked them to the side. The angry look in his eyes was back again, and it made her stomach come alive with butterflies as she watched him pull his cock out of his boxers. He wasted no time lining the tip against her entrance, hell; she didn't want him to take his time at all. She wanted it fast. *Hard.* She just wanted him.

She was soaked from the moment he had said his little speech inside.

His jaw fell open as she eased herself down onto him, starting slow until forcefully burying his cock inside of her completely. A moan escaped his lips as his fingers tightened around her throat.

"*Fuck*, baby," he breathed shakily. "If you keep doing things like that, I'm not going to last very long."

She bit her lip as he stretched her out, the stinging only lasting a few seconds as she began a steady rhythm on top of him. Her knees dug into the seat belt buckle as she bounced on top of him eagerly. As his fingers squeezed her throat, applying just the right amount of pressure, his other hand gripped her waist—his fingers pulling her hips towards him with every lift of her body.

"Good," Ophelia panted breathlessly, slamming down onto him, gliding her body back and forth as he twitched inside of her.

His eyebrows knitted at her words, his mouth agape as she rode him. The way he was looking at her alone made her want to come.

He pulled her face towards him by the hold his fingers had on her throat, smashing his lips against hers as he lifted his hips to meet hers. Their moans reverberated through their mouths as they kissed feverishly.

It was like they couldn't get close enough, couldn't get *deep* enough. He was pounding into her so hard that even her moans were breathless. The car was shaking from the momentum as he thrust into her repeatedly. She never wanted this to end, the feeling of him ravishing her in such an animalistic manner in her parent's driveway.

It was like a big *fuck you* to them. And she loved every second of it.

"*Ah*, Lia baby, I'm so close." He moaned weakly, his forehead pressing against hers.

Her fingers gripped onto his leather jacket as she bounced on him sloppily, her body suddenly feeling tired as the pressure built inside of her core. He sensed it, his hand leaving her throat as he cupped her ass, lifting her like she weighed nothing at all—thrusting himself inside of her so she could take a break.

"Just like that," she squeaked. "You're going to make me come."

Slamming into her one last time, his hand tangled in her hair, pulling her to his chest as he spilled inside of her. They reached their peaks simultaneously, both of them gripping each other in a sweaty, euphoric daze as their moans echoed throughout the car.

"Jesus Christ, Ophelia," James whispered into her hair.

She giggled weakly, unable to form words yet as their chests heaved in sync. After a few moments, she leaned back against the steering wheel as her fingers brushed along his bottom lip. Smiling softly, she examined the smeared blood that she knew was probably on her mouth as well.

His eyes scrutinized her face as she caressed his lips, blinking tiredly as his hands held onto her waist.

"James," she said quietly.

He hummed gently in response, leaning into her palm as it cupped his cheek.

"I care about you, too."

"Yeah?" he breathed.

She nodded. "Yeah. And thank you for standing up for me back there. You didn't have to do that, but I appreciate it more than you know. It felt good to have someone in my corner."

His features somehow softened even more at her words, his eyes closing as he smiled, turning to press a kiss into her palm before he leaned his head back against the headrest.

"What are you doing to me?" he wondered out loud, his eyes still shut.

As simple as the words were, they still ignited the growing flame inside of her stomach, the one that continuously grew every time she was around him. It spread throughout her chest, her lungs, and through her veins.

He was like an addiction that she couldn't shake and didn't want to.

After tonight, seeing the way he stuck up for her and defended her—

He had moseyed his way into her heart, too.

CHAPTER NINETEEN

Ophelia bit her lip as she watched James nod his head to the beat of the music emanating from the karaoke machine. Wiping down the bar as his lips mouthed the lyrics, his hips swayed playfully.

It was closing time, and the bar had been fairly empty all night, so there weren't any straggling customers to shoo away. Sean had gone home early since it was so dead, leaving Ophelia and James alone to close up.

Her heart ached inside of her chest at the thought of having to leave this guy in almost three weeks. What did that mean?

The fact that she felt this deep, penetrating twinge in her chest every time she thought about going back to Georgia. The fact that it only seemed to disappear when she was with him. When they were so absorbed in each other's presence that they didn't have time to think about anything else.

"What are you thinking about, pretty girl?"

His voice tugged her from her thoughts, not even realizing that she had been staring down at her fingers that were messing with the wooden bar, digging into a crevice as she zoned out.

Flickering her eyes up to meet his, she smiled as she hopped from the bar stool she had been perched on, walking backward towards the tiny area in front of the karaoke machine.

"Nothing," she said, shrugging innocently. "Just that you should dance with me."

Flinging the white rag on the counter, James scrunched his nose as he laughed softly. Walking from behind the bar as he approached her outstretched hands, resting them on her hips as they rocked back and forth to the smooth beat. She wrapped her arms around his shoulders, pressing kisses to his bearded chin, the tip of his nose, and his lips, eventually laying her cheek against his chest.

She wished they could stay in this moment. That time could stand still. That the circumstances were different.

"You can say nothing," he murmured after a few moments. "But I know better. You get this crease between your eyebrows when that brain of yours is working too hard."

Ophelia furrowed her brows playfully as she jutted her bottom lip into a fake pout. "Like this?"

"Yep—exactly like that."

Laughter burst through both of their mouths as she pressed her forehead against his burly chest, feeling the melodic sound reverberate through them in natural sync. She sank deeper into his hold as he rested his cheek on top of her head.

"Three weeks." He sighed into her hair.

"Hmm?" she hummed tentatively, lifting her head to glance up at him curiously.

"I only get three more weeks of you."

His hands gripped her waist firmly as he spoke, pulling her

tightly against him as they swayed slowly in a circle with the music. He leaned into her palm as she cupped his bearded cheek.

"Better make the most of them, then," Ophelia cooed teasingly, biting her lip as she blinked up at him.

His hands trailed up the sides of her body, cradling her face as his thumbs caressed her cheekbones. His eyes flickered back and forth between hers, scrutinizing her features; the unspoken hanging in the air once more.

His eyes always said everything that his lips couldn't.

"*My* Ophelia," he whispered so low that she could barely hear.

And then he was pressing his lips against hers, not in a hungry manner—but sweetly. His mouth molded with hers gently as if she would shatter from the pressure, holding her face carefully, his beard scratching against her skin. He breathed her in with every movement. Her head was spinning as he claimed her mouth, and her knees practically buckled from the kiss.

Who knew a man like him could feel so *soft*? His rugged exterior, and his complicated history. It all seemed to vanish as he delicately devoured her mouth.

She took it back. Now his lips were saying everything.

Her fingers knotted in his hair, tugging him down as she stood on her tiptoes, allowing herself to melt further in his arms. Pulling away for air, he pressed his forehead against hers, his eyes still closed.

"What was that?" She panted weakly, her heart thudding harshly against her chest.

"Me making the most of it."

Pounding on the front entrance shattered the moment, their heads turning toward the sound as James sighed. Ophelia followed closely behind him as he went to unlock the doors, and her neck craned as she peered over his shoulder to see who was demanding entrance after closing time. Her heart felt like it was descending into the lowest pits of her stomach when the door swung open to reveal two LAPD officers standing on the other side.

"James Benton?"

Their happy moment came crashing down, smashing against the ground in tiny fragmented pieces.

"Yes?" James answered quietly, his hand reaching back to find hers, giving it a squeeze.

He knew. They both knew what was about to happen. The faint squeeze apologized and comforted her all in the same movement. She wanted to protest when his hand dropped back to his side.

"I need you to turn around and place your hands behind your back," the taller officer ordered gruffly, whisking the handcuffs from his belt.

"What for?" Ophelia questioned loudly, her eyebrows knitting.

Her chest heaved as James turned towards the wall, crossing his wrists behind him. His eyes stared down at her meekly before he faced forward. She gaped at the officer before glancing at James, her hands shaking as she brushed her hair behind her ears.

This couldn't be happening.

"James Benton, you're under arrest for the assault of Martin Clark."

The blood rushed from her face, and her breath halted inside of her throat as her lips parted in shock.

"No!" she yelled loudly as the officer shoved James against the wall firmly, handcuffing him. "This is a mistake. *I'm* Martin's daughter. I was there. My dad punched him first—look at his lip!"

Adrenaline pulsed through her veins as they pulled him outside of the bar by the cuffs, completely ignoring her pleas. Rushing after them, Ophelia flung herself in front of the officers as she held her trembling hands up.

"Please, listen to me," she croaked. "This isn't his fault. He didn't do anything wrong—"

"Lady, you need to move or I'll be forced to bring you in as well," one of them grumbled, slinging James around her as they whisked open the back door of the patrol car.

"But—" she stopped, her mouth agape as she watched them read him his rights, shoving him down into the car by the top of his head. "James!"

He turned to look at her as they slammed the door in his face, flinching as his jaw clenched. His eyebrows pulled together as he stared at her through the window. She ran up to the car breathlessly, tears pricking her eyes as she placed her palm against the glass, mouthing *I'm sorry* over and over again.

How could her parents do this?

She knew they were on the verge of crazy, but this? Sending a man to jail over something that her father started? The anger that bubbled inside of her only made the tears well up faster, falling from her eyes as they trickled down her warm cheeks. The ache in her chest was back with full force.

James shook his head faintly as he watched her cry, his shoulders moving as he struggled against his restraints. Pressing his forehead against the window, he bit down on his lip.

"*Please,*" she squeaked. "This is a mistake."

But her voice came out in a whisper.

The squad car pulled off, ripping her hand away from the window as it drove down the street. Placing her palm against her forehead, Ophelia started to panic, watching the car disappear around the corner with James inside of it.

Spinning around feebly, she looked around the dark streets, searching for the answers she already knew that she wouldn't find. Shakes had set in from her adrenaline rush, and nausea settled in the pits of her empty stomach.

The muffled music could be heard from inside the bar as she whisked out her phone, dialing her mother's number with shaky fingers.

Julie picked up on the second ring like she was expecting the phone call. Probably because she was.

"Ophelia," she greeted coolly. "To what do I owe the pleasure of getting a call from the person who never answers their phone?"

"You fix this," Ophelia urged. "You call the police department and you tell them you made a mistake."

"Oh, we were hoping you wouldn't have to witness that." She sighed. "We were *hoping* you had made the right decision to stop seeing him."

"Mother—"

"He left bruises on your father's neck."

"Dad punched him in the face!" Ophelia shouted heatedly, pacing back and forth on the sidewalk. "What did you expect to happen? He was just defending himself. He didn't do anything wrong."

"This all could've been avoided if you had just taken the internship that I offered you, Ophelia," Julie lectured in a condescending tone. "If you're looking for someone to blame, find a mirror."

"Please," she begged, her anger faltering as she thought about James's face in the back of the police car again. "Please, for once, do something for me. He doesn't deserve this, don't do this to him. Don't do this to *me*."

Tears welled up in the corner of her eyes once more as her voice broke.

This was more than just James going to jail. This was everything—her childhood, her future, her whole life. She was begging for all the times they had put her through hell and back, all so they could control her. Control who she grew up to become. She was begging for just a sliver of what they owed her. Although nothing could amount to what she deserved from them.

"This *was* for you. This is the best thing for you. You don't need to be involved with a grown man. You have a future to be focused on."

"This was for *you*," she gritted her teeth, biting back a sob. "Just another thing to throw in my face. Trying to control every aspect of my life, just like you always do. You're messing with more than just my life, Mother, you're messing with his."

"Ophelia," she tutted. "You're being dramatic. You'll thank me for this one day. You'll see."

"I'm not being dramatic."

"James is a grownup. He will be fine."

"That's not the point!" Ophelia hissed, tears trailing down her cheeks again. "You know, one day you'll get what's coming to you for all the shitty things you have done, Julie."

Hanging up, Ophelia growled as she pressed her palms to her temples, shuffling back inside the bar as a sob erupted from her chest.

Gripping the wooden counter, she clamped her hand over her mouth, squeezing her eyes shut. Her chest bobbed so harshly that she was gasping for air, gripping the bar until her knuckles were white. The void in her heart had turned into an endless black hole, sucking her in until there was nothing left as she wept.

The fleeting image of James' somber expression, handcuffed in the back of a squad car, staring at her like *he* was the one who was sorry.

Another sob racked through her chest.

CHAPTER TWENTY

A WHOLE DAY HAD passed since James was taken away in handcuffs.

Wren and Sean picked Ophelia up from the bar last night, not sure what to do with the state she was in, sobbing and blubbering about what happened with her parents having James arrested. Wren wrapped a comforting arm around her the entire night—eventually, she had cried herself to sleep in the guest bedroom.

Wren never left her side. In fact, she was sandwiched between Ophelia and Sean until morning because he was worried about James, too. He wanted to make sure they were okay just as much as *he* needed to be okay.

The feeling of no control, not being able to do anything that very second, *that's* what ate Ophelia alive inside. She wanted to fix it as fast as she possibly could. To find James and get him out of there. He didn't deserve to spend one second in a jail cell because of her father.

At the end of the long night, as she cried in Wren's arms, she had ultimately decided that this would have never happened if he had never met her. If she hadn't walked into his bar that first night. He would just be James Benton—the owner of *The*

Beer Lounge, living his life without her poisoning everything she touched.

Sean had figured out that they had taken him to the local precinct downtown, holding him there for the night until the judge decided what his bail would be set at. It should've felt comforting that she at least knew a piece of information, but it only made it much worse.

So now, here they were, back at the bar as they waited around for *something*—Ophelia throwing back shots of tequila like her life depended on it.

It felt better to be numb than to be sad. The more upset she felt, the more she was reminded of how she didn't follow her own rules. *No feelings.*

Sean emerged from the back, rounding the bar as he approached Wren and Ophelia with an unreadable expression on his face. His hand found Wren's, squeezing it slightly as he sighed.

Looking up from her soon-to-be fourth shot, Ophelia bit her lip. "What did they say?"

"His bail was set at $50,000," he said, swallowing thickly as he crossed his arms in front of his chest. "Which, in California, means that you'd have to pay ten percent of that to bail him out."

Ophelia gulped.

"But he's not there."

"What?" she squeaked.

"Someone bailed him out, but they wouldn't give me any more information than that," Sean said, sliding his palm down his face. "I don't know where he is."

A million questions clouded her mind, making her feel dizzy. Or maybe it was the liquor. Why wouldn't he come back if he was bailed out? Who bailed him out? Was he upset with her? Maybe he never wanted to see her again.

"Don't do that," Wren scolded softly, her hand rubbing Ophelia's back. "Don't let your mind tailspin right now. Thinking the worst. I'm sure he has his reasons for not immediately showing up. A lot is going on right now."

"He hates me," Ophelia mumbled.

"Ophelia," Sean cut in, leaning against the bar as his dark eyes leveled with her own, sliding the shot far away from her reach. "I know Jam, and I know that there's no way that he could ever hate you."

"Then where is he?" she groaned quietly, letting her face fall into her hands. "He should know that I've been worried *sick* about him—"

The jingle of the front door opening interrupted her, and everyone's heads snapped up to see James walking through the entrance. The flame ignited in her stomach at the sight of him, but the look on his face extinguished the blaze.

He didn't smile. He couldn't even look at her. The frown lines on his forehead looked permanently etched in.

And as the door swung open again—it all clicked.

Gemma, his ex-wife, waltzed in behind him, looking just as striking as she remembered. Her black, stick-straight hair fell around her shoulders, silky smooth and perfect. She was beautiful, her cheekbones prominent, her full lips painted in red lipstick, and her thick eyebrows framing her green eyes. She was a goddess. She was tall, her long legs only making

Ophelia feel more sick to her stomach.

She wanted to throw up and scream all at the same time, but her voice was stuck in her throat as she watched the two of them approach the bar slowly.

"*Jesus*, James," Sean said. "We were worried about you."

"You should've been," Gemma snapped, her arms crossed in front of her chest. "He should've never been in there to begin with."

"It's not their fault," James said, his eyes cutting to her irritably.

"You're right. It's hers."

Her eyes narrowed at Ophelia as her lips pursed in distaste. Her heels clicked on the floor as she approached Ophelia, towering over her petite height as she glowered down at her. It's like she had lost the ability to speak, lost all ounces of confidence she had left—her mouth opened to say words, but none came out.

What was happening?

"Aren't you a little young to be frolicking around with grown men?" Gemma seethed.

Ophelia immediately regretted the alcohol she had just consumed. It was suddenly not settling right in her stomach, which churned uneasily as she swallowed the thick lump in her throat. She felt puny in front of the tall, statuesque woman that was glaring down at her.

Wren stepped forward, her arm cutting the small space between them, as she pushed Ophelia a few steps back.

"And *who* are you?" Wren asked, a thick layer of attitude lacing her tone.

"Gemma Benton. Catch up, babe."

As chaos ensued, Wren stepped forward to yell at Gemma—who gave it right back. Ophelia could only hear the loud ringing in her ears as she stumbled away from the mess that had unraveled in front of her. Her chest heaved quickly as she grabbed the bar stool for support, heat creeping up the back of her neck as the nausea took over.

"I need some air."

Her voice came out in a whisper as she booked it towards the door, darting around the impending catfight. As she brushed past James' outstretched hand, she burst through the door into the night air. Bending over with her hands on her knees, Ophelia sucked in a deep breath as she waited for the next wave of nausea to hit her.

And it did.

Her stomach heaved as she threw up into the middle of the street, her hand grasping the lamppost as she doubled over. She suddenly regretted all of the shots she had consumed while on the verge of a nervous breakdown.

A hand rested on her back comfortingly, making her peek up to see James staring down at her with concerned eyes. Stumbling backward, she swatted him away, pressing up against the brick of the building.

"*Don't.*"

"Are you okay?" he mumbled softly, stepping toward her. "Have you been drinking?"

"No, I'm not okay. I'm far from okay." She hiccuped, turning away from him as she placed her forehead against the brick. "Please, just go away."

The nausea was creeping up again.

"Ophelia," James murmured, his hand finding her back again. "I'm sorry, this isn't what I wanted to happen—"

"Did you call her?" Ophelia cut him off, shrugging his hand away as she backed up again. "To come bail you out? *Her*?"

"I know what this looks like—"

"Did she bail you out?"

He paused. "Yes, but—"

"No, no buts," she whined, throwing her hands up in aggravation, turning to walk down the dark sidewalk. "I cried over you for hours. I cried myself to sleep because I was worried sick about you."

He was suddenly next to her, matching her pace as she stomped forward. His hands grasped her shoulders to stop her as he darted in front of her. His eyes were wild and his chest heaved like he had just run a marathon.

"She knows someone at the precinct," he cooed, his hands cradling her face. His eyes watered. "They called her. I would never call her. You know I would never do that. I wouldn't do that to you."

Ophelia took a shaky deep breath as she peered up at him through her damp lashes, tears already streaming down her cheeks from her outburst. His thumbs rubbed the salty tears into her skin as he took a deep breath, too.

"You didn't call her?" she asked, her voice cracking as her eyebrows knitted furiously.

"No, Lia. I didn't."

"Why is she so adamant about being a part of your life?" Ophelia ran a palm down her face tiredly. "You're *divorced*."

His head dropped as he looked down at the ground, running his tongue along the front of his teeth. "Because she knows that she fucked up massively. She's just trying to get in my good graces again, even though I've told her over and over again that I want nothing to do with her."

"Because she slept with your best friend?"

"Because she slept with my best friend while my sister died. While I was on the verge of losing my fucking arm. On the worst night of my existence, she was screwing him in our bed."

Sighing with an audible whimper, she shoved her face directly into his chest, inhaling the scent that she had missed over the past twenty-four hours. Her fingers gripped his shirt as she pressed against him, relaxing as his arms enveloped her.

"That's why I live *here*. I can't afford to live in my own place, but I refuse to live where my ex-wife cheated on me," he continued. "And I could've moved into Brianna's apartment but I can't wrap my head around doing that, either. So I stay *here* in my bar."

"I'm so sorry," she sniffled, her voice small. "I'm sorry that she did that to you. And now *this*. This is all my fault. Just another bad thing to happen to you. James, please, don't hate me."

"Pretty girl," James breathed sweetly, tugging her face up to look at him, brushing her hair back as he examined her closely. "I could never hate you."

She leaned into his palm as another tear slipped down her cheek.

"You didn't deserve that. It's my fault."

"*Shh,*" he cooed gently, his lips pressing to her forehead. "Ophelia, baby, stop."

"I'm just sorry." Ophelia dropped her head.

James tucked his finger underneath her chin, tilting her head up, forcing her to look at him now with her red, puffy eyes. Swiping his thumb across her bottom lip that she had tugged between her teeth, he shook his head softly.

"You have nothing to be sorry for," he murmured. "It breaks my heart that you're so predisposed to think that everything is your fault when it's not. I would do it over again, the same way, if that means getting to know you. Meeting you."

And just like that, the flame had reappeared, stronger than it was the last time. Her entire body felt like it could burst into flames at any second, melting under his gentle gaze. The liquor only amplified the fuzzy warmth in her chest.

"Leaving you here is going to break my heart, James Benton."

She hiccuped nervously as she realized she'd spoken her thoughts out loud.

His lips parted faintly. "Then don't leave."

Don't leave.

Jeez—those words sounded so good coming from his mouth.

In her inebriated state, staring at him through watery and buzzed eyes, she had never been more tempted to stay. His eyes begged her, speaking everything that he couldn't say once more.

But perhaps she needed to hear the unspoken. Needed to

hear it coming from his lips.
    That would be her undoing.
    That would be her reason to stay.

CHAPTER TWENTY-ONE

Walking out of the bathroom wrapped in only a damp towel, Ophelia peeked over at James' sleeping figure on the bed, sprawled out amongst the pillows. Looking as cozy as ever.

He hadn't left her side last night, not once. He demanded to take her home, crawled into bed next to her, and pulled her in close until they both passed out. She woke up early this morning with his arms still enveloped around her waist, his face buried in her neck, snoozing softly. It had taken her a while to muster the motivation to leave the warm bed for a shower.

It was the most tranquility she could remember feeling for the first time in a while.

Brushing through her wet hair, Ophelia peered at her reflection in the mirror. Her eyes were still slightly puffy from crying, and her face flushed from being intoxicated last night. Frankly, she looked like a complete mess.

"*No*," James grumbled from his pillow sanctuary, making her glance at him in the mirror with a smile. "Come back to bed."

"I needed a shower," she murmured, turning to walk over to the bed. "I was a hot mess."

As she approached his sleepy figure on the bed, he crawled forward, grasping her hand and yanking her down onto the fluffy comforter. She giggled as he pulled her flush against his chest. His lips pressed sweet, lazy kisses on her shoulders as he wrapped his arms around her.

"Hot? Always," he said against her warm skin, his beard tickling her. "But a mess? Never."

She hummed in response as she tilted her head sideways, allowing him to trail kisses up to the sensitive spot beneath her earlobe. Twisting until she was underneath him now, he left sloppy kisses along her jaw. His lips found hers as his hands gripped her thighs—spreading them as he pressed his abdomen between them.

"Take this off," he demanded, his fingers tugging at the towel still wrapped around her body.

With a soft chuckle, Ophelia placed her hands on his chest as she shoved him away, her foot taking their spot as she pushed him off of her. Playfully tugging the ends of the towel up, exposing her inner thighs, she bit down on her lip.

"After you," she said, her foot still against his chest, keeping him at a distance.

With a low groan, he whisked his shirt over his head, tossing it into the floor without hesitation before unbuttoning his jeans and kicking them off as quickly as he could. Scrambling back on top of her, he slid down his boxer briefs.

"You're such a tease," he mumbled, his fingers yanking the towel from her body as he rested himself between her legs.

His lips smashed into hers, maneuvering hungrily against them as his hand tangled in the hair at the nape of her neck.

She took his bottom lip between her teeth as he tightened his grip. His other hand hiked her leg around his waist as he pressed himself harder against her, rolling his hips as a moan escaped his mouth. His tongue flicked between her lips as he tasted her.

"And what are *you*—" she paused, her fingers grasping his chin as she twisted his head sideways, peppering kisses underneath his ear. "Going to do about it?"

A raspy moan rumbled through his chest as she took his earlobe between her teeth, tugging gently as her fingers knotted in his hair. Arching her back, she bucked her hips against the hard length between her legs. His fingers dug into her hips as they moved, guiding them slowly in a steady rhythm.

"I'm going to fuck you so hard that you won't be able to walk straight for the rest of the day."

The flutters exploded inside of her stomach, descending into her core as they ground against each other slowly. Her skin pricked with goosebumps as his breath fanned over her. His hands trailed down to her thighs, hoisting them up as he positioned himself at her entrance.

Pressing her legs back until her knees rested on either side of her, he stared down at her as his jaw went slack.

Slowly pressing the tip of his cock into her, his gaze darkened. Her fingers gripped the blanket as he stretched her out. A tiny whimper escaped her lips as he thrust into her fully.

It was so deep, it almost took the breath from her lungs—he was hitting places she didn't even know existed as he started a steady rhythm. Resting his weight against her legs, his fingers dug into her skin as he gripped her for leverage.

"Fuck," she panted, her eyebrows cinching. "It's so *deep*."

"You can take it, baby," he encouraged, his hips lifting and connecting with hers over and over again. "*Just* like that. Such a good girl. Take my dick."

Her hands gripped his forearms as he pounded into her. A string of moans left her lips as she threw her head back against the pillows, the pressure in her core building rapidly with every thrust.

Clenching wildly around him, her pussy throbbed as he slammed himself into her. Her clit ached for touch.

"I'm gonna come," Ophelia whined, biting down on her lip. "Jamie, *please*—oh, *fuck*."

And then he pulled out of her, making her cry out in protest at the empty feeling. Narrowing her eyes up at him, she gripped his forearms.

"*No.* No, don't stop."

Flipping her over, a squeak left her lips as he shoved her face down in the pillows, lifting her hips so that her ass was in the air. His hand came down on her cheek as he smacked it, plunging himself back into her without warning, making her legs quiver as the coil tightened inside of her.

"Tell me it's mine," he growled into her ear, grabbing a fistful of her hair as he yanked her head back. "Tell me this pussy is mine. I want to hear it."

"It's yours," she mewled, her breath taken away with every thrust. "God, it's *yours*."

His hand came down on her ass again.

"Louder," he demanded raspily.

Her legs were shaking madly now, and her eyes rolled back as her eyebrows knitted together furiously. Her hand snaked between her legs to rub fast circles against her swollen clit.

"Fuck, it's yours!"

The pressure was so strong that she felt like she was going to combust any second. Rocking her hips back against him to meet his thrusts, she didn't care how eager she seemed for release.

"Come, Lia," James breathed next to her ear, his arm wrapping around her waist to force himself deeper into her. "Come for me."

Her body did as it was told, exploding like tiny little fireworks, trembling weakly as her climax racked through her. She gasped for air as he continued pounding into her, making her vision speckle with stars as he pressed soft kisses down her back.

She struggled to catch her breath as she writhed beneath him, overly sensitive from her orgasm.

"I *can't*," she panted breathlessly. "I can't take it, James."

Pulling out of her once more, he fell onto the bed next to her, his chest heaving as beaded sweat trickled down his skin. Pulling her into his lap, he brushed her hair from her face, cradling her cheeks gently as he stared up at her.

"We'll go slow this time," he whispered, lifting her as he slid his cock inside of her gently.

"My *legs*," Ophelia murmured faintly, grasping his shoulders for leverage. "They're shaky."

"I've got you," he said, holding her in his hands like she weighed nothing at all, gradually pushing himself inside of her before pulling out completely—only to repeat the process over and over.

He pressed kisses against her chest as he pumped into her, and his cock twitched as she weakly clenched around him. His moans vibrated through his lips as he helped her bounce on him.

"I've always got you, Lia baby."

Her eyes fluttered open to peer down at him. Her mouth popped open as he fucked her gently, her fingers caressing his cheekbones. They stared at each other for a while; shaky breaths, heavy eyes.

He looked at her like she was the last thing on this planet that he would ever get to see, savoring her, drinking her in.

She could feel him twitching inside of her every time the tip of his cock penetrated her. He was close. The flicker of need in his eyes told her so.

Using the last bit of strength she had left, Ophelia shoved him back against the pillows, bouncing on him slowly. Forcing herself down on him as she ground against him shakily, she watched his mouth pop open as he stared up at her. His eyes darted between her face and her body as his hands gripped her thighs.

"Oh my *God*, Ophelia," he rasped. "Don't fucking stop. Don't—*ahh*, fuck, fuck, *fuck*."

"Come on, baby." She lifted her hips to smash back down on his cock, biting her lip. "Come inside of me."

A strangled moan escaped his lips as his hips jerked; his orgasm washing over him as he pulled her down against his chest, burying his face into her hair as expletives left his mouth. His chest heaved underneath her as he came down from his high, holding onto her tightly as he rubbed her lower back.

They lay like this for a while in silence, recuperating from what had just occurred. Gripping each other as if one of them were to let go—then the other would slip away.

Eventually, James pulled the comforter over the top of them, snuggling down into the bed as he turned sideways. He cradled Ophelia against his warm chest with a content sigh.

She wished she could stay like this forever. Unmoving. Not a care in the world.

"I love how I feel when I'm with you."

She lifted her head to meet his gaze, pressing a kiss to his jaw before nuzzling into his neck. "And how do you feel?"

His fingers tickled the small of her back, drawing tiny circles on her skin for a moment before responding.

"I feel like I'm home."

Goosebumps spread across her exposed skin like wildfire, engulfing her in the warmth that emanated from his body. Her head spun as she breathed him in. Pushing away to prop up on her elbows, she licked her dry lips, examining his features as he stared back at her.

"I feel it, too," Ophelia spoke softly.

His fingers entangled with hers as his thumb rubbed the back of her hand.

"I don't want to be where you're *not*, Ophelia," he mumbled, his eyes averting down to their hands. "I don't know if I'm supposed to say that, but I am. I'm rooted here. My bar, my life, Brianna, *everything* is here, but it's not going to feel like enough without you."

And there it was.

A small fragment of the unspoken.

And just as small as it was—it felt like everything.

CHAPTER TWENTY-TWO

Two and a half weeks until Ophelia's summer in Los Angeles was officially over.

Two and a half weeks until she had to make the biggest decision of her entire life. One she would rather hide from than face; one that she was scared to death of. There were so many reasons to stay, but there was also *one* reason to leave.

And that one was her natural, undying instinct to please her parents who couldn't care less about her happiness.

Funny how that worked.

Was something wrong in her brain? A loose screw? Did she function differently from normal people?

She'd always been this way. Ophelia remembered the first time she had gotten in trouble during school. It was second grade and she had met another girl who she wanted to be friends with more than anything. The pair had gotten scolded for talking during nap time, and of course, the teachers always filled her parents in on every move she made. She distinctly recalled walking in the door after school had ended that day, excited to tell them about her new friend and all the adventures they talked about, only for her mother to demand that she never speak to the girl again.

And she didn't. Because she wanted to please her parents more than she wanted to make a new friend.

All she had ever wanted was acceptance.

After so many years of yearning for approval, wanting to see how proud they were of her—it was permanently stamped into her brain. She did it without thinking sometimes, even though every time she was reminded that nothing she did would ever make them proud.

Ophelia flinched as a hand rested on her shoulder, tugging her back to reality where she was packing a bag for the weekend trip that Wren and Sean had orchestrated as a last group activity before she had to go back to Georgia.

The four of them, plus Paul, were taking a road trip up to Joshua Tree, where the Michaels' owned a family vacation home.

"Lia, you've been staring at the same sweater in your hands for like five minutes," Wren murmured with a concerned expression, her perfectly plucked eyebrows pulling together. "Talk to me."

"Just not ready to leave yet," she smiled sheepishly. "That's all."

"Two and a half weeks from now, you're not going to be any more ready, you know."

Ophelia nodded, shoving the lightweight sweater into her bag before she brushed her hair behind her ears with a sigh.

She wanted to beg her best friend to tell her what to do and make the decision for her, but she knew that wasn't the right way. Not that Wren would ever tell her what to do, anyway.

"Do you think I messed up?" Ophelia asked quietly, looking

up at her friend. "I told myself I wouldn't let this become anything more, but look at me. And now I've pulled him into this with me. It's unfair to him."

"He's a big boy. You didn't force him into anything. And babe, I don't think either one of you actually had a choice." Wren shrugged. "Have you seen yourselves? You're both totally smitten."

"Yeah," she whispered. "I've noticed."

Wren clicked her tongue as she groaned sympathetically, wrapping her arms around Ophelia's shoulders in a gentle hug. "It's okay if this seems scary, Ophelia. I think anything worth keeping is scary because it also comes with the possibility of *losing* it."

"There isn't a possibility," Ophelia exhaled slowly. "It's a fact. There is no happy ending for us. It'll end—it's inevitable."

Everything always came to an end. Especially in Ophelia's life. Maybe she wasn't cut out for happy endings; *maybe* they just weren't in the cards for her.

"Hey." Paul knocked on the doorframe, interrupting their conversation as his eyes flickered between them. "Sean and James just got here. Want me to start loading up the car?"

Wren bounced on her heels excitedly at the mention of Sean, nodding quickly as she shooed Paul from the room. Sending her a reassuring smile, she left Ophelia alone once again to stare down at her bag that she had procrastinated packing all morning. Perhaps she was procrastinating because if she put off the trip, she could magically put off going back to Georgia.

"Please tell me that your best friend's handsy sibling is not coming with us."

Ophelia twisted to see James walk into the bedroom with a sour look plastered on his face, making her giggle. She enveloped her arms around his large waist, leaning into his bearded lips as they pressed against her forehead.

"Paul?" she questioned. "He's harmless, you'll see."

"*Harmless*," he repeated. "Right. The guy who ogles at you, calls you pretty, and spins you around like you're in some goddamn *rom*-com."

"You know what a rom-com is?"

His eyes narrowed down at her, his lips twitching. "That's not the point, Clark."

She bit down on her lip. "Are you jealous, James?"

He swallowed thickly, not saying anything for a moment. His lips pursed as he gnawed at the inside of his cheek. The gears were turning in his head, that much was apparent in his eyes. His fingers brushed the waves from her face as he glanced down at her hesitantly.

"I guess I am jealous. He's more suited to you than *I* am. If anything, you should be with a guy like that."

Her eyebrows knitted.

"What are you talking about?"

"Someone your own age. Someone who won't be a grandpa by the time you have kids. He's obviously into you. He'd probably follow you like a puppy to Georgia if you asked him to."

Ophelia blinked slowly, pulling away as her hands rested on his firm chest.

She'd seen him vulnerable before. The time he didn't want to expose his arm, but never like this. His eyes averted hers as he chewed at his lip.

"*Jamie,*" she whispered, lulling him to look at her.

He sighed, shaking his head. "No, I'm sorry. That wasn't fair—"

"I'm not interested in Paul at all," she interrupted, her hand reaching to caress his cheek. "He's like the brother I never had. I'm only solely interested in *you*."

The relief visibly washed over him, his shoulders relaxing as he practically melted against her palm.

"Yeah?" he mumbled.

"Yeah," she cooed. "And you're not *that* old, you know."

"You don't think so?"

"Nope."

Standing up on her tiptoes, Ophelia pressed her lips against his gently as she grasped his hair at the nape of his neck. His hands tugged her closer by her waist, deepening the kiss as he breathed her in.

Was he her puzzle piece?

Because she felt like she was perfectly molded with him in every aspect. Their lips moved in sync, his hands were the perfect size to grip her waist.

A low groan escaped his lips as she pressed her abdomen against him, her other hand gripping his leather jacket, pulling him flush against her.

Ugh.

Two and a half weeks.

The four-hour car ride to Joshua Tree proved to be more eventful than Ophelia had expected. Wren and Sean sat up front in their blissful bubble—fingers intertwined together as their hands rested in the center console between them. Meanwhile, her stomach hurt from giggling at James' annoyed expression every time Paul would engage in conversation with her.

His hand gripped her knee a few times, only when Paul's eyes were on them like he was marking his territory, claiming her as his own.

She thought it was hot.

So much so that she initiated a secret text conversation with James.

OPHELIA: *If you grip my knee any tighter, you might just leave a bruise.*

Ophelia stifled another laugh as she watched him check his phone out of her peripheral vision, biting back a grin as his hand slid toward her inner thigh. She wanted to laugh even more at the fact that everyone else was oblivious to what was going on.

JAMES: *If it's not your scrumptious ass legs, I'm going to* *squeeze him by his throat until he stops talking.*

Biting her knuckle, Ophelia held her breath, suppressing the laughter as hard as she could.

OPHELIA: *You might as well leave a hickey. I don't think he's paying much attention to the way you're gripping my thigh.*

JAMES: *Do not tempt me, Ophelia.*

The thought of him leaning over and suckling her neck with everyone else sitting in the car turned her on more than it probably should have. Her cheeks flushed as she stared down at her phone, averting his curious eyes as she typed back.

OPHELIA: *No? I don't think you'll actually do it.*

Her heart hammered against her chest as she watched James lift his head to finally acknowledge Paul, who was turned around in his seat, talking to them from the middle row of the three-row SUV. As Paul's eyes lit up, his hands moving around animatedly as he spoke, James cupped his hand around the side of her neck. Tugging her against his lips, he kissed her neck like there was no one else in the car at all.

Her face felt like it was on fire as he suckled the sensitive spot beneath her ear, wondering if he could feel her pulse thudding below the skin.

Paul's eyes widened like they were about to pop out of his

head as he quickly shuffled around in the seat, facing forward. His story was suddenly not important anymore as he clamped his mouth shut.

The seconds felt like minutes as he left his mark on her skin, his lips smacking as he pulled away from her. A cheesy grin plastered on his face.

Ophelia's jaw was slack as she stared over at him, rendered speechless as she watched him look down at his phone, typing away at another message.

JAMES: *That was fun. Tempt me to do something else.*

Her heart felt like it had dropped into her core as she clamped her hand over her mouth to keep from bursting into laughter, shaking her head as she peeked over at his proud smile.

OPHELIA: *I am not scarring everyone in this car, mister.*

JAMES: *When we get to the house, then?*

She got butterflies at his persistence.

OPHELIA: *Maybe. If you say please.*

JAMES: *Pretty please, baby? With **me** on top?*

CHAPTER TWENTY-THREE

Scrutinizing her floral dress in the full-length mirror, Ophelia twirled around slightly as she watched the hems flare out before they fell to her mid-calf.

It was a cute piece. The fabric scrunched up around the chest and arms, showing off her tanned shoulders. Her blonde hair cascaded down her skin in perfect waves, and her cheeks were dusted pink from being out in the desert sun all day.

The group had decided to throw a little party tonight—Paul pulling out a stereo system that their parents had in one of the guest rooms, along with a beer pong table out by the pool. It was one last *hoorah* before everyone went back to their normal life after the summer was over.

Brushing her hair over her shoulders, she smoothed out her dress one more time before leaving the bedroom she was sharing with James for the weekend, and descended the lavish staircase of the Michaels' vacation home. It closely resembled a mansion; the ceilings were tall, peaked, and the staircase spiraled all the way down to the first floor.

The sun had just started to set, painting the barren land of Joshua Tree in hues of orange and pink. Fairy lights were strewn up around the pool, illuminating the backyard as music emanated from the speakers set up right outside the patio doors.

Ophelia could see Wren and Sean dancing together playfully as she approached the glass doors, her lips lifting into a smile as Sean twirled Wren around, her copper hair whooshing around her shoulders. Paul was sipping on a beer as he set up a game of beer pong.

And then her eyes fell on *him*.

James was standing off to the side, watching the pair as they danced, too. A look she didn't quite recognize flickered in his eyes. She couldn't stop to figure it out because she was so focused on how handsome he was—donning a navy-colored button-up, cut-off sleeves, jeans, and dress boots. A necklace was hanging from his neck, rings perched on his tattooed fingers, and his beard was full from not getting a trim.

As she walked out into the patio, his eyes flickered towards her, his face softening as he examined her with parted lips. His throat bobbed as he swallowed thickly, rubbing his palm on his beard as he walked towards her.

Her pink cheeks flushed a couple of shades darker as she ducked her head, her hands intertwining behind her back as she peeked up at him.

"You look—" He hesitated, gulping. "*Gorgeous.* You look really fucking pretty in this dress."

She grinned widely as she lifted onto her tiptoes, pressing a kiss to the corner of his mouth to stop his nervous rambling.

"You don't look too bad yourself," Ophelia teased, her hands grasping his arm as they traveled down to hold his hand.

"Jesus, Ophelia," he continued, shaking his head as he pressed a kiss to her forehead. "You're stunning."

The butterflies torpedoed inside her stomach at his words, making her flush even more.

Tugging her along with him, James guided them over to the long table. Wren and Sean took a spot at one end while Ophelia and James took the other. Paul had decided to dive into the pool in his drunken haze, climbing onto the pineapple float with an unopened beer, and cracking it open with a grin as he propped his feet up.

"I don't know about you guys." Sean pursed his lips, rubbing his hands together. "But I may or may not have been the beer pong champion in college."

Wren scrunched her nose as she reached up to squeeze his shoulder. "I think the title doesn't stand after so many *years*, Sean."

He gave her a pointed look.

"Me too," Ophelia piped up, pulling her hair back into a loose bun. "Mine was given a few months ago, so I think my title still stands."

"Really?" James questioned with a smirk.

She nodded proudly.

"Jam, you better get your girl," Sean warned flippantly, flicking his wrist as he tossed the first ping-pong ball to start the game.

"Hear that?" James said under his breath.

Ophelia peeked up at him as he chucked a ball directly into one of the red solo cups. She raised a curious eyebrow as he tore his gaze away from the pouting pair across from them. With a proud smile, he gently poked his chest with his finger.

"*My* girl."

She couldn't help but giggle as she shoved his arm playfully, facing forward just in time for Wren to miss the cup she had been aiming for.

James had his eyes on her the entire time she made a winning shot into their cups, laughing mischievously as she watched them chug their beers. If she wasn't studying, the only other fun thing to do at college was to perfect her ping-pong ball-slinging technique. It only took her roughly seven minutes to win them the game. James only had to drink two times—officially making them the world's best ping-pong partners.

Even after the game ended, Ophelia snatched one of the cups anyway, emptying it in record time before she flashed James a toothy grin.

He was still marveling at her like she was a rare diamond that he couldn't take his eyes off of.

"What?" she chirped, blinking up at him.

"Do you have to pee?" he questioned softly, licking his lips.

"No, why?"

"Are you sure?" he raised a brow, his lip tugging between his teeth as he cocked his head at her.

Oh.

Peeking over at the rest of the group to see that they were still very much occupied, Ophelia nodded slowly before glancing back at him. "I meant *yes*, I do have to pee."

A snicker escaped her lips as he hurriedly pulled her behind him, making his way toward the patio and through the glass doors until they were inside the dark kitchen. All the lights were turned off, and the sun had already set, so the only glow came from the light above the stove.

James whisked her up onto the cold marble countertop before she could even manage to get out a word, her floral dress riding up her thighs as he pressed himself between her legs.

"I like you, Ophelia," he breathed, his beard grazing her jawline as he whispered against her ear. "A lot."

She hummed, her hands trailing up his muscular back, wrapping her legs around his waist.

"Show me?"

He pulled away for a moment, his eyes finding hers, and his lips parted as his chest heaved. The smell of beer filtered between them, making her head spin as his fingers gripped her thighs. He always smelled of vanilla and faint sandalwood; it was her favorite smell in the entire world at this point. Pecking her lips softly, his mouth lingered over hers as he tugged her bottom lip between his teeth, eliciting a tiny moan from her mouth.

"I'd show you every day for the rest of my life if you'd let me, pretty girl."

The gasp that bubbled up her throat was muffled by him colliding his lips with hers, his hands sliding up her thighs as they gripped her waist. Pulling her closer toward him, his mouth molded with hers hungrily. His beard scratched against her skin as he pressed himself deeper into her.

One hand traveled up her toned stomach, through the valley of her breasts before shoving her down against the countertop, her legs splaying out as a squeak left her lips. He held her down against the marble while his other hand whisked her lavender panties to the side, his eyes flickering up to meet her excited ones before his mouth connected with her glistening clit.

Ophelia's back arched against the counter as his tongue flicked between her folds, tasting her as his hand gripped her thigh to keep her legs from closing.

"*Yes*, Jamie," she cooed breathlessly as she closed her eyes, her fingers interlocking in his hair.

The possibility of someone walking in on them only made shivers shoot up her spine, a stark contrast to his beard against her skin.

He suckled her sloppily, his lips smacking loudly as he devoured her. His chin bobbed wildly as he pressed his tongue against her throbbing clit.

She could feel the coil tightening in her core. The pressure swelled so intensely that she was sure that she was going to burst, mewls leaving her lips with every move of his tongue against her.

"*Please*," she panted.

She wasn't sure what she was begging for, but she needed more.

"Come on, baby," James murmured against her slick, making her writhe underneath him. "Come on my tongue. I want to taste you."

His arm circled her thigh, his thumb pressing against her clit as it rubbed slow circles, making her buck furiously against his mouth.

A moan reverberated through his lips against her cunt, making the coil snap as her orgasm washed over her. Her legs twitched as she rode his face through her high, and her toes curled as she shuddered beneath him.

"Good girl," he said, standing up as he tugged her toward him, her ass lined up with the edge of the marble countertop.

She watched him through heavy lids as he unbuttoned his jeans, pulling them down just enough so his cock could spring free. Positioning it at her entrance, he slid the tip through her folds, lubricating himself before gently pushing into her.

Both of their jaws popped open as they watched him thrust inside of her, their moans in sync as he began a slow rhythm of stretching her out.

She squeaked, gripping the edge of the countertop for leverage as he pumped in and out of her. "So *big*."

"Yeah?" he questioned breathlessly. "You like how big my cock is, baby?"

Her eyes rolled at his words, and her back arched as her head nodded weakly.

James growled as he pounded harder into her, pushing her dress up with his hands until her breasts were visible, his hands kneading them gently. Leaning over as he fucked her, he encased her nipple into his mouth, swirling his tongue around it as he listened to a sweet sigh leave her lips.

And then the muffled sound of the music outside suddenly grew a lot more clear as the patio door whisked open.

Ophelia's head turned to see Paul strolling into the kitchen, and her hands tugged down her dress as quickly as she could. Sitting up rapidly, her hair fell from her loose bun.

His blue eyes widened as they fell on her and James. A strangled choke erupted from his lips as he turned around, his hand flying over his eyes.

"*Sorry*!" he said nervously, waving his hand in the air. "So sorry. I'll just—*uh*, I'll go."

Chest heaving, Ophelia's lips thinned into a line as she watched him walk back outside through a pitiful grimace. Squeezing her eyes shut, her head fell as she palmed herself on the forehead.

"Oh my *God*, James," she whispered.

What she hadn't expected was to hear James chuckle, which turned into an uncontrollable laugh as he leaned his forehead against her shoulder. His body racked with laughter that felt contagious—a giggle slipping through her lips at the sight of him losing it.

James finally sucked in a deep breath, grinning madly as he pulled his jeans back up. Adjusting her panties, he pressed a kiss to her cheek as he slid her dress back down her legs.

"I'm sorry," Ophelia sighed, licking her dry lips.

"*Sorry?* For what?"

"He interrupted our moment."

"There's nothing to be sorry about, Lia," he cooed softly, brushing her hair behind her ear. "I have you all to myself tonight."

She peeked up at him through her lashes, her cheeks flushing crimson.

"Lucky you."

Whisking her down from the counter, James wrapped his arms around her, pulling her against his chest as he buried his face into her warm neck.

"I do consider myself pretty damn lucky," he agreed in a mumble.

Pressing her face against his chest, she enveloped her arms around his waist, melting into his hug.

"Jamie?"

He pulled back, his eyes curious as he stared down at her now, waiting for her to continue.

"I like you, too."

And as she watched the adoration creep into his features, his eyes lighting up as his lips twitched with a smile at her words—she knew that he had his hooks so deep into her that she wouldn't be able to escape them without getting hurt in the process. But she didn't want to escape. She wanted to fall. Spiral hopelessly down into the hole with him until they weren't able to climb out again.

"I knew it," he teased, wrinkling his nose.

Ophelia rolled her eyes. "Shut up."

He chuckled as he kissed her forehead. "Seriously. I know every thought behind those beautiful eyes, Clark. You can't hide from me."

"Who said I was hiding?"

He narrowed his eyes teasingly down at her. Her cheeks ached as she fought against the grin that threatened to spread across her lips.

"You were hiding." His tone was confident.

"I think I can see your head inflating," she snorted playfully, jabbing his ribs with her finger. "It can't hold all of that *ego*."

James pressed his tongue to his cheek as he snickered again—and it was the cutest thing she'd ever seen. His smile had the ability to bring her to her knees, especially when it was one of this size.

"Not ego," he said. "*Confidence*."

She hummed skeptically.

"You can deny it all you want, baby. But I can read you like an open book. I have memorized every wrinkle between your eyebrows, every shade of pink that paints your cheeks, and every way your body reacts to any situation," he shrugged flippantly with a prideful smirk. "Sorry."

Yep—the cutest.

CHAPTER TWENTY-FOUR

The getaway weekend had passed incredibly fast, making Ophelia's nerves feel like a giant pile of chaos as the days crept closer to the end.

And now—as she walked down the sidewalk hand in hand with James towards a fancy Italian restaurant—she tried ineptly hard to push the fact that she had less than two weeks left toward the very back of her mind. She wanted to enjoy this night with him; she wanted to enjoy every night with him for the next twelve days.

She couldn't pass on a date with a handsome, tattooed bartender who looked at her like she was the last girl on Earth.

Ophelia wanted to soak it in.

James looked mouth-watering tonight as he held the door to the entrance of the restaurant open for her to walk through. Not a hair was out of place on his head, his beard was perfectly trimmed, and his tattoos peeked out the top of the sweater he donned underneath his blazer.

He kept his hand hovering over her lower back, guiding her towards the hostess stand to check in for their reservation, and her body buzzed from the proximity.

"Hi," he spoke lowly, making Ophelia wonder if the hostess

was as dazzled as she was by his voice. "I have a reservation for two under Benton."

The brunette checked her list, nodding with a friendly smile before glancing up at them. "Yes, Mr. Benton. If you'll follow me."

James linked his fingers through hers as they followed the hostess to their private, dimly lit booth—a bottle of Pinot Noir already waiting for them on the table. He guided Ophelia into her seat before releasing her hand to sit down across from her. His lips lifted into a tentative smile.

"Someone will be right with you to take your order," the hostess murmured sweetly, shuffling out some menus before disappearing.

"You look beautiful, Ophelia."

She flushed as she peeked down at her outfit one more time, suddenly not feeling so doubtful about the form-fitting dress that she had changed out of three times before she eventually didn't even have time to look for another outfit anymore.

The struggle of being a girl.

Her eyes flickered up to his, and her cheeks ached as she attempted to hold back her wide smile.

"Says you," she teased softly.

He always looked drool-worthy, but something about tonight was different. She couldn't quite put her finger on it, but as soon as he had picked her up, it was as though she was seeing him for the first time. Except this time her heart hammered so harshly inside of her chest that she was sure she was going into cardiac arrest.

Like she was being drowned in her serotonin boost. It wouldn't be a bad way to go.

His lips twitched with a smile at her words, and his hand came over the table to caress her open palm as he stared down at their hands. He looked like he was contemplating what to say, but the waitress had arrived to take their order before he could open his mouth to speak.

After ordering and filling their wine glasses almost to the brim, James cleared his throat.

"This is a date, right?" he asked hesitantly.

Ophelia giggled.

"Of course, old man. Catch up."

A pained laugh escaped his lips, making her smile falter as her eyebrows knitted. She observed him as he took a long sip of his wine. His throat bobbed as he swallowed thickly. Something was wrong.

"Ophelia," he continued, clearly struggling as he licked his dry lips. "What are you going to do?"

Now it was her turn to swallow the lump in her throat.

She knew what he meant by his question, but she wanted to avoid the conversation altogether. She wanted the last few days to be *happy*. It was an admittedly selfish thought, but she wanted to preserve the last bit of their blissful bubble.

"What do you mean?" Ophelia asked.

His lips pursed as he gnawed at the inside gently.

"There are hardly two weeks left."

She nodded, her eyes dropping to her finger as it circled the rim of her wineglass slowly. "James, can we not talk about this now? Can we just enjoy tonight, please?"

It sounded so selfish as it left her lips, but it wasn't what she intended.

"When do you want to talk about it, then?" His tone was firmer this time, his eyes staring over at her. "What's a good time for you? Will there ever be one?"

Her lips had parted at his crass words, the sting settling in her bones, just as the server walked up to the table once more. It was awkwardly silent as she placed their food in front of them, asking if they needed anything else before disappearing again.

Ophelia jabbed her fork into her noodles, twisting the silverware around quietly as she sucked in a deep breath.

"I'm sorry," he muttered.

"Is it so bad that I just want to enjoy the last few days that we have left?"

"So you *are* leaving."

She glanced up at him as she chewed a bite of her pasta, swallowing thickly. "I *have* to go back, James. I only have a year left before medical school. I've spent *so* much time working towards this. Wouldn't it be stupid of me to just drop it?"

It wasn't what she wanted to do, deep down. It wasn't even remotely close. But it would've been wasted time appeasing her parents that she would never get back. It would be like suffering for nothing if she just threw it all out of the window. And not to mention the endless nagging and lifetime of disappointment that she would never hear the end of.

James was rigid in his seat now as he gripped his wine glass, his jaw clenching as his nostrils flared. He stared down at his untouched food. He was clearly upset, which Ophelia didn't want either—there was no happy ending to this situation. Either way, someone wasn't going to feel satisfied.

"You're going to leave?" He sounded defeated now. "Just like that?"

"I don't want to leave, Jamie, but I have to."

"You *have* to," he repeated.

"*Please*," she begged in a rasp, clenching her jaw. "Please try to understand where I'm coming from. I'm not purposely trying to hurt you."

Downing the rest of his wine, he nodded slowly. She gawked at him as he rested his elbows on the table, completely ignoring his food.

"Are you going to eat?" she questioned meekly.

She wanted this night to be happy. But perhaps the happiness ended here.

"I'm not hungry."

Pressing her tongue against her cheek, Ophelia stared over at him for a few seconds, trying so hard to understand where he was coming from without getting angry with him. But she couldn't help the rage that flowed through her veins. She had just wanted to enjoy their night together.

"Okay." Her tone was clipped as she pushed her plate toward the middle of the table. "I'll wait in the car while you get the check, then."

His eyes swiftly flickered towards her, the regret pooling in them as his mouth parted to speak. Climbing out of the booth, she raised her hand in the air as if to shush him, not wanting to hear him say that he was sorry again.

She just wanted to go home.

Her heels clicked against the floor as she hurried out of the restaurant, tears stinging her eyes as she found the car and climbed inside it. As she sat in the leather seat, the silence deafening, she fought the urge to cry. Her chin wobbled despite her efforts.

Ophelia couldn't even be mad at him—if there was anyone that she needed to direct her frustration towards, it was herself. She was the one who ultimately allowed it to get this far. She should've known better than to think something good could come from anything in her life. It wasn't out of the ordinary for her to ruin things for herself.

The driver's door opened, but she turned her head to look out of the window. She didn't want James to see how upset she was. To see the tears that trickled down her cheeks. It would only make him feel even worse, and she had done enough damage as it is.

"Ophelia."

She bit her lip.

"Ophelia, *please*, I'm sorry."

"Just take me home, James," she whispered softly, her hands shuffling in her lap.

"I'm sorry. I shouldn't take how I'm feeling out on you," he muttered, starting the car. Two more beats passed before he spoke again. "This whole thing is just fucking with me more than I expected, and I told myself I wouldn't show that because ultimately it's your decision. It's *your* life. I think I just hoped I'd be a part of it, too."

His words felt like a punch to her stomach. Gripping the fabric of her dress in her hands, she watched the streets of Los

Angeles pass in a blur through the window as she sucked in a shaky breath. Her nostrils flared faintly as she struggled to compose herself.

"I want you to be a part of it," Ophelia sniffled. "I'm not just going to leave and forget about you, James. This hurts me, too."

More tears stained her cheeks.

Stupid traitor tears.

It was quiet for a while before he cleared his throat, and she could have sworn she heard him sniffle, too.

"I didn't mean to ruin our date."

"You didn't," she whispered. "I just want to go home. Please, take me home."

That was all she could manage to muster up as she leaned back against the leather. The energy that she had ten minutes ago had completely depleted, and now all she was left with was exhaustion. What she wanted felt so far out of reach that it was impossible to grasp in her fingers.

But that's how she had felt for her entire life. So here she was again, *settling*, not having what she really wanted because that meant she would be a failure. She'd be the black sheep of the family, the loser, the girl who flunked out of college and didn't get into medical school because she wanted to be with him.

Who knew what her parents would do next if she were to choose to stay? What else would they do to try and ruin his life more than she had already ruined it for him? They had gotten him arrested; the boundary line didn't exist for them. Nothing would stop them from getting their way.

Her head felt like it was going to explode the entire way back to Wren's apartment. Neither one of them spoke another word for the whole ride, not even as she hopped out of the vehicle and slammed the door behind her. Even as she walked into the apartment building without a single glance over her shoulder.

She knew she'd see the saddest man on Earth if she did, and she couldn't handle the thought of failing one more person in her life.

CHAPTER TWENTY-FIVE

It had been an entire day since James had dropped Ophelia off at Wren's apartment.

It was eating Ophelia alive, their conversation flickering through her mind over and over again, thinking of all the things she would've said differently. She could hardly sleep last night from all the overthinking. Her thoughts were too loud—she couldn't turn off the noise.

She should've comforted him. She should've hugged him. She should've reassured him.

Should've. Should've. *Should've.*

Had her parents really desensitized her to being a decent human that cared about other people's feelings? Made it impossible to see the signs of someone hurting? Had she been damaged so much that it was all she was used to?

Wren had spent the weekend over at Sean's, leaving Ophelia alone to wallow in self-pity as she listened to the silence echo throughout the apartment. She was currently curled up on the couch, true crime documentaries flashing on the TV screen that she wasn't paying any attention to, bundled up beneath a blanket.

She stared off into the distance at the darkness in the corner of the room.

What was *wrong* with her?

Sloppy knocks resonated from the front door, tearing her from her droning daze as her head snapped over toward the direction of the sound. Her eyebrows pinched together tightly.

Wren wasn't supposed to come home until tomorrow night, and surely, she would've texted if she had changed her plans.

Crawling from the couch, Ophelia readjusted her loose t-shirt that fell to her mid-thigh. Brushing her hair over her shoulder, she walked towards the door and swung it open carefully.

Her heart palpitated at the sight of James standing there, leaning against the doorway with one hand. His other hand rubbed his beard as his eyes flickered up to her. There was a gloss in them, indicating his drunken state almost immediately, and if that hadn't caught her eye—the smell would've. The liquor invaded her nostrils, strong and pungent, as her face fell.

Not only were his eyes glossed over, but they were also red like he had been crying. His hair was disheveled, as were his clothes, which appeared to be the same outfit he was wearing last night.

He had gone to the bar after he dropped her off.

Had he been drinking all day?

"James," she mumbled somberly.

"*Ophelia.*" He hiccuped, swaying slightly as he stood up straight. "I had to come see you. I couldn't spend 'nother night without you."

She could practically hear her heart breaking at his current state, knowing she had put him there.

Her hands grasped his shoulders gently, allowing him to put most of his weight on her as she tugged him inside, closing the door behind her with her foot. She shuffled him to the couch, plopping him down carefully. Sitting down next to him, she reached up to caress his bearded cheek.

"You're a mess," she concluded quietly, her head tilting sideways as tears stung her eyes. "Have you been drinking all day?"

James nodded slightly, leaning back against the couch as he rubbed his palm down his face.

"I'm such an idiot, pretty girl." He groaned, his eyes squeezing shut as his head fell back. "Always ruining everything 'cause I can't keep my mouth shut."

"You didn't ruin anything, James."

"I made you upset," he whined softly, his voice cracking as his eyebrows knitted.

Ophelia took his hand, pulling it to her chest as she rubbed her thumbs along his palm. "Last night was my fault. I'm the one who should be drunk at *your* doorstep."

His cerulean eyes flashed open; his pupils dilating as he examined her through his drunken haze. Sitting up abruptly, he buried his face into her neck. His weight caused her to fall back onto the couch. Her arms enveloped him, rubbing comforting circles on his broad back.

"Don't go," he mumbled into her hair, squeezing her tighter as he spoke.

His words were like a knife through her chest, the stinging shock rippling through her body as she blinked away the tears that threatened to spill.

"I'm here," she whispered softly, pressing her cheek against the top of his head. "I'm right here."

She hated herself for doing this to him.

"*Please* don't leave me."

Her eyes squeezed shut at the broken tone in his voice. Her stomach sank as she listened to him sniffle, and felt his tears soaking into her neck. A few tears of her own slipped down her warm cheeks, her chin trembling as she pulled him closer to her. He was twice her size, but she cuddled him anyway.

"*Shh,*" she cooed, her hand trailing up to hold the back of his neck.

He pulled away suddenly, staring down at her lips through wet lashes. His blue eyes were a bright contrast to the redness from crying.

"Please," James begged, pressing his lips against hers. His arms tugged her into his lap as he twisted them around on the couch.

She could taste the saltiness of their tears and the liquor on his breath as his mouth molded against her own. Her knees were on either side of his waist as she straddled his lap. Gliding his hands up her back, he gripped her neck as he pulled her down deeper into his kiss. The ripple of heat between her legs made her involuntarily roll her hips against him as their lips devoured each other needily, earning a low groan that vibrated through his chest.

"You're drunk," she hesitated, breaking their kiss as her

chest heaved shakily.

"I'll always want you, *need* you," he murmured, pressing his lips against her neck. "Sober, drunk, in every lifetime. Nothing will change how much I'll always need you, Ophelia."

She arched into him as he spoke, allowing him to pepper sloppy kisses to her skin, her hands gripping his shoulders as the butterflies erupted in her stomach.

His hands traveled underneath her t-shirt, gripping her waist as he guided her hips to grind against him. A strained moan escaped his lips as she felt him harden underneath her. Whisking the shirt over her head, her hair cascaded down her shoulders, and her nipples hardened from the cooler air as she straddled him.

"Fucking hell," he groaned, enclosing his lips over one of her hard peaks, swirling his tongue.

Ophelia's head fell back as he licked at her skin, her hands threading through his hair as his beard tickled her. Grinding against his erection, she bit her lip as a growl reverberated against her nipple before his eyes flickered up to meet hers.

He was so beautiful.

It was unfair.

"I want to make you come," James breathed against her chest.

"What about you?" she squeaked, flushing as she glanced down at him, observing her crimson-colored skin as he nipped at it.

He shook his head, lifting his chin to press his lips against hers. "Lemme make you feel good, baby. Please."

She could feel herself trembling at his words. Her stomach

twitched as his fingers trailed down toward her navel, caressing her panty line slowly as his lips parted in awe. His thumb rested against her clit through the pink fabric, rubbing lightly as his tongue flicked out to wet his bottom lip.

Her hips bucked in response as he teased her. Her hands gripped his shoulders as she pushed herself against his thumb, needing more.

"*James,*" she whined gently.

Pulling her panties to the side, his bottom lip tugged between his teeth. His eyebrows knitted as he stared down at her glistening cunt, and his thumb glided between her folds as he moaned.

"Come here," he panted. "Sit that pretty pussy on my face, sweet girl. I wanna drown in it."

Her legs wobbled in anticipation as she climbed from his lap, the ache in her stomach deepening as she slowly perched herself down onto his full lips. Her eyes rolled as his tongue flicked out, tasting her, making her shudder against him. His hands gripped her hips, holding her steady as she bucked against his mouth.

The mixture of his tongue swirling against her clit and his beard scratching at her sensitive skin made her jaw pop open as she stared down at him. A strangled moan escaped her lips as he suckled at her.

"*Fuck,*" she breathed. "Fuck, *yes.*"

His lips smacked as he released her clit, her body jolting from the sensation, as his hand reached around to rub circles against her with his thumb. Staring up at her, his wet lips curved faintly as he smirked proudly.

"Are you gonna come for me?"

She nodded frantically.

"That's a good girl. I want you to come all over my tongue," James rasped, rubbing his thumb faster as he spoke. "Don't look away. Keep your eyes on me. I wanna see you fall apart."

His slurred speech only turned her on more, the words tumbling from his lips without a second thought. She wanted to listen to them all night.

James lapped at her once more, his thumb still rubbing circles. The wet sounds made the coil knot tightly, to the brink of snapping as she struggled to hold her eyes open.

"*Please,*" she squeaked.

He moaned against her, and the vibration of his lips on her made her jolt.

Ophelia could feel the pressure building intensely between her legs, rising higher and higher with every flick of his tongue. And just as she thought there wasn't anything else she could take, he lifted his head just slightly as four little words left his mouth.

Four words that would send her world crashing down around her, the remnants ablaze as she basked in the flames.

"I love you, Ophelia."

A strangled cry burst from her lips as her orgasm rippled through her, her face pinched so harshly that it almost hurt. She gawked down at him as his mouth connected with her heat once more. Her hips rocked sloppily as she chased the high. Chest heaving, her hands gripped his shoulders to keep herself from buckling.

His eyes never wavered as they stared at each other for a

few long moments, until his hands tugged her down into his lap, cradling her against his chest.

And despite feeling the happiest she could ever remember feeling in her life, tears trickled down her face as a sob racked through her chest. Her fingers knitted into his shirt as she buried her face into him, crying uncontrollably as his arms enveloped tightly around her.

She didn't deserve his love, as much as she wanted to hear it. As much as she wanted it from him, it only made her sad because she knew that it was her parent's fault for making her believe something she was unlovable.

As quickly as the sadness appeared, it was gone, and replaced by relief. Reassurance. *Acceptance*. She was crying because she was happy.

All the years of trying so hard to earn the love of her parents felt like it was melting away, seeping out of her through her tears. He was there to pick her up again, take her pain as his own, and hold her as she released something that had been pent up inside of her for her entire life.

He loved her.

"I can take care'a you," James mumbled against the top of her head. "You're safe with me. I can keep you safe. You don't have to be scared with me."

Leaning back, she looked up at him through watery eyes. "James, I..."

She what?

Did she even know?

She shrugged faintly, burying her face into his neck, unsure. How could she put into words what she didn't even know herself? How could she begin to explain something she'd never felt before?

Even in his drunken state, he knew.

His hand crept up the back of her neck, his thumb caressing her skin reassuringly as if to say it was *okay*. His other hand held her against him. Their chests bobbed in sync with each other. It was like he knew without her having to say anything at all.

The unspoken.

It was always there, and perhaps it never actually needed to be said at all, because it was like he could read her mind. And that made all the difference.

James was always picking her up, making her understand her worth, and helping her discover things about herself.

Perhaps he was showing her how to love him, too.

CHAPTER TWENTY-SIX

Waking up next to James the next day felt like Christmas morning as a child. The butterflies fluttered around Ophelia's stomach as she watched him sleep, already bouncing with anticipation for his eyes to open as she nibbled at the end of her thumb.

Would he remember last night? What he had told her? Because that was something she was never going to forget, not that she ever wanted to.

Sneaking out of the blankets that shrouded their tangled bodies, she crept into the kitchen to make him breakfast. It was the least she could do, but he deserved some form of an apology for the way she had handled their date.

And it was time to open up. He had been nothing short of vulnerable with her, and his efforts merited reciprocation.

Ophelia may not have been an expert in the *letting down your walls* area of life, but she would try her hardest—for him.

And she decided she would start by telling him what she actually had wanted to do before her parents had forced her to follow in their footsteps.

As she whisked the ingredients for blueberry-lemon scones into a bowl, she smiled faintly at the thought.

The only person on the planet that knew about her love for baking was Wren. There wasn't a single soul other than her best friend that knew. She had never felt comfortable enough to tell anyone else before. Not until now.

Her parents would never approve of her passion—it wouldn't be something as admirable as being a surgeon in their eyes. They expected their only child to be as successful as them. Live up to the Clark family name. It was all about looks. They had always cared about what others would think. When it had come time for applying for college, her mother had practically done all of it for her—the decision had never been in her hands.

Never.

So she shoved her passion deep, deep down. She had tried making her parents happy her entire life, so much so that she put her love for certain things aside. And now she was ready to share them with James. That meant something. It had to.

As the scone mix chilled in the refrigerator, she chopped up a fresh bowl of fruits, swaying her hips softly to the music that poured from the speaker in Wren's living room—careful not to make it too loud so that she wouldn't wake James.

Wearing only his button-up from the night before, the hem of the material tickled her thighs as she danced, swiftly slicing strawberries as she simultaneously brewed some coffee. Her hair was pulled back into two braids along her scalp, cascading down her shoulders behind her, some loose strands falling around her face.

It wasn't until she was sliding the tray of scones into the oven that she felt a pair of arms envelop her waist. James' face buried into her neck, his beard scratching her skin in a way that made her want to sigh out loud.

"Good morning," he mumbled in a husky tone, still sounding half asleep.

Jesus Christ.

The morning voice.

"You look too fucking good in my shirt."

Ophelia giggled softly, leaning her head back against his shoulder as he peppered kisses along her skin. His hands traveled to her hips as he pulled her flush against his chest.

"*Our* shirt," she corrected teasingly.

"You can keep it." He chuckled, his teeth nipping at her earlobe. "It looks better on you, anyways."

He continued to gently bite her ear, sending her butterflies spiraling to her core as his hands crept underneath the button-up.

"No," she squeaked, twisting out of his grasp with flushed cheeks. "*No.* I'm making you breakfast. I have to focus."

His lips lifted into a smile as his eyes trailed over her.

It was extremely hard to focus when he was only wearing a pair of sweats that hung low on his defined hips—his bare, tattooed chest looking undeniably hot as he leaned back against the counter. His muscles flexed as his arms crossed. His brown hair was still disheveled from sleeping, and his eyes were still puffy from his slumber. It was ridiculous how attractive he was. Who just woke up looking like that?

"*Mmm*, breakfast?"

She nodded, quickly turning her attention to the coffee she was still brewing before she started drooling, pouring him a hot cup.

"You can cook, too?" he asked, his head tilting sideways.

Ophelia shrugged, rolling her eyes playfully as she carefully handed him the cup of coffee. "I may or may not dabble in it from time to time."

His tongue flicked out to wet his lips before bringing the mug to his mouth, taking a quick sip as his eyes stared at her the entire time overtop of the cup. Somehow his gaze was the hottest thing she'd ever seen in her life.

Focus, Lia.

"Is there anything you can't do?"

She pursed her lips. "I can't sing."

James laughed, his head tilting back as his nose scrunched slightly, shaking his head as he took another sip of his coffee. "Somehow I highly doubt that, pretty girl."

The pair stayed relatively quiet as Ophelia started to make scrambled eggs. The sounds of her whisking everything together in a bowl echoed around the apartment along with the music as James examined her every move, perched against the counter as he sipped at his coffee. She felt faintly anxious with his eyes studying her the entire time, but she made sure she didn't let it show.

As the eggs finished cooking on the stovetop, she pulled the tray of scones from the oven, setting them on the marble island next to him.

His eyebrows raised as he glanced down at the unfamiliar pastry before peeking back up at her.

Ophelia gave him a nonchalant grin as she poured a sweet glaze over the top of the scones, fluttering around the kitchen swiftly as she got everything prepared for breakfast. It was oddly nice to feel his eyes on her as she worked, knowing that his gaze was more curious than anything else. Knowing the last thing he would ever do was judge.

Once his plate was made, she placed it in front of him at the bar, and her lips formed a thin line as she sucked in a quiet breath.

She watched him lift the scone to his lips, his eyes never wavering from hers, before biting into it. His eyes widened for a fraction of a second, and his eyebrows raised profoundly as he chewed the bite thoroughly before swallowing.

"You made these—"

"Did you mean what you said last night?" she interrupted suddenly.

Great timing.

Setting the scone back down, his eyebrows pulled together as he looked at her. Walking around the bar, his hand grasped her face gently, whisking her hair behind her ear as he cocked his head.

"Yes."

She hadn't expected the wave of relief to wash over her the way it did, or the warmth to pool in her stomach as she leaned into his palm.

"I bake," Ophelia blurted.

His blue eyes searched her face.

"Sometimes," she murmured softly. "I like to bake."

Her nerves felt like they were swallowing her whole as she fidgeted underneath his gaze now. The words were bubbling out of her mouth like vomit.

James studied her closely, gauging her reaction as he held her face in his hands now, allowing her a few moments to gather her thoughts—to speak.

"Is that stupid?" she asked in a whisper.

His thumbs caressed her cheeks as he pressed a brief kiss against her forehead. "Ophelia, I could never think anything that you enjoy doing is stupid."

With a newfound sense of acceptance, she lifted her head to smile widely up at him, her shoulders relaxing. She could bask in the way he looked at her forever, never getting tired of his eyes examining her as if she was the only girl on the planet. He always made her feel wanted.

"I would've gone to culinary school if my parents hadn't decided my career for me."

His eyes softened. His hands trailed down her neck until they were grasping her shoulders, tugging her against him as he embraced her.

"You say that as if you still couldn't go," James murmured into her hair. "You're young. You have all the time in the world to change your mind. What your parents chose for you isn't set in stone. It doesn't have to be that way, Lia."

She gnawed at the inside of her lip. "It feels so out of reach. I only have another year left. I've put three years into college already."

"You should do what makes you happy, not what makes your parents happy."

Ophelia pulled away gently as she stared down at her intertwined fingers, taking her bottom lip between her teeth as she mulled over his words. Why did doing what made her happy seem so scary? It ignited a fury of nerves in the pit of her stomach just thinking about telling her parents off.

"I'm scared of what makes me happy," she admitted softly, goosebumps rising along her skin as she spoke the words out loud.

It was like a revelation that needed to be said, not only in her mind, but she needed to hear herself.

James placed his finger underneath her chin, tilting her head up as his eyes trailed across her features. His full lips parted as he looked down at her, and his finger lingered as it grazed across her jawline.

"What about it scares you?"

She swallowed thickly.

"For me to be happy, someone else is going to have to deal with the consequences," Ophelia mumbled, her eyebrows pulling together. "No one is going to get out of this unscathed."

"Me?"

She blinked slowly up at him, taking a shaky breath. "I don't know what my parents would do if I stayed here with you, and I don't want to find out. I don't want them to make your life any more complicated than they already have."

He reached up tentatively, the tip of his finger resting on the wrinkled skin between her brows, rubbing it gingerly.

"You're worrying about everyone else before yourself. There are two sides to every coin, but you can't change that," he said. "Stop trying to please everybody, pretty girl. This is about *you*."

She pouted. "I'm mostly worried about you. You don't deserve the baggage that comes with me. Shouldn't being with the person who's meant for you be *easy*?"

"I never expected this to be easy."

Ophelia raised her eyebrows. "You didn't?"

He shook his head, a faint smile dancing along his lips. "Nope, I knew I was done for the moment you walked into my bar."

She couldn't help but reciprocate his smile as her cheeks flushed.

"I would walk through fire for you, Ophelia," James continued softly. "Choke out psycho parents. I would do that for you. And I know you're not used to hearing these things, things you *deserve* to hear, but that's okay because I'll remind you every day until you tell me to stop."

Her heart thudded harshly against her chest, stalled even, beating unevenly as she struggled to compose herself under his gaze.

"Your parents don't scare me," he breathed, his fingers brushing against her flushed cheek. "Nothing scares me enough to keep me from you. The only thing that scares me is the fact that you're going to leave. Not seeing you again scares the shit out of me."

Ophelia wasn't sure what it meant as the surge ripped through her chest, through her rapidly beating heart, and her veins.

But she had an inkling that it was love.

CHAPTER TWENTY-SEVEN

Normally, seven days would feel like an ample amount of time—but not with James.

One week felt like one second.

And one second was not long enough for Ophelia, not when it came to spending time with the guy she was hopelessly falling head over heels for. James came like a whirlwind into her life, knocking her on her ass and leaving her head spinning. Each day that they spent together only solidified his grip on her heart. He was everywhere all at once. There wasn't a single part of her that didn't feel the lasting effects of his presence.

For the tiniest, measly second—she had contemplated staying.

She felt hope that something could work out, especially if it was meant to. But then her phone screen lit up as her mother sent her a message, and it only took six words to destroy any hopes she had started to create in her mind.

SATAN: *I got you into medical school.*

I got you.

Like she wasn't capable of getting herself into a decent medical school. Her parents had so little faith in her that it made her feel physically ill.

OPHELIA: *What does that mean?*

Ophelia shoved her face into the pillow as she sat on the bed, yelling loudly into the plush as she squeezed the sheets so hard that her knuckles ached. She hated how harshly her heart started to pump inside of her chest as she waited on her mother's response; hated that she allowed her to affect her this way.

SATAN: *After this next year at college, you'll have a full ride into medical school. I spoke with the department head at the University of Oxford.*

OPHELIA: *In England?*

The University of Oxford was one of the best medical schools in the world, but it was located in the UK, which was quite a distance away. If she had thought Georgia was too far...

SATAN: *The acceptance rate for their medical school is 9%, Ophelia. You'd be out of your mind to refuse such an amazing opportunity. England is an exquisite place. It would do you well to get away for a while.*

Julie couldn't care less which medical school Ophelia had gotten accepted into. All she cared about was that she wouldn't ever have the chance to even think about staying here in California. The farther away she was, the farther away from *him* she was.

That's all her parents wanted.

And it was soul-crushing.

OPHELIA: *And if I say no?*

SATAN: *You won't. What do you think happened to the charges? They were dropped. For now. We will only keep them that way as long as you agree to go to England next year.*

A knock against the doorframe to her bedroom made Ophelia jump as she jerked her head up to see James smiling at her, but his grin faded slightly at her befuddled expression. His eyebrows cinched as he slowly stepped into the room.

"Everything okay?" he asked, his eyes searching her frantic ones.

Shit.

Shit.

"*Yes,*" she squeaked, swallowing thickly. "I'm okay. Everything is great."

Walking quickly over to her now, James sat next to her on the bed, the mattress sinking slightly as his head lowered to meet her worried gaze. His hands slid up her thighs, squeezing them gently as he cocked his head.

"Ophelia, please don't lie to me."

Her heart dropped into her stomach.

"If it's about the fact that we only have a week left—" He paused hesitantly, shooting her a reassuring smile before continuing. "Well, I think I can help. I've been looking into culinary schools around here, and there are so many that offer financial aid. You could apply and do what you want to do. It wouldn't be that expensive with the aid—"

"James."

"You wouldn't have to leave," he breathed, his eyes glistening brightly. "You could stay here with me. I could take care of you. Baby, *please* let me take care of you—"

"*James.*"

His bearded lips clamped shut at the urgency in her voice, his fingers digging into the flesh of her thigh as his throat bobbed. His faint smile resided on his mouth, not quite reaching his eyes, trying its best to cling on for dear life.

"The upcoming term is already paid for," Ophelia murmured steadily, taking a deep breath.

She watched his shoulders rise and fall slowly as he mirrored her breathing before his tongue flicked out to wet his bottom lip.

"I can pay your parents back. I'll take more shifts at the bar."

Her heart was sinking further and further with every ounce of hope he had been desperately trying to grasp onto, each word feeling like a jab to her ribs. Her parents were crushing her happiness, which only made her have to crush his. A devastating domino effect that would leave everyone scrambling to pick up the pieces.

"My mom got me a full ride into medical school. She just messaged me before you got here."

"Whoa."

His voice was hoarse.

Her ribs ached. Her heart was shattering in her chest.

"Yeah," she croaked quietly, staring down at his hands on her thighs.

"Where?" James asked faintly, his voice still hopeful. It only felt like he was ripping her heart from her chest and stomping all over it.

Her eyes stung as the tears welled up inside of them. Nausea rolled through her body, strong ripples of uneasiness churning in the pits of her stomach as she forced her chin up to look him in the eye. As soon as his eyes found hers, his jaw clenched. His nostrils flared.

Stomp. Stomp. *Stomp*.

He was unknowingly crushing her soul and her spirit, all while she was obliterating *his* for the rest of time.

"In England."

A ragged exhale left his lips as his eyebrows faintly raised, his teeth biting on his bottom lip as his head dropped. Loosening his grip on her thighs, he rubbed his hand down his face. His shoulders rose and fell with each meticulous breath he took.

"Are you going to go?"

She gritted her teeth to keep her chin from trembling as she struggled to compose herself. "I don't have a choice."

His head lifted quickly as he stared at her in bewilderment.

"You always have a choice, Ophelia."

Not this time. Not when they were threatening to continue to make his life hell if she chose to stay.

Ophelia could feel the bile rising in her throat as she watched the sadness wash across his features. She swallowed it back down, blinking carefully as the tears blurred her vision.

"If I don't go—" She hesitated, biting at her quivering lip. "My parents are going to charge you with assault. And I don't know if I could deal with me being the reason your life is ruined, James."

"They said that?" His voice was hoarse.

She nodded.

"You could never ruin my life," he whispered despondently after a moment.

He placed his finger underneath her chin, forcing her to look up at him again as a tear trickled down her warm cheek. His thumb brushed it away, tucking her hair behind her ear as he examined her.

"I feel like I already have."

Her voice cracked at the end of her sentence. Her eyebrows pulled together as she choked up, more tears falling down her cheeks—betraying her. She couldn't even look him in the eye. She didn't want him to see her like this. She didn't want to make him more sad than he already was.

His hands were suddenly cradling her face, his eyes flickering back and forth between hers as she peeked up at him.

"You didn't ruin my life, pretty girl," he said. "You saved it."

A sob fumbled out of her full lips as it racked through

her chest, her head dropping as she avoided his gaze. His hands immediately tugged her against his chest, his warmth radiating through him and enveloping her, just as his arms wrapped around her. She never wanted to leave them. She'd rather die peacefully here than ever have to leave them behind. She found solace in his touch.

"I'm so sorry for all of this," she cried.

Her chest shook violently as she tried to catch her breath, and her hands held him tightly as she sobbed. The salty tears drenched her flushed cheeks, trailing against her lips, and dripping down her chin.

"*Shh*, baby," James rasped, pulling her into his lap, cradling her like a child as he pressed his cheek against the top of her head. "*Please* don't cry. I don't want you to cry."

"I'm sorry," she said, sniffling. "I'm sorry for making you love me. I'm sorry for making you sad. I'm sorry that I ever made you—"

"No, Ophelia," he interrupted firmly. "You don't apologize for any of this. This isn't your fault."

She didn't know what else to say, if there were even words that could fix the way he felt. All that made her feel even the slightest bit better was crying in his arms, sitting in his lap as he brushed her hair from her face, and shushed her gently in her ear. She'd never felt more comforted and devastated at the same time.

Minutes had passed, but they had felt like hours as they sat in silence—listening to her sniffle into his chest.

"I can come with you."

She pulled away slowly, looking at him through puffy eyes.

"I would never want you to uproot your entire life here just to follow me to another country, Jamie. Your life is here," she mumbled. "And you following me wouldn't stop my parents. It would only fuel their fire."

His lips pursed as he chewed at the inside of his lip, nodding faintly as his hand found hers.

"I don't want you to leave."

She pressed her forehead against his shoulder.

"I know," she whispered.

"I could come visit you," he scrambled helplessly, his voice shaking. "You could still come back during the summers, right? You could do that."

"That would be a long time of just seeing each other during summers or Christmas break. Medical school is another four years." Ophelia sighed, squeezing his hand. "And while I would love to see you anytime I possibly could, I don't think it would be fair to either of us to only be able to see each other a few times a year *if* that."

James' lips stayed parted as he glanced down at her, the realization cascading across his face, only making him look even more sad. She wondered if he could hear her heart exploding into a million tiny pieces as she watched him come to terms with the end.

She wondered if he ever would.

"I hate this."

He sounded raspy. Broken. Each word was like a deep slice to the chest.

It was the right person, but at the wrong time. A lose, lose situation. It was the first time she'd ever felt like this for someone.

"You should hate *me*," she whispered.

His thick brows furrowed deeply at her words as he gaped down at her, his hands cradling her cheeks without hesitation.

"Don't say that." His eyes were firm. "Don't ever say that. There's not a single fiber of my being that could hate you."

It wasn't hard to decipher after that. Ophelia had fallen in love with him—descended into the black hole that she couldn't see the bottom of. Not until she was crashing into the ground without warning, remnants of her heart and soul scattered around her as she struggled to pick up the pieces.

CHAPTER TWENTY-EIGHT

Forty-eight hours.

That was all that was left between now and her flight back to Georgia.

Ophelia sucked in a shaky breath as she shoved more clothes into her suitcase, packing what she didn't need ahead of time so that she wouldn't have to cram it all into one day. It felt like each piece of clothing she placed inside was a nail in the coffin. A death sentence.

As much as she was falling apart on the inside, pieces of her happiness chipping away, she refused to let James see it. He had spent every night with her since she had broken the news of medical school to him, so she had to plaster a smile on her face constantly—it was exhausting, but she wanted their last few days to be peaceful.

Happy.

Picking herself up from the floor, she twisted on her heel to see James watching her from the doorway. His body leaned against the doorframe as his arms crossed over his burly chest.

"Hi," she murmured.

"Hi."

He pushed off of the frame, his hands dropping to his sides as he walked over towards her. Her mouth parted to say something as he approached her but was quickly muffled as he grasped onto her arms—tugging her against him as his lips smashed into her own. His hand traveled up her arm until he was gripping the hair at the nape of her neck, pulling her deeper into the kiss as his tongue dipped between her lips.

Her legs felt like jello as his mouth moved with fervor against hers. Her hands rested on his chest weakly.

When his lips left hers, she could feel her swollen pout. Her neck craned as he peppered kisses down her sensitive skin.

"What was that for?" Ophelia rasped.

His beard tickled her as he brushed his lips against her earlobe. "Did you think I was going to let you leave without a proper goodbye?"

A squeak escaped her lips as his hands hoisted her up by her thighs, wrapping her legs around his broad waist as he walked them over towards the bed. Carefully plopping her down on the mattress, he pressed his abdomen between her legs, forcing them apart as his lips found her collarbone.

"I want to taste every part of you," he breathed, his breath fanning across her neck. "Lick every inch of your skin. Make you feel me everywhere. Make it impossible for you to forget about me."

Her skin felt like it was on fire, buzzing underneath every kiss on his path down her chest. His hands whisked her shirt over her head, and her blonde waves splayed out across the bed as he crashed on top of her with his muscular chest.

Her fingers entangled in his hair, tugging him back faintly

as her chest heaved.

"I could never forget about you, Jamie."

A growl reverberated through him as he ripped his sweater from his body, his tattooed abdomen illuminating in the glow of the lamp on the bedside table. Every detail and crevice of muscle was outlined with a shadow, allowing her to see just how defined he really was.

"No one will touch you like I do, Ophelia," James said breathlessly, his hands gripping her thighs to spread them, pressing himself against her core. "No one."

She mewled softly at his assertiveness, and her back arched into him as their skin collided.

She wanted to feel him everywhere, all at once.

"*Say* it, baby," he demanded, softer this time, pulling back so that his desperate eyes met hers. "Say that no one else will touch you like me. That you don't want them to."

Ophelia reached up to hold his face in her hands, her thumbs brushing his cheeks as she pecked him on the tip of his nose.

"No one else will touch me, James. I don't want anyone else's hands on me unless they're yours."

An airy moan left his lips as he pressed his erection against her through his pants. She rolled her hips to meet his, tugging him down by his hair to crash her lips into his. His fingers dug into her waist as he fumbled to unbutton her jeans, yanking them down partially.

"Because you're mine," he panted, pressing sloppy kisses through the valley of her breasts. "All of this." Another kiss. "Is mine."

"Show me," she rasped in a whine.

Her stomach twitched underneath him as he trailed kisses toward her navel, his fingers pulling down her pants the rest of the way until he was tugging them from her ankles. She could feel how damp her panties were against the warm contrast of his breath as he hovered over her, caressing her panty line with his finger.

Whisking his finger underneath her panties, he tugged them to the side. His eyes observed her beneath him as he licked his lips.

"This," he cooed lowly, sliding his finger through her folds. "Is because of *me*."

Ophelia shuddered as he pressed his mouth against her, lapping her clit slowly. His beard rubbed harshly against her skin—the sting only turning her on even more.

"*Yes*," she murmured shakily, staring down at him as he flicked his tongue against her.

She would willingly swear off men for the rest of her life underneath his skilled tongue. She'd sign her soul away to him if he asked her to. It was mesmerizing, making her head spin madly.

"Moan for me, baby," James urged. "I want to hear you. I want the fucking neighbors to hear you."

His mouth connected with her again, making her choke mid-breath. Grasping the bed sheets tightly as he devoured her, a string of mewls left her lips in staccato pants. Her core tightened under the pressure of his tongue.

"James." Ophelia moaned loudly. "Oh, God."

"That's it." He growled against her, pulling back until he

was towering over her. His jaw slack. "I *am* your God."

Ophelia bit her lip as she peeked up at him.

"Shall I worship you, then?"

His eyebrows twitched as they pulled together, his lips parting.

Pushing herself up until she was perched on her knees, she trailed her hands down his burly chest. She didn't stop until they had reached the button of his pants, flicking it open and tugging them down his waist as she stared at him unwaveringly.

"Is that what you want?" she questioned in a gentle tone, shoving her hand inside his boxers, encircling her fingers around him. "Me on my knees? Worshipping you as I suck your cock?"

His breathing was shaky as his eyes grew heavy from her touch, his mouth agape as he bucked against her hand.

"*Fuck,*" he breathed. "Yes, fuck, *yes.*"

Stepping from the bed, Ophelia kept her hand secured around him as she kneeled down on the floor. Yanking the rest of his boxers down with her other hand, she took his cock inside of her mouth. Peering up at him, she forced him deeper between her lips.

His mouth popped open as she swirled her tongue around him, lubricating him with her saliva as she stroked gently with every bob of her head.

Pressing down further, she sputtered slightly as he jabbed the back of her throat. A string of saliva streamed from her lips as she pulled his cock from her lips with a loud *pop*.

"You look so pretty sucking my dick," he praised weakly, his hips jerking involuntarily as she continued to stroke him.

"Yeah?" she breathed.

As he went to speak again, she took him in her mouth once more, making him moan raspily. His hands brushed her hair from her face as she bobbed up and down, gagging as she forced him down her throat.

"So, so pretty," James panted heavily. "Come here. I want to fuck you, pretty girl."

The flutters were in a frenzy inside her stomach as he pulled her from the ground, shoving her onto the mattress. Pressing himself between her splayed legs, he slid his cock through her slick folds. A moan bubbled from her lips at the sudden contact, her hips rolling into his.

Her hands gripped his shoulders as he thrust into her, stretching her out. Pulling out slowly, he slammed back into her again.

"Oh my God, *please*," she begged, unsure of what exactly she was begging for.

James moaned at her pleas, his hips bucking at a rapid pace. Pressing kisses along her chest, he encased a hardened peak between his lips as he fucked her.

Ophelia's eyes fluttered closed at the sensation of his warm mouth overtop of her nipple.

"My girl. My Ophelia."

Burying his face into her neck, he bit down into the crevice gently. The sting of his teeth sank into her skin, making her clench tighter around him. He growled as her cunt milked him; her moans mixing with the sound of their skin making contact over and *over* again.

Her breath halted inside of her throat as she ran her fingers through his hair, pulling him closer.

"I'm yours," she urged shyly next to his ear. "I am yours."

"M-more," James pleaded weakly, his movements getting sloppy as he slammed into her. "I need more, baby. Please. Keep talking to me. I'm going to come."

The sound of him begging made the pressure swell between her legs. Tugging his head down even more, her lips pressed against his ear.

"You feel so fucking good, baby," she purred. "So big."

James whined, pulling away slightly to peer down at her. His jaw was slack, quick pants rolling from his lips that matched his thrusts as he continued to slam into her.

She loved the way he looked when he was at her mercy.

His forehead connected with hers, and his eyes trained on her still, unblinking.

"I love you."

His voice was urgent, pleading for more. There was a hidden gravity behind his words.

Ophelia was seconds away from her orgasm bubbling over the edge, the pressure built so high in her core that she could hardly breathe as he pumped into her. Tears pricked the corners of her eyes at the overwhelming sensation. The words fumbled out of her full lips before she could even process her thoughts.

"I love you, James," she said.

And that was all it took for her climax to ripple through her as a sob left her mouth. Clenching tightly around him, she felt him twitch inside her as his orgasm reached him, too.

Slamming his face into her neck, he groaned; his movements jerky as he spilled inside of her.

They were gripping each other so harshly that she was sure there would be bruises left after.

And then James stilled—unmoving as he lay gently on top of her for a few moments in complete silence. All that could be heard was their ragged breathing as they came down from their highs together.

Beats passed.

Her heart thudded against her chest harshly from the adrenaline that was pumping through her veins. For a moment, she wondered if maybe she had said the wrong thing. Made everything worse, somehow. And then she felt it.

Warm tears soaked her flushed skin as she felt him tremble. He sniffed quietly, and his jaw clenched as he tried to keep the tears at bay. His heart was pounding through his chest, reverberating against hers.

He was crying so hard that the bed was practically shaking.

Water welled up in her own eyes as she wrapped her arms around his broad shoulders, twisting her body sideways as she cradled him against her, shushing him quietly. Tugging the comforter over their bodies, she cocooned them in the blanket, creating a fortress around him.

She didn't know how many minutes passed as she rubbed the back of his neck with her thumb.

She worried that she had only upset him more by telling him how she felt—and she wanted to cry along with him. She had almost started to before he pulled back gently to meet her eyes.

His blue ones were swollen and red from crying. His face was damp, but somehow still seemingly beautiful. His freckles stuck out along his flushed skin.

"Tell me again," he croaked.

Reaching up to swipe the tears from his cheekbones, she murmured, "I love you, Jamie."

His shoulders relaxed.

He released the breath he had been holding.

His puffy eyes softened.

It was like the words were his kryptonite. Solace pooled in his eyes as he examined her features, his arms wrapping around her waist.

"You're the best person I've ever known, Ophelia Clark. My favorite girl. My Lia. I'll love you in every lifetime, every *universe*, every afterlife. As much as you're breaking my damn heart, I'd gladly rip it out of my chest and hand it over to you—it's yours. Break my heart a thousand times. I don't care, as long as you know that it beats for you."

CHAPTER TWENTY-NINE

THROWING ON A LIGHT jacket, Ophelia locked the door behind her as she left Wren's apartment.

She was meeting Wren at the coffee shop around the corner of the building for one last coffee date before she flew back to Georgia tomorrow. To say that she was sad would be the understatement of the year. Leaving her best friend every summer wasn't an easy task.

The chilly morning air nipped at her cheeks as she walked down the sidewalk toward *Cuppa Coffee*. She shoved her hands inside the pockets of her jacket, licking her dry lips.

Wren was perched in the corner of the cafe when she entered, sitting in the worn, brown booth that was their spot every time they met here. Her waves cascaded down her shoulders as she sipped at her warm coffee, a mug resting across from her, waiting for Ophelia.

Sliding into the booth, Ophelia let out a playful sigh.

"What am I going to do without you for another school year?"

Wren rolled her eyes, waving her hand dismissively. "*Don't* remind me. I don't need to remember that this is our last time hanging out for a while."

Scooping up her coffee mug, she sipped the warm beverage slowly.

"On the bright side, I was thinking of coming home for Christmas this year."

"I don't suppose that is because of me." Her best friend smirked. "Now is it?"

Partially, of course, it was. Ophelia would be lying if she said that it wasn't also because she wanted to have any excuse to come back to Los Angeles to see James. It wasn't possible to stay, and he couldn't come with her, so maybe she could just...what? Tease him more by popping in now and then.

Ugh.

"Lia," Wren continued, pulling her out of her overwhelming thoughts.

"*Hmm?*"

"Tell me what's going on."

Ophelia set down her mug, allowing her chin to rest sullenly in her palm as she stared out of the front entrance window. Her eyes didn't rest on anything in particular—kind of in a daze. Staring, searching for the future, wanting her eyes to fall on it so she could see exactly what was supposed to happen.

"I'm leaving James behind," she said, her finger tracing the outline of the engraved pattern on the booth table. "And I may as well be leaving my heart behind with him."

Her eyes observed Ophelia closely, lips pursing, all traces of playfulness gone from her features as she rested her hands on the table.

"You love him."

So much.

Ophelia nodded.

"Listen, I have watched enough crime documentaries to know how to commit the perfect murder," Wren whispered. "Say the word, and I can just kill your parents. You and James can live happily ever after."

A giggle slipped through her lips. It was times like these when she was eternally grateful for Wren's sense of humor and undying protectiveness. She always knew just what to say to make her crack a smile when she felt like doing anything *but* smiling.

"Even in the afterlife, my mother would still find some way to haunt me."

"You're right." Wren sighed, her hands finding Ophelia's and giving them a gentle squeeze. "That bitch."

She relished in the comfort that Wren's hands brought to her, fighting the urge to shut her eyes and let the tears stream down her cheeks. The fear of leaving everyone she cared about behind made her want to crawl out of her own skin.

"How did I get here?" she whispered shakily, her voice sounding strangled as it left her mouth. "How did this happen? Why can't I have the things that I want?"

Wren's eyes glazed over as she blinked away the tears, her head tilting sympathetically as her eyebrows cinched.

"You can always have the things that you want, babe," she encouraged. "No one can take that from you."

"They already have."

"Then you take it *back*."

Her shoulders lifted as she inhaled a deep breath, exhaling

steadily through her nose.

"I don't know how," Ophelia confessed in a small voice. "It feels too far out of reach to even grasp anymore. And at what cost? Just so they can get him arrested again? Or something worse?"

James had already been through too much in his life. Car accidents, his sister's death, his ex-wife—she didn't want to add to the growing list of hindrances he already had. She didn't want to be another problem. And so far, it seemed as though all she had done for him was make his life more difficult. The first time they met, he was having to drive her home because she was intoxicated. She should've seen it then. Should've been smarter.

"Have you asked him how he feels about all of this?"

Ophelia drew her bottom lip between her teeth.

"He would drop his entire life here to come with me, but he knows I would never allow it. He wants me to stay, but he knows that's nearly impossible. There's no happy ending here, Wren."

"There would be if your parents took the time they've wasted controlling your life and applied it to pulling their heads out of their asses," Wren grumbled.

"That would be too much." Ophelia rolled her eyes. "No, instead, they'd rather ship me off to another country for medical school. So they don't have to deal with me, and so no one else has to either."

"Bitches."

"Bitches," Ophelia agreed.

"I'll just have to uproot and move to England with you. We

could be roomies."

Her lips formed an appreciative thin-lipped smile as she sipped at her coffee again, the idea settling into a spot in her brain for safekeeping. She was desperate for anything at this point.

"That would be perfect if I actually wanted to go to England."

Wren's jaw clenched as she gave her a disapproving look, her round eyes softening shortly after. "You do realize how that sounds, right, Ophelia? You're not doing anything that's making *you* happy. That's not how anyone should live their life."

She knew exactly how it sounded—she was giving up her happiness for the sake of James. To make her parents happy, or at least satisfied temporarily. They were always going to want something else from her, wanting to strip away more and more of her happiness until she had nothing left.

"I'm okay with giving up my happiness if it means that James will be okay," she mumbled softly, drinking the rest of her coffee before setting the mug back down in front of her.

"And I would bet that he would say the same thing about you."

Dammit. He would.

"I should've just stuck to tequila," Ophelia whined, letting her face fall in her hands. "Tequila never lets me down like men do."

"You don't mean that, though," Wren said. "Because he hasn't let you down."

Silence fell between them, shrouding them in a dark, thick

cloud as they sat across from each other. There weren't words that would make Ophelia feel any better, and the more she talked about the situation, the more exhausted she felt. She wished she could crawl under the booth and never come out again.

Maybe she could just fake her death.

"You need a hug," Wren said after a moment, pushing up from the booth. "Come here."

Ophelia didn't hesitate to stand up and allow her best friend to engulf her arms around her, burying her face into Wren's sweater as she fought against the stinging behind her eyes. What would she do without these hugs? FaceTime, texts, and calls weren't the same as this. And she would need this.

"On the bright side, I'm glad you found someone to keep you company while I'm gone," Ophelia teased.

"Yeah, yeah. Sean could never compare to you."

It grew quiet as they hugged each other.

"This sucks," Ophelia grumbled after a few moments, her voice cracking.

"Good luck tomorrow," Wren said comfortingly, squeezing her tighter. "I know it's going to be hard, and I wish I could be there."

Tomorrow.

Her flight back to Georgia.

James was taking her to the airport to drop her off. Her stomach churned uneasily at the thought of how that was going to go.

They pulled away simultaneously, Wren grasping Ophelia's face in her hands as she looked at her with glossy eyes.

"Please, promise me that you'll take care of yourself."

"I promise."

"And promise me that you'll start doing what makes you happy. I know that day might not be today, but soon, you'll have to choose *yourself*. And I hope when the time comes, you don't hesitate," Wren whispered, her lips forming a thin line as she cleared her throat. "You better not hesitate. I'll come find you and beat your ass."

"I love you." Ophelia laughed breathlessly.

She inhaled the flowery scent of Wren's perfume, storing it away in her brain to pull out again on the days when she missed her best friend the most.

"I love you, brat."

Ophelia missed her soul sister as soon as she left the coffee shop. Tears nipped at the back of her eyes. Her chin trembled with the warning of a sob forming inside of her chest, but she buried it as far as it would possibly go.

She wanted to have one day where she didn't cry.

And that day would have to be today because *tomorrow* —

Tomorrow she'd be leaving every ounce of her tears, her heart, and her soul in the sunny state of California.

Her home.

She may have grown up in that miserable house that her parents still resided in, but her home was in the arms of *him*.

CHAPTER THIRTY

JAMES LOOKED PALE WHEN he arrived to pick up Ophelia. He kept fidgeting with his rings, rubbing his hands on his jeans, and palming at his beard. It was as though his hands constantly had to be doing something—and if that didn't tell her how anxious he was, his eyes did.

His pupils were dilated, fixated on her suitcases and duffel bag by the front door, blinking slowly before they eventually lifted to meet hers.

His brown hair was tussled like he had run his fingers through it about a dozen times.

His frantic state only made Ophelia feel even worse. Her stomach twisted into a knot as she struggled to keep her composure. She hoped that her friendly smile didn't look as strained as it felt as she reached on her tiptoes to plant a kiss at the corner of his lips.

"Hi," she greeted softly.

"Hi."

His voice sounded hoarse. Thick.

"I thought we could stop for coffee on the way," Ophelia said gently, her hand finding his as he walked inside. "We have some time to kill."

He nodded, his throat bobbing as he swallowed.

A frown was permanently etched into his brows, wrinkling his forehead as his lips sat in a faint pout. His nostrils flared with every breath as if he was struggling to keep it together, and his composure faltered slightly as his jaw clenched.

"James," she cooed tentatively, reaching up to place her palm against his warm, bearded cheek.

"Hmm?"

"Look at me."

His eyes immediately flickered up to meet hers as he leaned gently into her hand, a wince flashing across his features as he studied her.

Ophelia could see the turmoil in his irises. Her heart fell into her stomach because of it; the nausea bubbled in the depths of her intestines. She could feel the bile rise in her throat, choking her, rendering her speechless as she stared up into the war that was happening behind his eyes.

This was because of her.

"Maybe I should just get someone else to take me to the airport. I don't want it to be any more difficult than it already is."

"No," he stated firmly. "No one is taking you but me. I want to see you off. I have to."

Perhaps it was the crack in his voice. The need. The pleading tone laced his words. Ophelia wasn't exactly sure what made her stand on her tiptoes and crash her lips against his. Her arms wrapped around his neck as she leaned into him. A low groan rumbled through his chest as his arms enveloped her waist, pulling her deeper into him as their lips molded together.

His hands traveled up her spine until they were holding the back of her neck, and his fingers entangled in her hair as they kissed.

"We could skip coffee," she panted breathlessly as she pulled away, her lips already swollen from his touch.

"Ophelia." James sighed quietly, hesitating. "As much as I love the idea of having you underneath me again, I don't know if I would be able to let you leave after."

"I know."

It was the last thing that either of them needed, but she couldn't stop herself from pulling him towards her once more, pressing kisses along his jawline slowly. His shoulders went rigid as she peppered her lips down his neck, and his fingers dug into her waist.

"*Ophelia,*" he warned.

She knew. But she was afraid to let go, afraid he would disappear forever, and she wanted to touch him for as long as she could.

And *maybe* she was stalling.

Unraveling her arms from around his neck, Ophelia flattened her feet on the ground as she pulled away. His arms remained wrapped around her waist as his chest heaved. Peering down at her, the unrelenting turmoil hid behind his eyes once more.

"It's not that I don't want you, baby," he whispered. "Because, fuck, there's nothing I'd want more. But I don't think I have any more energy left inside of me to ravish you the way I want. It's all going towards keeping my shit together."

It made complete sense. But why did it hurt so much?

Ophelia nodded, gulping down the thick wad in her throat. Pulling away from him, she watched as he picked up her duffel bag and tugged the suitcase towards the front door.

"Ready to go?" she asked.

"Yeah."

It was excruciatingly silent the entire walk toward the elevator. The only sound came from the faint hum as they descended to the main floor.

This was never the way that she had wanted this to end. She didn't want what they had to turn into this—both of them awkwardly quiet because they didn't know what to say to each other. Because they were too sad to say anything at all.

Ophelia only had herself to blame.

So instead of crying, she stayed quiet. She would save her tears for the plane ride back to Georgia.

She wanted to shrivel up into the corner and sob every time she snuck a glance over at James. Her eyes stung each time she watched how glum he appeared on the way to the car. It made her feel physically ill when she remembered that it was all because of her.

She disappointed everyone in her life. This shouldn't feel like anything new.

But it did.

And it all hurt just the same.

No wonder her parents wanted to send her far away; no wonder they never bothered forming a normal relationship with her as a child.

Ophelia's shoulders sagged as she observed James load her baggage into the trunk of the SUV, pleading for his eyes to look her way—but they didn't. Her chin trembled as she walked around the car to climb into the passenger seat, and her hands fidgeted in her lap.

Could she blame him?

She strung him along only to stomp his heart into the concrete in the end. If she were in his shoes, she probably wouldn't want to look at her either.

She faced forward as James climbed into the car next to her, her lips pursing as she chewed at them inside anxiously.

"We don't have to stop for coffee," she murmured, staring out of the windshield. "If you just want to get this over with, which I don't blame you if you do—"

"I don't want to get this over with, Ophelia," James snapped, his hands gripping the steering wheel as he grit his teeth. "I don't want to do this. I don't want to drop you off. I don't want to watch you walk away from me knowing it's the last fucking time. I'm sorry that I'm not particularly chipper on the day I have to watch the girl that I'm in love with *leave me*."

Knives, straight into her chest. Piercing her heart hundreds of times.

That's what those words felt like.

She twisted her head away from him as a tear slipped down her flushed cheek, holding her breath to keep a sob from slipping from her lips.

"That came out harsher than I meant," he mumbled after a few moments. "I'm sorry."

Ophelia couldn't speak. She didn't know what would come out if she even tried.

She wanted to scream at her parents, scream at...everything. Anything to release the pent-up emotions inside of her, because crying just wasn't cutting it anymore.

"Ophelia, I'm sorry."

She bit her quivering lip.

"Baby, please," James cooed, his hand resting on her thigh. "I'm sorry. Please look at me."

His arm wrapped around her shoulder, pulling her gently towards him before she tugged out of his grasp. Finally, peering over at him, she shook her head as more tears fell down her cheeks.

"I'm sorry, you know," she croaked, shrugging away as he went to put his arm around her again. "I'm sorry that I made you feel like this. I feel like I ruined everything for you."

"Lia, don't," he pleaded quietly, his eyebrows knitting. "Don't do that. You didn't do anything wrong. When will you realize that none of this is your fault? You can't always take the blame."

"I can't help it, James!" Ophelia cried out loudly, the shrill sound echoing in her ears. "My entire life, I've been made to feel like everything is always *my* fault. My parents don't love me? That's my fault. People don't put me first? *My*. Fault."

His eyes were wide as he stared at her, taken aback by her sudden emotional outburst.

"All I've ever done is do exactly what they ask of me and it's still not good enough."

His hand found hers, squeezing hard enough to where she

couldn't yank it away this time.

"And the one thing—the *one* thing I wanted was to be good enough for *you,*" she cried, her voice breaking. "And I can't even do that. I'm always going to disappoint you, James. That's why I have to go."

Forcefully this time, he tugged her against his chest, cradling her head in the crevice of his neck as sobs racked through her. His hands held her comfortingly, but firmly at the same time, as if to say that it was okay to break down.

"You have never disappointed me, pretty girl." His breath fanned across her ruffled hair as he rested his chin on top of her head. "You've amazed me, shocked me, made me so proud of you—you're so resilient. Your strength astounds me, sometimes. I wish that *I* could be like you."

His words only made her cry even harder as she gripped his shirt in tight fists.

She always wanted to be like *him*.

"I don't feel very strong right now." Ophelia sniffled.

"I'll be strong enough for the both of us."

She lifted her head. "I thought you couldn't be strong enough today? Not when I'm leaving."

He brushed a lock of her hair behind her ear, his thumb catching a tear that escaped down her cheek, swiping it away. "The world could be ending, and I could be on my last breath, but I would still be here to hold you. I may not be strong enough for myself, but I will *always* be strong enough for you."

Her skin felt like it was ablaze from his words, buzzing everywhere as warmth encapsulated her entire body. It encompassed her heart last, surrounding it in a veil of comfort as it swelled inside of her chest, making her melt further into his arms.

He held her there for the entire trip to the airport, nestled in his neck, one hand on the wheel while the other was wrapped around her—giving her reassuring squeezes now and then.

Those squeezes were everything.

Ophelia tried to cling to every little thing, etching them permanently into her brain for safekeeping when she wanted to remember him.

The walk inside the airport felt like it had taken a fraction of a second, time seeping by in the blink of an eye. James accompanied her until he didn't have any other choice, all the way up to the security check.

This was it.

This was the moment she had tried so hard to avoid and push towards the back of her mind.

The end.

"*Ah*, fuck," James hissed, pinching the bridge of his nose as he sucked in a deep breath. "I don't want to do this."

Ophelia peeked up at him through her damp lashes, taking one of his hands as she gave it a gentle squeeze. Her thumb rubbed the back of his hand as she licked her lips.

With watery eyes, he finally looked down at her, clearing his throat.

"Do you want to know the moment that I knew I was going to fall in love with you?"

The question took her breath as she furrowed her brows up at him. Nodding gently, she blinked back the familiar stinging behind her eyes—already knowing that what he was going to say would rattle her to the core.

"When you took me to that pool and told me that my arm made me unique," he mumbled, a breathless laugh escaping his lips as he swiped a tear that was trailing down his cheek. "I think at that moment I fell *hard* for you."

Ophelia smiled sweetly.

"No one has ever made me feel the way that you do." He paused, shaking his head. "I am so lucky to have met you. You've changed my whole life in just a few short months."

"It might have taken me a while to realize it, but do you want to know my moment?"

His somber eyes immediately lit up at her question, like he had wanted to know the answer his entire life. His hand gripped hers in anticipation, his chest even heaved a little harder.

"Please," he whispered.

"The moment you stood up for me in front of my parents." Ophelia flushed slightly, looking down at her feet. "I didn't realize it then, but you made me feel safe. You made me feel like I was worth fighting for."

"Well." James bit his lip to bite back his smile. "You did jump me in the car right after, so I kind of had an inkling."

"Shut up."

They laughed in sync for a moment before silence followed, reality setting back in.

"But maybe—" she paused, blinking up at him. "Maybe I knew it all along. The feeling in my stomach every time I look at you. Every time I talk to you. It's always been there. I don't think I knew what it was until now."

She could see his chest shakily rise and fall as she spoke.

"I was too busy trying to fight it off instead of embracing it," Ophelia said softly. "If I had just accepted it from the start, I would've figured out sooner that I am so, *so* in love with you."

James reached up to brush her hair behind her ear, his fingers caressing her cheek, her jaw, and her bottom lip. Like he was memorizing her. Taking her in. His eyes were glossy as he observed her.

"I'm going to miss you so much."

She sighed, gnawing at the inside of her lip. "I'm going to miss you, too. You've become my best friend, you know?"

He nodded slowly, trying his best to smile even though his eyes were watering again.

"Flight 1034 to Atlanta, Georgia, is departing in twenty minutes. Flight 1034 to Atlanta, Georgia, is departing in *twenty* minutes."

The voice over the intercom was the closing statement to their love story.

Standing on her tiptoes, Ophelia pressed her lips against his, squeezing her eyes shut as she kissed him gently. Once. Twice. Three times.

"I am in love with *you*, pretty girl," James rasped.

Chin trembling once more, she wiped at her damp cheeks as the tears fell again. Taking her bag and suitcase, she licked her lips, the salty liquid seeping into her mouth—tasting like the worst day of her life. One last longing look lingered between them before she sucked in a deep breath.

Twisting on her heel, she turned to walk away from him, tears streaming down her cheeks. Dragging her suitcase along behind her, she hurriedly walked towards the security checkpoint, afraid if she didn't hurry, she wouldn't actually go. But she stopped—peeking over her shoulder to see James staring hopelessly after her, tearing her heart in two.

Dropping her bag to the floor with a loud smack, her legs started moving underneath her as she ran back towards him, smashing against him as she wrapped her arms around his neck. Pressing her lips against his feverishly, she basked in the feeling of his hands on her waist for the last time.

"Wait for me?" Ophelia asked selfishly, kissing him again, and again, and *again*.

Say yes.

"I'll always wait for you, Lia."

CHAPTER THIRTY-ONE

JAMES

James didn't know why on Earth he had allowed himself to actually consider showing up at Ophelia's parents' doorstep. It was fucking dumb—they hated him. They had literally gone to the greatest of lengths to make his life a living hell. But here he was, pacing back and forth in front of their front door, chewing at the inside of his lip.

The last two months had been the most excruciating, miserable weeks of his entire life. Texting Ophelia felt like a tease. It only made his heart shatter inside of his chest with every message he received from her. He always wanted more. He wanted *her*.

James couldn't focus at work. His head was never in it while bartending. Even the customers had started to notice. When he wasn't working, he was holed up inside his room in the back—he basically never left *The Beer Lounge*. Sean continuously tried to get him out of his depressed funk, but it never worked. He'd slip back into his vacant haze in a matter of hours. It always came back.

He missed his pretty girl.

So, he'd ultimately gotten so tired of himself that he decided he was going to go change her parents' minds.

Or try.

Fuck.

This had to be the dumbest fucking idea he'd ever come up with.

Running his fingers through his hair, which was significantly longer because he'd even stopped getting it cut, he let out an exasperated groan before rapping his knuckles against the front door. His heart hammered against his chest, and it was the first time it had felt anything but broken in months.

James had almost turned and high-tailed it back over to his motorcycle, but the sound of the door unlocking told him it was already too late to run.

The door whisked open to reveal Julie, who laid her narrowed blue eyes on him as she pursed her faintly wrinkled lips. Her arms crossed in front of her chest as her chin tilted upward.

"James."

"Mrs. Clark," he responded. "I need to talk to you."

"If you're here to talk about my daughter, you have truly lost your mind—"

"*Five* minutes." James cut her off, licking his lips. "All I need is five minutes. And then if you don't want to hear anything else I have to say, I'll leave."

He shuffled backward as she stepped out of the house, closing the door behind her as she flicked her hair behind her shoulders. Her grimace told him that she wasn't looking forward to his words in the slightest, but hell, at least he had gotten her out of the door.

He hadn't actually thought this far ahead. He had no clue what was about to leave his fucking lips. He thought she'd slam the door in his face.

"What's Ophelia's favorite color?"

Real smooth, dumbass.

Julie's mouth hung open in confusion before clamping it shut again. Squinting, she shook her head at him. She looked like she was about to say something absurd before he interrupted her.

"She would tell you that it depends on the day," he quipped, rubbing his palm down his face. "But I know better. She wears pastel pink all the time. Pastel pink shirts, pastel pink hair clips. She even has pastel pink *shoes*."

His fingers were running through his hair again, irritating his scalp which was sensitive from repeating the same action all day long.

Julie's eyes rounded, but she stayed quiet.

"Did you know her favorite color was pastel pink?"

"What does this have to do with anything?" she snapped lightly.

"That's what I thought," he grumbled. "What's her favorite movie? I'll spoil it for you. It's *13 Going On 30*. She said she watched it with you when she was a kid. She loved how you guys laughed at the part where the girls sing Pat Benatar together. It's been her favorite ever since."

Julie swallowed thickly, shuffling back and forth on her heels as she averted his gaze. Her once penetrating stare had dwindled. She knew he was making a point here.

"And did you know she still has the first A+ homework she

ever received? It's stuffed in her closet in her old room because it makes her happy that she made you guys so proud," James said breathlessly, his eyes stinging. "She clung to that homework like it was fucking gold. Because it made *you* happy."

The words were fumbling from his mouth before he even had the chance to think about whether he was saying the right or wrong thing.

He just needed to say it.

"And she does this thing when she's listening to you talk like she's so invested in every word that leaves your mouth." He laughed earnestly, gritting his teeth. "She rubs the back of your hand with her thumb. It's small, I know. Minuscule. But it feels like everything."

Julie's eyes flickered back up to observe him silently. Her thick eyebrows wrinkled deeply as they knitted together. This was news to her.

"She's so forgiving. Even when she has no reason to be," he hissed. "Her heart is the size of the goddamn universe and you guys take advantage of that. She'd do anything to please you and you don't even see it."

"I don't know what you're talking about."

The statement was meant to be powerful, blowing off his words, but he heard the faltering tone behind them.

"She doesn't want to be a surgeon. She wants to *bake*," James whined in frustration. "But she feels like she can't have that because you wouldn't support her decision. You would tell her it's not good enough. You would rather do everything in your power to keep her away from anything that could be good for her."

James didn't want to lose his cool, but the more he opened up about his feelings, there was no such thing as containing the abundance of emotions that were stuffed deep down. They were pleading to be set free.

"Your own daughter thinks that she will never be good enough in your eyes."

"That's not true," Julie argued, a softness creeping into her voice before she turned away, staring down at the driveway with her hand hovering in front of her mouth.

"I love her," James rasped. "I love her so much. And it kills me that she's so busy trying to be perfect enough for you that she's sacrificing her own happiness in the process."

His chest heaved as he struggled to compose himself, swallowing down the sob that he would allow himself to feel later when he was alone in his room again. Interlacing his fingers behind his neck, he sighed deeply as he waited for Julie to react.

She continued to face away from him. Her fingers fidgeted with her chin shakily. He could see her shoulders rise and fall with each calculated breath.

Say something.

"I think you should leave."

Closing his eyes tiredly, he nodded slowly, peering down at his leather boots.

"Okay," he said lowly.

It wasn't the reaction he was hoping for, but at least she wasn't cussing him out or trying to get him arrested again. She seemed genuinely bothered by his words, whether it be because she felt bad or because she didn't like someone calling her out, he wasn't entirely sure.

As he walked past her, bounding down the front porch steps, he hesitated slightly at the bottom. His heart skipped as he twisted to observe her red eyes, and her chin that trembled the same way Ophelia's did when she cried.

She was *crying*?

Fuck.

"I know you don't like me," James whispered, swallowing the lump that had formed in his throat. "But for what it's worth, I would do anything for her. I mean, I'm here, aren't I?"

Julie sniffed, blinking back more tears as she straightened her shoulders.

"And why would that mean anything to me? What makes you so special, Mr. Benton? Any boy could waltz up here talking about how he'd do anything for our daughter. And much less, ones who didn't choke out my husband."

As much as her indignant need to fight back and be stubborn pissed him off, she was right.

"I would do anything she asked me to. I'd be anything she needed me to be. I already have—I've picked her up time and time again when she was broken because her parents instilled the fear inside of her heart that she would never be good enough. I have and will always love her the way she deserves to be loved, exactly the way she is. *That's* the difference."

Her face softened.

"Indeed it is."

The words were barely audible, but he heard them.

"You can fix this," he murmured. "There's still time. You can change. For *her*."

She nodded. "Goodbye, James."

It was a dismissal, that he knew, but he was at peace with it because she had heard him out. She had listened to his wild rambling, his pleas, and she didn't immediately shut them down.

Which meant she was thinking about them.

And that was more than he could ever ask for. Even if his attempts today lead to nothing, he could say he had tried.

"Goodbye, Mrs. Clark."

Turning to walk down the driveway, his lips twitched in the corners as he threw his leg over his motorcycle. The bike roared to life, and for the first time in two months, *he* felt alive again, too.

CHAPTER THIRTY-TWO

Halloween in Georgia didn't feel the slightest bit spooky. Nor did it even feel like it was October. There were leaves on the ground, sure, but they were saturated with rainfall from the gray clouds that had hung around for the last four days. Which meant it was humid. The temperature was an uncomfortable seventy-five degrees and it was wet, everywhere.

This was the worst Halloween Ophelia could remember in a long time. And it just so happened to be her favorite holiday.

Perhaps it was just matching her mood.

She had been glum, like today, for the past two months. Since leaving James standing by himself in the airport. Every day was the same on campus, with a repetitive schedule of classes, studying, and more classes. She would come back to her dorm, sleep, and do it all over again the next day. Except today.

When she bounded down the concrete steps of her dormitory, her rain jacket sloshing around her noisily, she stopped in her tracks when she saw her mother standing at the bottom of the steps. Holding a black umbrella over her head, her hair was in perfect condition despite the dreadful humidity.

Ugh.

"What are you doing here?" Ophelia droned, peeking up at her underneath her hood.

"I was hoping you'd have a moment for some coffee."

She blinked down at her, her eyebrows knitting in confusion at her words.

"I have class," she said slowly, crossing her arms over her chest.

"You can't skip it for today?" her mother asked, glancing around them. "Just blame this dreadful weather. Seriously, Ophelia, I never knew why you picked Georgia of all places—"

Julie was complaining, per usual. But her tone had sounded different—she sounded pleasant, for once. And her mother was not pleasant.

"What do you want?" She interrupted her warily, swallowing the lump in her throat. "Why are you being...nice? Just tell me what you want now, not over coffee."

Julie sighed, not with an attitude, but in exhaustion. Her eyes were sympathetic. Ophelia couldn't remember if she'd ever seen her mother in this state before, which only rattled her that much more.

Had someone died?

"I'd like to talk about James."

Oh no.

"*God*, what did you do now?" Ophelia whined, her face falling in her damp palms as she started to panic. "Please tell me you left him alone. I'm here, like you wanted, without him."

"*No*, Ophelia," she hissed, pinching the bridge of her nose as she hesitated. "It's not bad, just—let's go get coffee. I'm not standing here in this rain any longer than I have to."

Ophelia gawked at her mother before nodding faintly, pointing at the campus coffee shop two buildings down from her dorm. Leading the way, her rain boots sloshed in the puddles on the sidewalk as she walked.

She couldn't fathom what her mother was going to tell her about James, but she could only hope the conversation wouldn't be as awful as the rain.

The aroma of coffee beans filled her nostrils as she stepped inside the coffee shop, holding the door open for her mother. The pair didn't say anything for a while. They had even ordered their coffees separately. It wasn't until they settled in a more private booth in the corner that they glanced up at each other.

Ophelia could feel her stomach churning in anticipation. The nerve endings in her fingertips were igniting as she waited for her mother to speak.

"James came to see me a week ago."

Ophelia could feel the blood draining from her face as she shakily picked up her coffee to take a sip, wincing as the warm liquid scorched her lips.

"I didn't know he did that," she whispered.

The thought made her heart skip inside her chest. She had no idea what gave him the courage to do something as incredibly risky as that, but it made her miss him so much more.

"He came to defend your honor," Julie said coolly, searching

Ophelia's face. "He had a lot to say about you. Surprising things. Things that *I* didn't even know about my own daughter."

Ophelia could feel the vice grip around her heart at the sound of her mother's voice cracking on the last word, and the way her eyes averted her gaze as she sipped at her own coffee. It was obvious that she was struggling to keep her composure, but it was also shocking.

The witch did care.

"What things?" she asked quietly.

"Things about you. Who you are as a person. What you're interested in. He knows more about a woman who he's known for a few months than I do about my daughter that I've known for twenty-one years."

Julie licked her lips as she dabbed at her eyes in humiliation—sniffling as she rolled her eyes at herself.

"I'm not trying to make you feel sorry for me," she rasped. "I don't deserve your sympathy. I have been a poor excuse of a mother, and I don't know if there's anything I can say to fix that. But, I brought this."

She pulled a white envelope from her purse, setting it on the wooden table as she slid it across toward Ophelia.

Staring blankly down at the envelope, Ophelia tucked her damp hair behind her ears before peeking back up at her mother in blatant curiosity. Even still, she felt inclined to question the judgment of the woman who gave her life.

"Are you paying me off?" Ophelia squeaked doubtfully.

Julie's shoulders sagged. "I'm sorry that I've failed you to the point of making you think that my every intention is malicious. It's a *plane* ticket, Lia."

"To England."

Was she rushing her off to medical school sooner?

"To *Los Angeles*."

Ophelia's head jerked up as she looked at her in bewilderment. "What does that mean?"

A plane ticket. Back home. To her best friend. The beaches. Him.

"Go bake." Julie laughed weakly, a tear slipping down her cheek before she swiped it away. "Go be with James. Go be *happy*."

Chills cascaded across every surface of her body, her heart thumped erratically against her chest, and she could hear the thumping in her ears. Her fingers had begun to shake as she set her coffee back down, tears stinging her eyes.

"But classes...the semester." Ophelia trailed off gently, sucking in a deep breath.

"I've already taken care of all that."

"I can't believe this," she whispered, biting back the tears as she flipped open the envelope and pulled the ticket out, running her finger along the print.

"Well, you better start." Julie sighed, dabbing at her face with a napkin as she clasped her hands together. "Because your plane leaves in a few hours."

Ophelia jumped up from the booth, gasping as she nudged the table with her rain boot on accident. The coffees swayed slightly as she hurried to keep them from tipping over.

"Oh." She rushed quickly, her chest heaving. "Oh my God, I have to pack."

"Yes, go pack a few things. I'll arrange to have the rest of it brought later." Julie waved her fingers towards the front entrance. "I'll wait here. I'll take you to the airport."

"You're not flying back?"

"Like I said." Julie swallowed. "I'll arrange to have your things brought to you. I'll stay and take care of everything."

Ophelia's hands hovered in the air as she shakily tried to contemplate everything running through her brain. An exasperated laugh left her lips as she ran her hands through her hair.

Julie was no saint. In Ophelia's book, she was far from it. But her mother having a change of heart was quite possibly the best thing that could have ever happened. And for that, she was grateful. For that, she was willing to allow her to redeem herself.

All she'd ever wanted was *this* mother.

"Thank you," Ophelia whispered as she wrapped her arms around Julie's shoulders, tugging her into a tight hug.

"Don't thank me yet. This is minuscule. I have a lot of making up to do."

She had so many questions. What exactly did James say? What was the turning point in the conversation? What did her father think? The questions were on a repeat inside of her head, but there was no time for questions.

She had a plane to catch.

"This is everything," Ophelia said softly, kissing the top of her mother's head before making a bee-line for the front entrance.

As she pushed out into the rain, she left her hood down as

she began to run. Her boots splashed against the sidewalk as she zipped towards her dormitory.

The rain stung her skin as she ran in the downpour, the water smacking her rosy cheeks as her damp hair whipped around her face.

The gloom was exuding from her, seeping down her skin like the raindrops that fell on her face.

Down. Down. *Down.*

Leaving the sadness in the dust behind her as she bounded up the steps of her dorm, she burst inside and fled up the stairs to the second floor.

She was going to see James again.

She was going to tell him how much she loved him. How much she has wanted to be with him. How she'd bake all the cakes in the world for him.

For the first time in Ophelia's life, the warmth spread throughout her body, like lava underneath her skin. Like the sun shining on a hot summer day. She was happy.

For the first time, everything was falling into place.

Like *puzzle* pieces. The puzzle pieces she had been so jealous of as she watched Wren and Sean together. Now she had her own.

CHAPTER THIRTY-THREE

Ophelia's knee bounced impatiently as she stared out of the Uber window, desperate to see the glowing sign of *The Beer Lounge*.

The driver had gotten stuck in five o'clock traffic as soon as he had picked her up from the airport, making their forty-five-minute trip turn into almost *two* hours, much to her chagrin. The sun had already set. Only faint rays of orange and pink darted across the sky before darkening completely. The inside of the car was illuminated in red from the taillights.

She couldn't even focus on the music she was shuffling through on her phone. She kept removing her headphones to focus on the traffic ahead of them. Frustratedly huffing each time the car came to a stop.

The poor Uber driver probably thought she was a major bitch.

Her patience only grew more thin as the traffic slowed to a complete stop only five minutes away from the bar. It was bumper to bumper, and horns blowing angrily at each other. Ophelia's overstimulated nerves couldn't take anymore.

"I'm so sorry, sir," she said quickly, gathering her duffle bag and scooting towards the door. "But I really have to go. Thank you for getting me this far. *So* sorry."

"Wait—"

But she didn't even hesitate to hear what he was going to say. She was whisking the car door open as she climbed out rapidly, her shoes hitting the pavement as she began to run as fast as she could down the street with her heavy duffel bag weighing her down.

She refused to let anything stop her from reuniting with James.

Even the damn bag.

Her hair whipped around her flushed cheeks as she pushed further, and her shoulder ached as the bag slammed into her side with every movement. People on the sidewalk were throwing her bewildered glances as she flew past them, but she didn't care.

She just wanted him.

James was just within her grasp, practically brushing against her fingertips. She could feel it. *Nothing* could pull her away. This was her moment.

Two months had felt like two years.

Wren had filled Ophelia in on everything that was going on since the day she had left. She was always in the loop about James. She knew how depressed he seemed, how he never left the bar most days, and how his hair had grown longer because he didn't have the motivation to cut it.

A loud horn wailed in her ears as she came to a halt at the edge of the sidewalk before crossing the street. Her heart thumped harshly against her chest as it heaved with each breath. She was so distracted and overwhelmed that she had almost run out in front of a car, which was accompanied by a not-very-happy, older man who threw his hands up at her.

"Sorry," she whined, wincing apologetically.

She avoided the old man's glare as he drove off, sucking in a deep breath before bounding away again, only seconds away from the bar now.

Ophelia exhaled slowly as she froze in front of *The Beer Lounge*. Her shoulders rose and fell shakily as she watched him through the window, through her reflection underneath the glowing sign. Relief pooled in her veins as she smiled to herself, observing his dark brown hair that was pushed back, and his full beard that she missed so much, still accentuating his jawline. The smile on his face didn't quite reach his blue eyes as he reacted to something Sean had said, cleaning the top of the bar aimlessly.

God, she had missed him so much.

She wanted to see the smile touch his eyes. She wanted to see them crinkle in the corners as his nose scrunched. She missed that nose scrunch.

Pulling open the door, she walked inside, music from the karaoke machine filling her ears as she approached the bar and dropped her bag to the ground with a loud *smack*.

Sean was the first to look up, already knowing that she was coming because she told Wren, as a cheeky grin spread across his lips. Reaching his hand up to grip James' shoulder, he chuckled.

James was seemingly unfazed at first, like he'd gotten used to not paying attention the past two months, before Sean nudged him gently with his elbow. He jerked his head up suddenly, inhaling to suck in a deep breath before freezing.

The rag in his hands dropped to the floor as his eyes softened, his fake smile disappearing as his mouth popped open.

"*Ophelia?*"

His voice was small, *raspy*.

"Hi," she said softly, her cheeks lifting.

He scrambled around Sean until he was darting quickly from behind the bar, colliding with her as his arms enveloped her waist. Burying his face in her hair, a breathy laugh escaped his lips.

Her arms wrapped around his neck as she breathed him in. Her eyes closed as she melted into his arms, basking in the scent of his cologne that she hadn't smelled in so long. It reminded her of home.

"You're here?" he whispered shakily, his voice muffled by her hair. "How are you here?"

"My mom." Ophelia laughed softly. "She came to see me. You changed her mind, James."

He pulled away suddenly as his hands came up to cup her cheeks in his palms, looking at her as if he couldn't believe that she was actually standing in front of him. His thumbs brushed her cheekbones, and his eyes darted across her features like he was etching it into his mind.

"I can't believe you're here, Lia."

"I want to stay here with you," Ophelia said sweetly, her eyebrows pulling together. "I want to bake. I want to find a cheap culinary school around here to go to. I want to be with you."

It was like those words rejuvenated something inside of him, making his shoulders lift as he sucked in a deep breath. His lips turned upwards. Each word that left her mouth breathed life back into him, every ounce of visible numbness washing away.

James pulled her toward him as he pressed his lips against her forehead. She could feel his breath fanning across her skin as he sighed in relief.

"I'm moving," he mumbled against her skin.

"Moving?"

"To San Francisco. I'm moving into Brianna's house. It's just sitting up there...empty. I've decided that it's time. I can do this." He hesitated briefly, swallowing the lump in his throat. "You could come with me. You could live there with me if you wanted to. I'd want you to."

Ophelia bounced on her heels as she reached up to press her lips against his.

"Yes."

Kiss.

"Yes. Yes. *Yes.*"

Two kisses.

Three.

It had been two whole months since she had felt his lips on hers. She was hungry for it. Locking her fingers in his hair, she pulled him deeper into her kiss as she arched her back. His hands were still cupping her face as he kissed her with fervor, inhaling her. A groan escaped from his throat.

"Let's go outside." James chuckled in between kisses. "I don't want to give these boozies a free show."

Ophelia bit down on her lip as she held back her wide smile. Grasping her hand, he tugged her behind him as he led her outside into the fresh air.

James didn't stop until they were in the dimly lit alleyway before he desperately pushed her up against the brick with a low growl. His hands were in her hair as he devoured her lips, down her jawline towards the sensitive spot on her neck, nipping and pecking her skin. Butterflies threatened to suffocate her completely as they soared inside her chest, filling her stomach and throat, making her skin buzz just beneath the surface from his touch.

The roots he had planted had sprouted into trees, growing throughout her body. She was blossoming like a tulip in the summer sun; her soul coming alive and basking in everything that was James Benton.

"I have wanted to kiss you since the moment you left," he panted against her neck, pressing himself against her. "I've wanted to taste you on my lips again. I dream about it."

She sighed softly as his lips pressed kisses down her chest, stopping at the valley of her breasts.

"I've missed you," she whispered. "So, *so* much."

He groaned at her words as he kissed his way back up toward her mouth, taking her bottom lip between his teeth.

"I missed you, pretty girl."

She shuddered beneath him as his hands traveled underneath her shirt, gripping her waist as his thumbs caressed her stomach.

Wrapping her arms around his shoulders, Ophelia ran her fingers through the hair at the nape of his neck. "Wren kept me updated, you know. She told me how you were *really* doing the whole time. I'm so sorry, Jamie."

His head cocked sideways. "Don't be sorry. It was fucking rough without you, yeah, but I would do it over a million times if it meant that you came back to me like this."

"It's because of you," she urged softly. "You fought for us."

His face softened as he grasped one of her hands, pulling it to his lips as he kissed her knuckles gently.

"I told you I would do anything for you, Ophelia."

She bit down on her lip before standing on her tiptoes to kiss him again. Kissing James was something she would never get tired of—the feeling of his lips molding with hers made her head spin each time. The way his hands held her like he never wanted to let her go.

"It's funny." Ophelia sighed playfully, leaning back against the brick as her hands slid down his muscular chest. "The night I walked into your bar for the first time, I had mentally sworn off men forever."

He hummed jocosely.

"How'd that work out for you?"

"It didn't." She shrugged casually. "Guess I should've emphasized the old men part."

James shook his head as a wide smile dimpled his cheeks, reaching up to brush her hair behind her ear.

"Fossils with scarred arms?" he scoffed teasingly.

"Yep—totally forgot to add that to my list."

"Thank *God* for that," James murmured, pulling her against his chest as he wrapped his arms around her, kissing the top of her head. "I don't know what crazy, desperate plan I would've come up with if you hadn't come back to the bar the next day."

"You wanted me to?"

"More than anything."

She leaned back to look up at him, secretly enjoying how he had to have his hands on her at all times. They were like magnets, gravitating toward each other without even trying. Like he had mentally decided he was never going to let her go again.

"You don't regret any of it?" she asked.

"*Hell* no."

A tiny giggle escaped her mouth as she pressed her lips against his briefly.

"I knew Gemma wasn't my person, almost from the start, but I married her anyway. I just thought that she was the best I was going to get," he said. "I came to terms with the possibility that maybe I didn't deserve better than her. Maybe that's just who I was supposed to be with."

Ophelia watched his eyes avert hers like he was humiliated by his own words, so she placed her hand over the top of his—rubbing the back of it with her thumb.

"Even after it was over," he continued in a hushed voice. "I thought that I had my one, and that was *it* for me. I wasn't getting another chance."

"You didn't think you deserved better?" Ophelia prodded gently.

He shook his head. "No. Not until I saw you walk into my bar, hoist your tiny ass up on my bar stool, and down shots of tequila better than me."

She smiled softly, her eyes flickering down to the ground before peeking up at him. "That night when you dropped me off, I never expected to see you again. I thought it was just a chance encounter, but then you remembered my name. You had taken the time to see what my name was on my license and I knew that I had to see you again."

Perhaps, unknowingly, that night—he already had her wrapped around his finger. Hell, it might've been from the moment she laid eyes on him.

"I love you, Ophelia Clark," James breathed, his smile fading as his face grew serious, but still soft.

God, she loved him.

She was in love with him. Her soul was irrevocably intertwined with his. She had crashed into him like a wave, cascading over him as if he was sand, bringing tiny bits of him back with her as she receded into the ocean.

CHAPTER THIRTY-FOUR

Last night was the first night that Ophelia had slept over in James' bed. And despite being surrounded by boxes of his things that he had already begun to pack, it was the coziest night's sleep she could remember having in a long time.

At first, in her sleepy haze, she contemplated whether yesterday had been real. But as reality oozed back in, and she felt a pair of muscular arms enveloped around her waist, the smile that spread across her cheeks made her face ache.

James was spooning her, his warm, bare chest pressed against her back, and his face buried in the crevice of her neck as he snored softly. His beard tickled her skin. His breath fanned across her neck and collarbone, making her nipples harden beneath the flimsy, oversized t-shirt she wore.

It had been two months since she had felt him pressed against her, and it was driving her crazy.

His breath made goosebumps rise on her skin, and her back arched involuntarily as she bit down on her bottom lip. Her thighs squeezed together as she closed her eyes, focusing on her steady inhale and exhale.

"Keep arching into me like that, Ophelia." James breathed against her neck, his voice raspy. "And I'm going to rip your panties from your body and show you just how much I missed you."

His words sent waves of butterflies soaring through her stomach, his morning voice only making them spiral directly between her legs.

"Is that supposed to scare me?" she teased, pressing her ass against him.

"It should."

His hands gripped her waist underneath her shirt, and his fingers dug into her skin.

"Because I missed you so fucking much."

Ophelia smiled wryly as she stretched, her oversized tee coming up over her hips as it exposed her panties. A tiny sound escaped her lips as she arched again innocently. Mimicking a bored yawn, she patted her palm over her open mouth before snuggling back into him.

With a frustrated growl, James twisted her until she was face down on her stomach, and her cheek pressed against his pillow as he pinned her down from behind.

"What did I say, Clark?"

She licked her lips in anticipation.

"You said you would rip off my panties if I arched my back again," she said.

His fingers hooked underneath her underwear as he pressed himself against her. "And what did you do?"

"I arched my back."

He didn't say anything as he sighed deeply, his fingers caressing her skin as he slid them back and forth beneath the waistline of her panties as if he was contemplating his next move.

Ophelia was practically panting in excitement because of his touch. She didn't need contemplation, she needed action—now.

"*Please*," she whined gently.

She listened to him hum quietly as the sound rumbled through his chest and reverberated against her back before his fingers gripped the fabric of her panties and tore them off of her with one sharp tug. Her skin stung from the action, but the pain only made her body shudder beneath him, rolling back against his erection that was buried against her ass.

Ophelia gasped when his palm came down on her cheek with a crack—her teeth digging into her bottom lip to hold back a moan.

"*Jesus*, Ophelia," he rasped. "You're fucking soaked. My boxers are drenched just from pressing against you."

She squirmed gently, throbbing between her legs just from thinking about what was beneath his boxers.

"*James*," she pleaded.

"Tell me what you want," he ordered, his legs straddling her as he pinned her to the bed.

She twisted her head to peek over her shoulder, her breath raspy as she observed him hovering over her, and the way his long hair fell past his forehead. Her ripped panties were still clenched in his fist, and it was the hottest thing she had ever seen.

She arched deeper, rolling her hips into him. "I want you."

His fingers gripped her hair, yanking her head back as his lips pressed against her ear. "Be specific, baby."

"I want you to fuck me."

Her voice was strained.

Her hands were already gripping the sheets eagerly as her stomach churned with fervor. She was clenching around nothing.

She could feel his fingertips trailing up her calf, goosebumps following closely behind, as he continued to pull her head back by her hair. She tensed as they crept up the inner skin of her thigh, her hips lifting slightly in urgency.

"And how do you want it?"

His thumb brushed over her clit, making her tremble as her chest heaved.

"Rough," Ophelia said shakily.

The moments after the word left her lips were almost a blur. They happened so quickly, so hungrily, that her head was spinning. Her breath had depleted from her lungs as she tried to keep up with his movements.

James had shoved her ripped panties into her mouth, gagging her and making her drip down her thighs from how wet she was from it.

And then he had tugged her up by her hips, propping her on her knees with her face smashed into the pillow. A muffled squeak left her lips as his mouth connected with her cunt, his tongue flicking between her folds as he sucked her clit.

"I could drown in this pretty pussy," he mumbled against her, the vibration of his voice making her toes curl. "You taste divine."

And then a finger slid inside of her, making her moan against the fabric of her panties. Her eyes squeezed shut as it curled inside of her—repeatedly hitting the sensitive spot over and over and *over*. His beard was a stark contrast to his smooth tongue, mixing with the sensation of him finger fucking her. The coil in her stomach was tightening, ready to snap at any second as he pressed his tongue firmly against her clit.

As he added another finger, her orgasm washed over her. Her loud moans were drowned out by the cotton shoved inside of her mouth as she writhed underneath him. She could feel herself soaking his fingers as they continued to pound into her relentlessly.

"I love watching you fall apart in my hand."

She craned her neck to peer at him in her post-climax haze, just in time to see him remove his fingers from her to pop them between his lips as he tasted her. His eyes fluttered closed as he groaned, leaning forwards and tugging the panties from her mouth as he pressed his lips to hers.

"As hot as this is," James chuckled breathlessly. "I need to hear my name leaving your lips as I fuck you."

Leaning back up, kneeling behind her, he tugged his cock from his boxers. Lining the tip up to her entrance, he slid it through her glistening folds slowly before pushing himself inside of her. Their moans came out simultaneously—echoing around the room as he started a rhythm inside of her.

Ophelia felt like she was floating as the electricity underneath her skin sparked everywhere—her fingertips, her chest, her veins. Her chest felt like it was swelling, and her heart pumped erratically as he buried himself inside her.

"Oh God, *James.*" She sighed softly, her hand trailing behind her to hook around his forearm, holding onto him for leverage as he thrust frantically into her.

"*Yes*," he panted. "Yes, baby. Say my name."

He released her hip to intertwine his fingers with hers, pressing their hands into her lower back as he shoved her deeper into the pillow. His tiny grunts floated through her ears, making her head spin as expletives left her lips. She could feel the pressure building once more, taking her breath away as she clenched around him.

And then he was pulling out of her, making her whine in protest before he flipped her onto her back, yanking the baggy t-shirt over her head. Crashing his lips against hers, he let out a heady sigh.

"I missed you," he mumbled into her lips. "I missed you so much, Lia. God, I missed *this*."

Spreading her legs apart with his hands, he maneuvered his mouth against hers heatedly. With one swift hip movement, he was inside of her again, pumping into her as he snaked his tongue between her lips.

Ophelia's hands grasped the sides of his face as he thrust deeply into her. His skin connecting with hers was the sweetest sound she had ever heard, and his moans were the cherry on top.

"*Ah*, yes, *fuck*," she cooed, her voice wavering with each thrust.

Their eyes connected as he pounded into her. The electric current flowed through their heavy-lidded gaze.

She'd never felt more alive. More in love.

"I love you," Ophelia rasped suddenly, her eyebrows cinching as her orgasm threatened to reach her again. "I'm in love with you, James."

A soft whine escaped his lips before he was kissing her again, moaning loudly as he pulled out. Thrusting the tip of his cock inside her, he teased her before slamming into her fully.

"Fuck, you're going to make me come."

He kissed her again.

"I love you."

Another kiss.

"I love you so much."

His voice was strained, breathless, *hot*.

"Say it again," Ophelia pleaded in a whisper, caressing his cheekbones.

He shoved his hips forward, hard. His hands gripped her hips for leverage as he plunged in deeper, and her legs wrapped around his waist as she bit into his shoulder.

"I—"

Thrust.

"Love you."

That was all it took for her climax to wash over her in sync with his own—feeling him twitch inside of her as he held onto her tightly. They gripped each other as their chests heaved, struggling to catch their breath.

Her vision was starred as she came down from her high; her lips trailing kisses down his jawline as he pressed kisses of his own to the crevice of her neck. It was one giant bubble of bliss that she never wanted to crawl out of.

"You're my favorite girl."

She paused, pulling away slightly to peer up at him with a soft smile.

"Be my girlfriend, Ophelia."

Her stomach fluttered at his words. It was just a title, she knew that, but her nerves were electric under her skin as if he'd just asked her to marry him. It wasn't as if they hadn't been acting like they were dating this entire time, anyway.

"On one condition," she whispered playfully.

"Anything."

"Open a wine and coffee bar with me." Ophelia bit her lip timidly, brushing his long hair from his face. "You can still sell your alcohol and I can sell coffee and bake pastries. Right near the beach you took me to in San Francisco."

James leaned back slightly, his eyes flickering across her features for any signs of her teasing. His lips parted when he didn't find any ounce of humor in her statement. He realized she was being deadly serious, making him sit up straight as the corner of his mouth twitched.

"Wait," he chirped. "Really?"

She nodded enthusiastically.

"You'd want to do that with me?" he asked in a small voice.

"Absolutely," Ophelia reassured with a confident smile, jutting her chin up. "I was up thinking about it all night. We could even name it *Bri's Boozy Cafe*."

His face softened exponentially.

"That's perfect," he whispered. "You're perfect."

And as he leaned forward to press soft kisses over every inch of her face, Ophelia sunk down into his pillows, feeling more at home than she ever had in her entire life.

CHAPTER THIRTY-FIVE

Taping up the last cardboard box of James' things, Ophelia sighed happily as she rubbed her hands against her jeans, wiping the dust and dirt away from the long morning of packing.

It had been a long week of preparing for the move to San Francisco, but she wouldn't change it for anything. She would take all the long weeks, months, and years if it meant getting to be with him.

Ophelia's mom had been in touch about all of her belongings back in Georgia, reassuring her that she'd have everything shipped to their new address promptly. Her father wasn't entirely on board with the whole thing. She hadn't heard from him once—everything was relayed through Julie. As much as it saddened Ophelia that only one of her parents was willing to accept how things were and let her be happy, she was finally done wasting time caring about what other people thought.

This was her life.

She was taking it back in full force.

Everything was falling perfectly into place. Wren was taking over the bar with Sean. James and Ophelia were moving into Brianna's house this evening, and they were going hunting for the ideal space to start their business together next week.

Julie had deposited every penny that was going towards college and medical school into Ophelia's bank account—with the firm words, "*I'm your mother. I was going to pay your way to become a surgeon, and I'm still going to pay for you to do whatever makes you happy, Ophelia.*"

She'd never asked her mother to do something like that, but the woman hadn't taken no for an answer before, which didn't seem to be changing anytime soon. Grateful didn't quite cut how that made her feel.

A pair of muscular arms enveloped her waist, pulling her from her train of thought as she leaned back into James' shoulder with a smile. He buried his face into her neck, pressing light kisses against her skin as he sighed.

"I still can't believe this is happening."

She twisted to peer up at him, tilting her head slightly as he placed her palm against his bearded cheek. "I know. It feels like some fever dream."

"You're not having second thoughts?" James asked quietly, his eyes averting hers as he had a second of self-doubt. "About moving in with me? Owning a business with me?"

"No, James." Ophelia gently cupped his cheek and forced him to look back up at her. "I want this. For the first time in my entire life, I feel like I can *breathe*."

His bottom lip disappeared between his teeth as he chewed at it nervously, his eyebrows cinching briefly as he gave her a fleeting look. Worry lines formed along his forehead as his shoulders rose shakily with each breath.

"It's just—" He paused, swallowing thickly. "I know this is a lot. Moving in together. Being together. It's a big step and if you're not ready for that, you can tell me. It's one thing to move home for me, but now I'm making you move away from your home and—"

"Jamie, you are my home."

She could hear his sharp intake of breath before he let it *whoosh* through his lips in a heavy exhale, his features softening as he pulled her into a warm hug. His arms wrapped around her shoulders as he pressed his cheek against hers.

"I grew up in Los Angeles, yeah," she continued after a few moments, rubbing his back gently. "But home is wherever you are. We could live on a boat out at sea, or a tent in the woods somewhere. I don't care. As long as you're there."

After spending two months away from him, Ophelia realized that was something she never wanted to do again. There was the male population that she had sworn off, and then there was him. He was in an entirely different category all to himself—different from anyone else she had ever come across in her life. He wasn't *a* man, he was *the* man. The man made specifically for her. She felt it in her bones every time she was around him. Her skin would come alive. Her body would feel as though it was buzzing with heat. Her heart would lurch at his every word.

The rest of the male population was subpar because he was the one for her.

She had fought her way through shitty relationships, bad hookups, and dumb guys to find him.

"I'm glad to hear you say that, because—" James stopped, licking his lips. "I did something."

She hummed curiously.

Holding his pointer fingers up in the air briefly, a nervous grin spread across his lips. Pulling an envelope from his back pocket, he handed it over to her as he ran his palm down his face.

"Open it," he ordered tentatively.

"What is this?" Ophelia murmured, her fingers running along the black ink on the outside that read *Diablo Valley College*.

"Wren helped me fill out an application at this culinary school up in San Francisco," he explained quickly as she tore open the envelope. "For you."

Ophelia's mouth popped open as her eyes read over the acceptance letter for their culinary degree program in baking and pastry, before gawking up at him. The paper trembled in her shaky hand as she stared at him for a few seconds, her eyes stinging with fresh tears as she struggled to form a coherent sentence.

"I—" she mumbled in shock. "I don't know what to say."

"It was my first idea before confronting your parents." He laughed nervously, his eyes searching her face thoroughly. "You could go to school while we open the cafe. I could take the brunt of it for a while so you can get your degree."

"You—I don't even—" Ophelia stuttered gently, shaking her head slowly. "*James*. You did this for me?"

Her heart felt like it was swelling inside of her chest as she held back the floodgates that had threatened to burst behind her eyes. She glanced between the letter and James as she clamped her palm over her mouth.

She'd never had someone care so much for her that they would go to the lengths that he had to ensure her happiness. He'd practically taken care of her from the moment they had met. He'd driven her home to make sure she'd gotten back safely, and he had only known her for ten minutes. The mere kindness that exuded from this man was astonishing. He had one of the sweetest souls she had ever met in her entire life.

"Of course I did," he breathed.

She slammed into him with a muffled squeak, wrapping her arms around his neck and nearly squeezing the life out of him as tears trickled down her warm cheeks.

"You're always taking care of me."

"You're my girl," he said in a matter-of-factly tone. "I'd do anything for you."

"Thank you," Ophelia mumbled against his neck as she pressed her face into him. "Thank you, thank you, thank you."

How did she deserve someone like him? Someone so selfless.

His arms wrapped around her waist as he lifted her up, her feet dangling as he squeezed her back. They embraced this way for a while—happy tears streaming down her face in what felt like waves as she held onto him for dear life.

"I've never had anyone come into my life like this and fight so hard to show me what I deserve," she sniffled as he set her back down on her feet. "I'm sorry I didn't make it easy for you, but I'm so thankful that you didn't give up."

"I could never give up on you, pretty girl."

His fingers brushed her hair behind her ear as they swiped away at her damp cheek. Leaning down, he pressed a kiss against her forehead.

She'd always loved how much he would kiss her forehead. How much he would touch her, period. His love language was undoubtedly physical affection because he never failed to consistently press kisses anywhere he could. He'd probably kissed her a thousand times, but she'd still feel a surge of electricity under her skin when his lips touched her. He was always leaving his mark, even if she couldn't see it.

"There aren't enough words to tell you how thankful I am for this." She gestured towards the paper.

James grasped her hand, intertwining his fingers with hers as his thumb brushed along the top of her knuckles gently.

"Let's go, Clark," he urged as he bounced on his heels, flashing her a smile. "I'm ready to show you our new home."

Our new home.

Ophelia loved the sound of that.

"Hmm, and our new bed," she replied cheekily. "I suppose I can show you how thankful I am when we're breaking it in tonight."

He groaned, throwing his head back. "It's almost like you read my mind."

Ophelia rolled her eyes, swatting at his shoulder as he snickered. Tugging her out of the room and through the entrance of *The Beer Lounge*, she sighed happily as they walked past the movers who were heading inside to grab the boxes.

She watched as he approached his motorcycle, and threw his leg over. The sun glistened against his brown hair, cascading rays of light across his features as he looked up at her. His eyes twinkled in amusement.

She had fallen in love with every part of him, and he had loved her just the same. Their love had been fiery, passionate, fervent.

Ten weeks of a love that had scorched so hot that she would be permanently burned forever.

A *red summer*.

EPILOGUE
ONE YEAR LATER

Pink and blue scattered along the top of the long table—plates, silverware, napkins, cups. There were even tiny pacifiers strewn atop the tablecloth that rippled in the cool November breeze that came through the open windows. Streamers and balloons sprinkled Wren and Sean's apartment, accompanied by a banner that read *Oh baby!* and a three-tier cake.

Ophelia's cheeks dimpled in the corners as she smiled softly, watching Wren as she bustled around the kitchen to prepare everything in time for the gender reveal party with the tiniest baby bump. Her swollen stomach protruded out faintly in her oversized cashmere sweater, and her skin glowed in the rays of sunlight cascading through the apertures.

Her heart swelled in her chest at the sight of her pregnant best friend.

"She's glowing."

Ophelia turned to see James perched against the doorframe of the bathroom, watching her with his hands stuffed inside his leather jacket pockets. His dark hair fell to his chin, tucked behind his ears, connecting with his full beard. Tattoos trailed up the side of his neck.

A whole year later and the sight of him still made her head spin.

"Yeah," she agreed gently, flicking her braid behind her shoulders as she approached him. "She looks beautiful. I'm so happy for them. They deserve this."

Ophelia thought back to the moment that Wren had told her that she was pregnant—rosy cheeks, a wide smile, and she was gripping her hand so hard that she thought she was going to break a knuckle. She had been nervous, but Ophelia knew that she was destined to be a great mom.

Sean and Wren would be the best parents. Their love for each other showed in everything that they did—the way they talked, and the way they moved around one another. It was practically instinctual, and parenting would undoubtedly be the same for them.

"Come here," James murmured under his breath as his eyes darted towards the kitchen to check if everyone was still preoccupied. Grasping her fingers, he tugged her with him inside the hallway bathroom.

"James, we are *not* doing it in the bathroom at Wren and Sean's gender reveal party."

"No." He snickered, his nose scrunching as he pressed her back against the sink. "Silly girl, I have something for you. A present."

"A present?"

He nodded enthusiastically, leaning down to peck her lips gently before he fished his hand back into his jacket pocket. His lips pursed as he gnawed at the inside of them, hesitating slightly.

"This might not be conventional. I mean, our entire relationship hasn't been conventional," he mumbled quickly, his throat bobbing before he continued. "And I was going to do this later, but watching you in there—all excited and happy, I couldn't wait."

Ophelia's brows furrowed as she grinned expectantly up at him, bouncing on her heels. "Do what, James? You can't get me all anxious like this. Spit it out."

Her heartbeat quickened as she watched him fidget some more, and their chests heaved practically in sync together. The nerve endings in her fingertips were buzzing in anticipation.

A nervous laugh escaped his bearded lips as he whisked something out of his pocket.

A box.

A tiny, *black* box.

Inhaling sharply, her lips parted in realization as goosebumps cascaded across her skin. The hair pricked on the back of her neck as she bit down on her bottom lip, and her hands trembled as she clasped them together in front of her mouth. Her heart thumped so harshly against her chest that she questioned if he could hear it.

"And now that I'm doing it." His voice shook. "I realize that it might not be the best thing to propose to you in a bathroom. Wow, I'm really fucking this up—"

"No," Ophelia blurted in a squeak. "Don't stop."

She didn't care where he proposed to her, she would accept him anywhere. She would say yes, always. There was no question about it.

If she could even speak by then.

She felt like she was spiraling all over again, falling for him ten times over, as she watched his hands shake holding the box. His entire body was trembling nervously as he perched himself on one knee. His head still came up to her chin with how tall he was, flicking open the box and holding it out to her.

"Ophelia Clark," James breathed. "I've been head over heels for you since the moment I laid my eyes on you. The very second I saw your blonde hair, your chunky Converse, and your oversized sweater that you were wearing in the middle of summer. I knew that I was wrapped around your finger, whether I liked it or not. It was like coming up for air. I love you senselessly. I'm *in* love with you. I saw this ring six months ago. It's been stuffed in my nightstand drawer ever since. It was beautiful, and I knew that you deserved to have it on your finger. So, pretty girl, will you marry me?"

The teardrop-shaped ring glistened in the light; the stone sitting inside of a rose-gold band. It was the prettiest ring she had ever seen. Tears stung the back of her eyes as she nodded, wrapping her arms around his neck with such force that they swayed slightly.

"*Yes.*" She sniffled. "Yes, yes, *yes.*"

Pressing kisses against his neck, his cheek, his lips—she let go briefly as she extended her shaky hand. She held her breath as he slid the ring onto her finger, rubbing her knuckle with his thumb sweetly as he peered up at her in awe.

"I'm sorry that it wasn't somewhere more special—"

She cut him off by wrapping her arms around him again, her lips smashing against his.

"Shut up," she mumbled against his mouth, smiling into his kiss as she sighed. "It was perfect."

"Are you sure?"

She giggled, cupping his cheek. "You did it in the heat of the moment. That *is* perfect."

His arms enveloped her waist in relief as he pressed his cheek up against her chest. Cradling his head, she brushed his hair behind his ear softly as they embraced for a while. She stared at the ring as her hand rested on his shoulder, and her cheeks ached from smiling so hard.

Commotion echoed in the living room, making them laugh in unison as James interlaced his fingers with hers. She could hardly contain the excitement that bubbled in her stomach as he guided them out of the bathroom, rounding the corner without anyone even noticing that they were ever gone. She felt like she had the world on her finger. She couldn't stop glancing down at it.

He'd decided he wanted to marry her six months ago. Her dream ring had been two feet away from her every single night as she was snuggled in bed with him.

Everything was falling into place.

It had been for a year, and it still was. Every time it felt as though things couldn't get more perfect, they somehow managed to do just that.

Their apartment overlooked the San Francisco Bay. They were able to watch the sun set and rise every single day over the vast ocean. Her heart had never been so happy before to be in one of the places she loved the most with the person she loved the most. Their cafe was a hit in town; she was only two semesters away from finishing her degree, so she had been able to be more hands-on with baking at *Bri's Boozy Cafe*.

Ophelia's eyes watered as she watched Wren and Sean get into position behind the table, confetti rockets perched in their hands that were ready to be shot off at any moment and reveal pink or blue shreds of paper. Glancing up at James, she blinked away the tears forming in her eyes as she sucked in a deep breath.

He looked down at her, his eyebrows cinching in concern as he cocked his head sideways.

"What is it, Lia?"

She shook her head, smiling meekly. "I'm just emotional. Ignore me."

His arm swung over her shoulder, tugging her toward him as he pressed his lips to her forehead.

And then they were popping their confetti rockets, Wren and Sean screaming in unison as they attempted to jump and hug at the same time. Confetti flew all around the apartment, settling on every inch of surface it could, coating the living room in a field of *pink*.

It was a girl.

Ophelia swiped at the corner of her eye to catch the tear from falling, smiling as she watched the pair embrace. Sean shot James an excited thumbs up as he swirled Wren around carefully. As he plopped her back down on the ground, his hands found her swollen stomach and he leaned down to give it a tiny kiss.

James placed his finger under her chin, pushing her head up to look at him as confetti fell around them.

"I want this with you."

Her heart skipped.

"Babies?" she whispered softly.

He plucked pink confetti from her hair, his lips lifting in the corners. "Yeah, babies."

"We would make some pretty cute babies."

Confetti swirled in the breeze from the windows. There were pieces in his hair, clinging to his jacket. Only he could look hot with pink confetti stuck to every surface of him.

The roseate shreds of paper fluttered around like the butterflies inside of her stomach as she peered up at him.

"After you're finished with culinary school. After a wedding," he breathed, his eyes flickering across her features. "Your dream wedding. After all of that, I want to make babies."

Swoon.

"Let's have a summer wedding," she urged, leaning against his chest as she pecked his lips. "This upcoming June. Two years from when we met."

"On the beach?"

It was a question, but it sounded more like a statement. He knew how much she loved the beach.

"The one you took me to on the way to San Francisco," she reminisced cheekily. "Where we skinny dipped together."

He hummed.

"That was a good night."

"Want to stop on the way back home?" she offered.

James pressed his tongue to his cheek as he wrapped his arm around her, pulling her back against his chest. His mouth hovered next to her ear.

"There's nothing I would want more, pretty girl."

Leaning her head back against his shoulder, she pressed her head into the crevice of his neck. With a happy sigh, she observed all the happiness around her.

And for the first time, she felt *good enough*. She deserved to feel so overcome with happiness that she could explode. She deserved to smile so hard that her cheeks ached. She wasn't the side girl anymore—she was the girl that his eyes would search for in a crowded room, the girl he had a specific smile stored away for, and the girl that made him belly laugh unlike anyone else. With James, she felt seen. He pushed her to love herself just as much as he loved her.

She'd found her puzzle piece.

Her soulmate.

Perfectly created and perfectly molded for her.

THE END

BONUS CHAPTER

JAMES

THE DAYS WERE LONG, and the nights were even longer behind the goddamn bar. It was all a blur of familiar drunken faces, slinging the same drinks, and still having absolutely nothing to show for it. James could work every day for the rest of his life and he'd still be looking *final notices* in the face on his twin-sized bed in the back when he went to sleep every night.

He needed a change of pace for his own sanity, that much he knew, but the problem was he had no idea what to change.

Cleaning some dirty shot glasses, he glanced up impatiently as a young, college kid slapped a twenty down on the wooden bar. He was clearly the frat boy type—expensive clothes, tanned skin, and the confident smirk plastered on his face. One that was undoubtedly popular with chicks; there was even a girl sizing him up from the other end of the bar right now.

"Can I get you something?" James forced out, sucking in a deep breath through his nose.

Frat boy flashed him an intoxicated smile. "A round of shots, my friend. Vodka."

These college kids and their vodka.

This would be his third trip to the back to grab some more bottles of liquor because of these fuckers.

"Sure," he said with false enthusiasm. "I'll be right back, *boss*."

Disappearing into the back, James took a second to run a palm down his face. He still had two hours of this shit. The music emanating throughout the bar was making his temples throb with a migraine, and the loud patrons tonight weren't helping. Saturday's were always like this; he should've known better than to think that this one would've been any different.

The truth was—nothing was going to help a headache stemming from burnout, which is precisely what he was feeling.

Fucking burnt out.

"Hey, Jam."

Jam. The nickname his best friend and coworker pinned him since they were old enough to talk.

Turning at the sound of Sean's voice, James watched as he entered the back room. His dark eyes gave him a once-over before he let out a low whistle.

"You look like hell." Sean winced.

"I feel like it, too."

A mischievous grin twitched on his lips before he grasped James' shoulder and gave it a squeeze. "I have just the thing you need. She's blonde, smoking hot, and sitting at the bar waiting on *you* to go make her a drink."

James gave him a pointed look.

Sean put his hands up innocently. "What?"

"Not this again," he groaned, turning to grab a few bottles of vodka from the shelf behind them.

"I don't know what you're talking about."

"Playing matchmaker has never suited you," James huffed, licking his lips.

Sean stepped toward him, taking the bottles from his hands. "I didn't say go marry the girl. Just...take a look. Do some window shopping. I've got the frat boy, don't worry."

"Wow." James feigned shock. "I'll be forever indebted to you."

His sarcasm didn't wound Sean like he had hoped, instead, he disappeared back to the bar as he snickered. Leaving James alone for a moment as he pinched the bridge of his nose, wishing he could hide in the back until closing time.

Sean had been trying to impersonate Cupid for months now. He was throwing potential hopefuls at him left and right, but what he didn't understand was that James was tired. Like permanently exhausted. Having a pretentious ex-wife would do that to a person. He couldn't muster up the energy to even *want* to date anyone.

With one last deep breath, which didn't make him feel better in the slightest, he left the back room and walked through the doorway—back into the annoying atmosphere of loud music and drunk college kids.

He didn't look up immediately. To be honest, he didn't want to give Sean the satisfaction of checking out whatever blonde was sitting at their bar, but he didn't have much of a choice as he walked right up in front of her. And as his head lifted, meeting a pair of blue eyes that mirrored his own, he wanted to kick himself for waiting to look at her in the first place.

She was *beautiful*.

An enigma of long, platinum hair that framed her pink cheeks, and cerulean eyes that peered up at him through thick lashes. Her features were soft, and her lips were full. Her eyes widened a smidge as she gawked up at him, but she quickly recovered as she straightened in her seat.

His lips twisted as he chewed at the inside of his mouth.

"Got an ID?"

Really fucking smooth.

A smirk flittered across her pink lips as she whisked her driver's license from her purse, sliding it across the bar toward him before tapping on her birthday playfully. "Just turned twenty-one this year, mister. I'll have a shot of tequila."

He glanced down at the license.

Ophelia Clark.

He'd hardly glanced at her birthday because he couldn't stop staring at her goddamn name.

Sliding the ID back to her, James turned to grab the bottle of tequila and poured the clear liquid into a shot glass. In a moment of fleeting curiosity, he peeked at her reflection in the wall behind the shelves holding all the alcohol.

She was staring at his ass.

Right at it. No shame. No hiding it. And then he realized that she had no clue that the wall of liquor was reflective. No idea that he was gritting his teeth so hard that he was sure one of his molars would crack just to keep from laughing.

"Want to open a tab?" he asked quietly, scared that she

would catch the shake in his voice.

Ophelia nodded as she flashed him the cutest smile he'd ever seen. "Keep them coming. It's been a long night."

That makes two of us.

"Did you drive?"

"No, I walked. Kind of." She sighed as she twisted her hair into a tiny, pastel pink hair clip. "It's a long story."

He wanted to know all about this long story. Hell, he'd pull up a chair and happily listen to her speak all night, if she'd let him. Her voice was velvety, *comforting*. Suddenly, his migraine had subsided. Stored away somewhere for another day.

"You walked," he repeated firmly as he placed the shot in front of her. "By yourself?"

He didn't like that thought.

She threw her head back as she downed the tequila like it was water, and he'd never seen anything more mesmerizing in his entire life. Was there anything this girl *couldn't* make look cute?

"Well, I was on a date." Her statement made his stomach churn. "But he started to show me pictures of his mom and talking about how he wanted to be with someone who reminded him of her, and uh—*yeah*. It was kind of weird. So I had him drop me off at the corner outside."

No doubt just like one of these drunken fuckers who were being a smidge too loud in the bar. He wondered if those types were *her* type.

"You know, for a bartender, you're not very talkative."

So fucking cute. The way she peeked up at him with a small smile. Like she was unsure if she was allowed to be that up-front with him or not.

James fought against a smile of his own. "How do you plan on getting home?"

He wouldn't normally care so much, but she was already getting the attention of the frat boy himself and some of his friends. Their eyes lingered on her for a beat too long. Waiting to swoop in at any moment like a predator with its prey.

"I haven't thought that far ahead," Ophelia admitted as she took her bottom lip between her teeth.

Jesus Christ.

It wasn't a big deal. It *wasn't*. But it was. His heart hesitated proper function inside his chest at the sight. It was becoming a hindrance just to form a coherent thought in her presence.

"Do you live in LA?" he asked.

Great. Small talk.

"I grew up here, but I live in Georgia on campus right now. I'm staying with my friend for the summer."

"Georgia is pretty far," he said, pressing his hands to the bar as he looked down at her.

"Yeah, that was on purpose."

James nodded before filling her shot glass for the third time. "Does your friend live within walking distance?"

Her pretty blue eyes were glossing over in an intoxicated buzz, and her cheeks were flushed now. It made him feel uneasy with the way the vultures were eyeballing her. Probably waiting on her to get drunk so that they had more of a chance of taking her home.

Over his dead body.

"I'll just call an Uber." She shrugged as she spoke, and it

wasn't hard to catch the way she swayed in her seat.

Getting in the back of a car with a total stranger didn't sound like the finest option either. From the looks of it, it was either her walking home, catching a ride from one of the douches, or calling an Uber. He didn't like any of those options. James knew he could get her home safely, that much was guaranteed. His mind had practically already been made up as he filled her glass again, furrowing his brows in thought.

"You don't feel weird getting a ride home from a stranger by yourself?" he asked, glancing at the clock on the wall behind him. "At almost midnight?"

"They're usually nice, old men."

He hummed.

Yeah, unless this time was the exception and she caught a ride with a serial killer.

"You're skeptical." There was amusement in her tone.

"*I* could take you home."

Ophelia's mouth popped open at his words, but her posture straightened. Her body perked up whether she realized it or not.

Throwing the rag down on the counter, James turned toward Sean and gave him a tiny nod. He resisted the urge to roll his eyes as Sean gave him a pointed look paired with an eyebrow raise.

"You don't have to do tha—"

"Sean, could you take over until I get back?" James blurted quickly.

The pointed look turned into more of a playful, narrowed

one as Sean's lips twitched in the corner.

Fucker.

"Sure thing, Jam."

Hurrying out from behind the bar, he watched Ophelia gulp down the rest of her tequila before wiping her mouth with the back of her hand.

"That's enough tequila for one night," he murmured, fighting the urge to smile once more as he extended his hand out for her to take.

"But I opened a tab."

Her bottom lip protruded into a pout. A teasing, adorable little pout. And his stomach had suddenly come alive with butterflies. The feeling had sucked the air from his lungs as he struggled to compose himself. It was a foreign feeling. He couldn't remember the last time he'd had *flutters*.

"Don't worry about it." He shook his head. "It's on me. Let's just get you home safely, yeah?"

Couldn't remember the last time he'd held someone's *hand* and damn near passed out from the contact. His chest constricted as she hesitantly placed her palm into his. Warm electricity ignited in his fingertips from touching her. He couldn't breathe.

Holy shit.

As he guided her outside of the bar, he took that moment to walk ahead of her—gather his bearings as he approached his motorcycle and threw his leg over.

"This is yours?" Ophelia hiccupped timidly.

He nodded. "I hope that's okay."

"More than okay," she laughed, hopping behind him and

wrapping her arms around his waist. "Let's go."

That was something he wanted to hear again. Her laugh. It was as soft as her voice, but sweeter, somehow. Her blue eyes crinkled faintly in the corners as the sound burst from her lips, and it was an image well deserving of being in an art museum.

"Are you ready?"

"As long as you drive responsibly—because I may be slightly inebriated, and I'm barely hanging on here." She tightened her grip around his torso. "Then I think I'm ready."

James couldn't help but laugh as he kickstarted the bike to life. He tensed slightly as she pressed her cheek against his back, but the sound of her gently yelling her address over the loudness of the motorcycle made him relax with a small smile. Another foreign feeling. It had been a while since anyone had touched him like this, as innocent as it was.

As he made his way down the streets of Los Angeles, he brought one of his hands down every so often, holding her intertwined fingers in his to make sure she was steady. The address she'd given him wasn't far off, luckily. Easing the worry in his stomach that churned at the thought of her tumbling off the bike.

The night had taken a turn that he hadn't quite expected. He was fully prepared to sling out drinks until closing time with a pounding headache, but yet, here he was with a beautiful girl that had her arms wrapped around his abdomen.

Sean is never going to let this one go.

The trip was over entirely too soon. James couldn't keep the disappointment from pouring in as he pulled up in front of the apartment complex, cutting off the motorcycle as she loosened her hold around his waist.

"Well, um, *Jam*?" she questioned meekly, squinting at him apprehensively as she hopped off to comb her fingers through her hair. "Is that your real name?"

The laugh escaped from his bearded lips before he could stop it. "Jamie. Um, James. Jam is just something Sean has called me since we were kids."

She hummed with a tiny smile. "Jamie. *James*, thanks for the ride home."

"No problem."

He wanted to say more. He didn't want to stop talking to her at all, but he had no clue what to say. Holding a conversation was never his strong suit.

"Thanks for not murdering me," Ophelia said.

He coughed into his fist to keep from choking at her words. "You thought I was going to murder you?"

"It was a joke, bartender boy."

So fucking cute.

"Yep." He nodded. "I knew that."

"I'll see you around." She grinned widely down at him. "Maybe?"

Still perched on his bike, he bounced his leg as he mirrored her smile. The bundle of nerves swirled around in his stomach at a nauseating pace. It made him feel like a teenage boy again that had just seen a pretty girl for the first time. The air constricted in his chest, making him feel speechless as he looked at her. What could he say? He'd forgotten how to do this.

She took a few steps backward as she threw her small hand in the air, waving at him. "Goodnight."

"Goodnight, Ophelia."

The look on her face was all he needed to feel like this was something he *wanted* to learn how to do again. Her features lit up at his remembrance of her name, and he knew that there was no possible way he could go without seeing that smile again.

Hell, it was the first time in a long time that *he* had smiled, too.

ACKNOWLEDGEMENTS

Thank you, reader. I will be forever grateful that you gave this book, and me, a chance. This story holds a special place in my heart, and I hope that it resonated with you somehow, too.

To my promotional team, thank you for being my biggest cheerleaders and supporting me every step of the way.

To my beta readers Grace, Lindsey, Siiri, Bianca, Lia, Cindy, Alison, Sara, Samantha, and Rooha, thank you for taking the time to read my book and helping me get it ready for the world to read. I couldn't have done it without your feedback and support.

To Jenni Brady, thank you for taking the time to proofread my book. Your feedback and critique were vital for this debut and I'm so grateful.

To Grace, thank you for always being a sounding board during my journey and never hesitating to offer your knowledge and kind words. I have learned so much from you, and I am so lucky to consider you a friend.

To Lindsey, thank you for being my number-one fan from the start. You've been so supportive, encouraging, and willing to read through the manuscript *twice* just to help me get this book ready for its debut. I am forever thankful.

To the book community, you have been abundantly supportive in ways that I could have never imagined. I feel so accepted here. Thank you.

To my parents, thank you for being so supportive. Every time I wanted to give up, you reminded me of how hard I worked for this. I love you so much.

And to my smoking hot husband, thank you for being my backbone, always. Through all of the sweat and tears that I have poured into this process, you've held my hand every step of the way and reminded me that I can do this. I would've never believed in myself enough to get me this far if it wasn't for you. Thank you, thank you, *thank you*. I love you.

ABOUT THE AUTHOR

Cassidy Hudspeth is an Indie Author who loves to read and write spicy romance books. She's been writing for twelve years and reading for as long as she can remember. She resides in Southern California with her husband, son, and fur child.

You can keep up with her on her Instagram (cassidyhudspethwrites) or visit her website at cassidyhudspethwrites.godaddysites.com for more information. You can also join her VIP Facebook Group "Cassidy's Bookish Babes" for sneak peeks at future novels and current works in progress.

Made in the USA
Las Vegas, NV
10 October 2023